LOS

LOS

A Cadence Turing Mystery

ROBIN JEFFREY

Robin Jeffrey

Books by Robin Jeffrey

The Cadence Turing Mystery Series

.exe: A Cadence Turing Mystery (Book 1)
R.A.T.: A Cadence Turing Mystery (Book 2)
LOS: A Cadence Turing Mystery (Book 3)

The Night Series

Hungry is the Night (Book 1)
Bloody is the Night (Book 2)
Lonely is the Night (Book 3)

Contents

I

Chapter 1

"I don't see why you're so upset," said Cadence, arms akimbo.

"I'm not...upset," I managed haltingly, breathless after traversing seven flights of stairs. Hands on my thighs, chest heaving, I shook my head from side to side. "I'm just... a little... disappointed."

Cadence shook her head. "Sinc, but why?"

I rolled my eyes. "Cadence..." Straightening, some of the strength returning to my overworked limbs. I cast my arms out to indicate the box-filled room in which we stood. "This is not a date."

Cadence's mouth hinged open and shut. She looked around the room, eyes wide, as if she might find the answer to my apparently incomprehensible objection somewhere in the mess of moving boxes that surrounded us.

When Cadence had invited me out for an 'afternoon date,'

I had hoped against hope that she had something appropriately romantic in mind. It was autumn on Arrhidaeus, and Römer boasted some spectacular botanical gardens that would now be bursting with colorful foliage. I had mentioned it to her only last week, thinking that perhaps we might take a stroll through one of the glass-domed biomes, hand in hand; maybe even picnic under one of the red and purple-leaved trees.

I should've known better.

"Of course, this is a date!" Cadence crossed the room to stand by me, throwing her arm across my shoulders. "We are engaging in a dynamic, entertaining activity together, which will bring us closer in both an emotional and physical sense."

"Then why is he here?" I countered, jerking my head behind me towards the figure struggling inside from the corridor.

Inspector Oliver Brisbois froze in the doorway, balancing a box full of assorted power cords on his hip. He looked decidedly unlike himself, having abandoned his usual secondhand suit for a pair of black jeans and a long sleeved dark green plaid shirt, unbuttoned at the neck. Cadence and I turned to look at him. His bright green eyes jumped between our appraising faces, and he shrugged, sharp shoulders brushing the bottom of his ears. "I hate to admit it, Cadence, but he has a point."

Cadence released me, her words rising in volume as if by saying them louder she could convince me of their rightness. "But there's no way that we could have handled everything by ourselves!"

"I understand that," I said, stepping to one side to allow Brisbois the space he needed to walk past with his burden.

"And if I don't have everything moved-in by tomorrow, I'll break the lease!"

I nodded, hands outstretched towards her. "I understand that as well, but–"

Cadence looked around at us, rubbing the back of her neck. "Henry assured me that things like this were typical activities for human couples to engage in."

"I did say that I'm afraid," admitted my dear friend, his voice suddenly in my ear.

Deflating faster than a punctured balloon, I rubbed at the bridge of my nose with my fingers. "Oh, for–" Turning, I didn't even bother adopting a more welcoming expression as I said, "Hello there, love of my life."

Henry Davers, my childhood friend and confidant, had also come dressed for physical labor, donning a multi-pocketed pair of tan trousers and a short-sleeved black t-shirt with the words "FREE WHISTON" emblazoned upon the front in light blue.

"Hello, Chance." He embraced me warmly, nodding to the man on the far side of the room as he did so. "Inspector."

Brisbois gave a wave, his brow furrowed as he dug through the box of equipment he had deposited on the reception desk. "Off-duty, it's just Oliver." He looked up, a slim rectangle in one hand. "Cadence, where do you want this computer?"

"Oh, let me show you..." Cadence crossed the room towards him, abandoning me to my irritation with a hurriedness that did not escape my attention.

Turning to Henry, I rolled my dress shirt sleeves back down my arms. I shook my head. "This is not a date," I repeated, anxious to prove my point to someone, anyone who might sympathize with my plight.

Henry nodded, his hands falling into his trouser pockets. "Yes, I can see that."

"If you can see it, and I can see it–" I waved my hand at Cadence, who was happily directing Brisbois in the perfect placement of her computer terminal. "–then why can't she see?"

Henry rocked back on his heels, chin lifting as he performed an uncanny imitation of his father mid-lecture. "As I understand it, romantic courtship is more group oriented in Animanecron society." The corners of his mouth pulled down into an exaggerated frown. "Less emphasis on one-on-one interactions, and more on how a potential partner fits in with day-to-day life as a whole. And family is often a big part of day-to-day Animanecron life." He patted my shoulder, smiling. "We're her family."

Snorting out a laugh, I pushed my hand through my sweat-soaked blond hair. "In that case, I'm surprised your parents aren't here."

"Oh, they were invited," he said, nodding. "But they had other obligations."

Eyes wide, my mouth opened to respond when Cadence cut neatly in between us, walking towards a pile of crates placed next to the front door. "Urio, Chance, do you know where that pack of blank docudiscs ended up? I can't find them."

"There are still a few boxes downstairs in the lobby," volunteered Henry. "Could they be in one of those?"

"Probably. I'll go–" She jumped, came to an abrupt halt, and pulled a buzzing mobile out of her pocket. Frowning, she placed the bud in her ear and answered the call. Her frowning face cleared into a bright smile. "Mr. Shine! Hello! Cy, yes, we're in the midst of finishing the move right now!" She spun one hundred and eighty degrees and paced back into the office. Nodding, she covered the bud with one hand and whispered to us as she passed, "Chance, Henry, could you–?"

"We've got it," said Henry, smiling. "Come on, Chance. No rest for the wicked."

Pulling my sweat-soaked shirt away from my back, I sighed heavily and followed my friend out the door, muttering, "Karma can be vicious, can't it?"

When I first met Cadence on the AN-GRAV coming from the Mawson Docks, I had no idea how completely my life would change. In the span of less than an Arrhidaean year, my father had been murdered, forcing me to take over the system-spanning company that was my family's legacy. That was only after, of course, Cadence had cleared me of all suspicion in his death and had brought his true killers to justice. Since then, from boardrooms to nightclubs, protests to galas, Cadence had been at my side through one adventure after another.

However, the war that had driven her from her home on the moon of Whiston, far on the other side of the Archerusia system, still raged. Animanecrons, artificial intelligence originally created by my family's company, Halcyon Enterprises, had lived on Whiston for over two centuries in peace, sent there by unanimous decree of the Interplanetary Council. That peace was shattered when their planetary neighbor, Charcornac, attacked the moon in a xenophobic frenzy, beginning the systematic destruction of all animanecrons they and their allies could find.

It was a miracle Cadence had survived at all. And now she was not just surviving – she was thriving.

"I have to admit," said Henry as we traipsed down the stairs. "I was surprised when Cadence didn't move back into the flat with you."

"We both agreed it was for the best," I explained. "She needed space to be herself, to be independent – live her own life. Especially after everything that happened with Elea Cerf."

Henry nodded, glancing at me from the corner of his eyes. "But you're still a part of her life, right?"

"Course," I said quickly, not meeting his gaze. "How is Ergo Sum treating you? They certainly seem to be keeping you busy these days."

There was a pause before he answered, and for a moment I wasn't sure he was going to let my obvious evasion slide. But then he smiled and said, "There's no end of things to do, that's for certain. But you know me: I'm happy to help however I can." He lifted his chin into the air, his smile widening. "It's good to feel like we're finally making some progress."

It was the work of Ani Rights organizations like Ergo Sum, sympathetic politicians, and the animanecron survivors themselves that had finally begun to turn the tide against Charcornac. As support for their plight spread across the system, the refugees had been allowed freer travel and access to aid on many more planets. However, they still faced discrimination and fear at almost every turn, which naturally led to the formation of places like the ani-friendly district in which Cadence's new premises stood.

I looked out the window on the second-floor landing, which

was mercifully open, a cool breeze licking at the back of my sweat-slicked neck. The walkways outside were bustling with PTs and people, many of whom I could now recognize as animanecrons. These former residents of Whiston favored bold, geometric tattoos, through which lights could often be seen coursing. But even those who were not marked in this way moved with an almost supernatural grace, and matched certain gestures with certain phrases, although few used the speech tags Cadence employed when speaking Common Tongue. Instead, Animatum could be heard flowing freely on the street outside; I let the strange guttural clicks and hisses of the language skitter into my ears like music.

We reached the ground floor, where a final pile of crates sat to one side of the inconveniently out of order elevator. I gestured to the pile, sighing. "Well, this should be the last of it."

"To think," said Henry, crossing the entryway towards the boxes, shaking his head. "She came here with hardly more than the clothes on her back... and now she has all this."

"To be fair, most of this she bought recently to support the new venture." I followed him at a reluctant stroll. "Though she has turned into a bit of a clothes horse, there's no doubt about that..."

As few humans had ever wanted to live in Districts 14, 15, and 16, the animanecrons filled in the gaps, linking unwanted city spaces into a new Ani community along the Mawson Docks. I had heard that more and more animanecrons were coming together to live and rebuild in similar forgotten and unwanted places.

It was fitting then, I supposed, that my beloved Cadence

should start her new professional life here. No longer as a simple story cube seller. Oh no. Cadence had something much grander in mind.

The last few moving crates awaited me and Henry under the building's glowing interior directory. In jittery illuminated pixels, the name of Cadence's latest venture reflected proudly in our eyes: *Floor Seven - Turing Detective Agency*.

"Wow." Henry stood in front of the sign, hands on his hips. "It's really something to see it made official like this." He reached up and tapped his finger against the letters, a half-smile lighting his face. "Whose idea was it, anyway?"

"The agency?" I picked up one of the boxes, frowning a little with the effort of holding the heavy container. "Hard to say. I think Simone may have given her the notion when she paid her for her work on Elea's case. But I suspect Brisbois encouraged her to go through with it, helping her get the necessary licenses and whatnot."

Henry took the box from me with a grunt, buckling a little under the weight before finding a better grip. "And... what do you think of it?"

I turned away from him, shrugging. "I support her one hundred percent, naturally." Lifting the second container into my arms, I started up the wide stairs. "Her story cube business wasn't taking off, so it made sense for her to make a change."

Henry fell into step behind me. "But?"

A dismissive snort was my initial response. "But nothing," I said after another floor. "She's sure to make a success of it. She's Cadence – the best."

"Something's wrong, though," said Henry at length, pausing

to balance his burden on the windowsill of the third-floor landing. He looked me up and down, chest heaving. "I can see it all over your radiantly red face. Is it work?"

I moved to stand next to him, rolling my sore shoulders. "Work is..." I cast my mind over the endless parade of meetings, reports, and bureaucratic mishmash that made up my days and sighed, shaking my head. "No. No, it's not work." I chewed contemplatively on the inside of my mouth. I glanced at him from the corner of my eye. "You... you promise not to laugh?"

He set his box down on the floor with a grunt and dusted off his hands. "Promise."

Hesitating, I mirrored his movement, pivoting on my heels so that I could lean back against the window. I pulled my arms high and tight across my chest, still avoiding his gaze. "Henry, it's been three months since Cadence and I decided to... you know, make a go of it. As a couple, I mean. Romantically. And..."

Henry grinned awkwardly, letting loose an uncomfortable chuckle. "And what, Chance?"

I ran my hand through my tousled hair, gritting my teeth together. "And... nothing."

"Nothing." He stared at me blankly.

I looked him in the eye at last. I lifted my brows but said not a word.

His brown eyes widened into pools of embarrassment. He pushed away from the wall, Adam's apple bobbing as he swallowed hard. "Oh! You mean...?" He winced visibly. "Seriously? Nothing?"

"Nothing," I drew the word out, emphasizing each syllable, hands sliding slowly through the air.

Scratching the back of his neck, the tip of his tongue snuck out to wet his lips. "Surely, you've–"

"I can guarantee you, whatever you're thinking, we haven't." I tugged at the bottom of my dress shirt. "Now, I know, the physical side of a relationship isn't everything, but with this new role of Cadence's, I haven't seen her these past six weeks. And now, for the first time in over a month, she wants to see me, and it's for...this."

Henry's gaze bounced around the landing before coming back to rest on me. He stared for a beat longer than was comfortable and then turned and picked up the box he had been carrying, letting out a low: "Hm."

I watched, dumbstruck, as he started up the stairs, leaving me adrift in his wake. I closed my gaping mouth shut so hard my teeth clicked together. I scrambled to catch up with him, remembering at the last minute to retrieve the box I had been transporting. "Hm?" I demanded. "Is that really all you have to offer?"

Several steps in front of me, he sighed, shaking his head. "Since when am I the relationship expert?"

"Since you started working at Ergo Sum," I said, referencing his do-gooding on behalf of the animanecron cause. I took the steps two at a time, insisting, "Surely you must have gained some kind of insight into the animanecron mind? Some special intelligence that you can share with me?"

"You want my advice?" He turned around on the next landing, so that he was walking backward. "Ask her about it."

"Ask?" I repeated, only slightly ashamed of the hint of panic in my voice.

Henry nodded. "Clear, forthright communication is always best." We started up the last flight of stairs and he lowered his voice so only I could hear him. "You do love her, don't you?"

"Of course," I said immediately. "I've never been more sure of anything in my life."

"Then talk to her," said Henry, struggling a little to push open the door to Cadence's new offices with the toe of his shoe. "And really, listen to what she has to say." He held the door open for me with his body and, as I passed, muttered: "Don't make the same mistake twice."

I bristled at his admonishment but held my tongue, settling instead for dropping the crate onto the floor more roughly than was strictly called for, directing my glare out into the open office. The seventh floor had, at one time, been the site of a mom-and-pop tech start up. There were no walls to speak of in the place, just a thousand square feet of open hardwood floor. There was a modest kitchen and closet sized washroom on the premises. A small loft was accessible from a short staircase in the front of the room, which I believed Cadence intended to use as a bedroom.

"Sinc, thank you so much, Henry," said Cadence, beaming at my lifelong friend as he placed the crate he was carrying at her feet. Looking past him towards me, she pointed up to the floor above us. "Chance, could you take that box up into the loft? And when you've done that could you come help Oliver with the story cubes?"

"Certainly," I said, picking up the crate I had dropped with a grunt. "What's in this anyway, Cay?"

"My personal computer and vertex module and things like

that," she answered. "I think some clothes as well, I ran out of boxes for all of those..."

I rolled my eyes, but smiled all the same as I trooped upstairs with my cargo. After depositing the box in the center of the loft floor, I paused for a moment, leaning over the balcony to catch my breath.

Watching Cadence direct the work below, I felt a surge of affection swell inside me that left me breathless. I loved her so completely, so entirely – in the almost year we had known each other, she had become the center around which all else orbited. So, what was wrong? Why did I feel like a dull asteroid to her brilliant star? Why was she so distant from me?

A buzzing in my trouser pocket drew my attention. I pulled my mobile out, glancing down at the blue flashing bud curiously. I accepted the call with a press of a button.

"Chance Hale," I answered, nestling the bud more firmly in my ear as I turned away from the hubbub of unpacking.

"Chance." A chipper, energetic voice greeted me. "So sorry to call you on your off hours."

"Miss Taylor," I said, sitting myself down on the crate I had just carried upstairs. I stretched my legs out in front of me and leaned back, fanning myself. "No need to apologize. I needed a break anyway."

"A break?" My executive administrator sounded thoroughly confused. "I... I thought you said you had a date this afternoon?"

"It's a long story." Straightening up, I shook my head. "What is it that you need?"

"Comms is trying to get ahead of any questions about Halcyon Enterprises restarting their defensive smart tech work, remember? They'll need a statement from you if the IPC gives the green light to military intervention in the Whiston Conflict."

I stood, moving away toward the windows. I kept my voice low as I asked, "Has there been any indication that the IPC is moving in that direction?"

There was a short spurt of tapping, fingers against a laser-projected keyboard before Lily Taylor spoke again. "Some new chatter, so the folks in comms think it's just a matter of time before IPC issues a declaration. The economic and political sanctions haven't done much to stop the Charcornacians from pursuing their 'solution to the Ani-Problem'; certain planets in the system are getting restless. Comms just wants you to be prepared when the IPC returns from its Summer Intersession next week."

I drew a hand across my forehead and closed my eyes. "Right. Well, tell them to send whatever they have to me, and I'll look it over as soon as I can. But nothing official goes out without my approval. Understood?"

"I'll make sure they toe the line."

I managed a weak, sideways smile. "You always do. Thank you, Miss Taylor."

"You're welcome, Mr. Hale. And... enjoy your date?" The upward inflection on the last word spoke volumes.

2

Chapter 2

I stepped back, wetting my lips with the tip of my tongue as I mentally scored my handiwork.

A fully assembled dresser now sat flush against the left wall. In the center of the small loft floor, I had also rolled out Cadence's futon, covering it with the secondhand bright yellow duvet she had purchased earlier, a single white pillow resting at its top. On the opposite side of the room, sat a spindly metal desk, just big enough for one person, with a vertex box attached to the underside and a single optric occupying its surface. A small optric, barely bigger than a human hand, it showed Cadence sitting in the middle of a group of laughing people, a person leaning in on either side of her. Two older men, William and Zachariah, the equivalent of Cadence's parents, stood in the back, crouching over, and smiling with manic brightness. The red-headed woman on her left, Cassandra, and the young man to Cadence's right, waving at the camera with an arm thrown over her shoulder, Iago, were her siblings.

All gone now. Killed by the Charcornacians. Gone, but never forgotten.

Content with my arrangements, I leaned over the banister that separated the loft bedroom for the rest of the space. "Cay," I shouted down into the office proper. "Can you come up here for a minute?"

A few seconds passed before I heard Cadence's tread on the staircase. I stepped back into the center of the room just in time for her to reach the landing. She gasped aloud, her summer smile rocketing across her face.

"Oh, Chance!" She looked around open mouthed for a moment before clasping her hands together. She rocked up onto the tips of her toes and bounced, smiling broadly. "Sinc, thank you! This looks perfect. How'd you know–?"

"Well," I admitted, sheepishness coloring my cheeks pink. "I remembered how you had your room set up when we lived together at the Feathers." Slipping my hands into my trouser pockets, I nudged the edge of the mattress with my foot, straightening the rectangular sleeping pad. "Wasn't hard to recreate."

As it so happened, I had spent as little time as possible in the flat since Cadence had struck out on her own. I didn't begrudge her leaving – under the circumstances, it was the only reasonable thing for her to do. But I couldn't deny that I missed her terribly, and that I'd much rather be here, with her, schlepping boxes back and forth, than relaxing alone in any of the sphere's luxury apartments.

Unsure how to express this sentiment without sounding trite, however, I settled for saying nothing, glancing at her through my eyelashes and luxuriating in her approval. I watched as she moved through the tiny space, stopping at the optric, picking it up and looking at it with fondness. After a moment she looked back at me and smiled again, but the smile was tinged with a weariness that plucked at my heart.

"Here: sit down," I said, stepping aside and gesturing to the bed. "You've been on your feet all day -- you must be tired."

She considered my offer, shrugged, and then made her way over to the futon, collapsing down on it with atypical graceless-ness. She ended up leaning back with her hands flat behind her, propping up her torso, while her legs splayed out in front of her, feet pointed towards the ceiling.

She looked straight ahead for a moment and then up at me, frowning. "So have you," she said. "Do you need to rest?"

I smiled and sat down beside her, crossing my legs at the ankles. "Well, if you insist." Glancing over at her, I reached up and rubbed between her shoulders.

The normally physically effusive woman I had come to love pulled away from my touch. Not violently, but with a firmness that was difficult to misinterpret. I looked at her, but she was staring straight ahead. She rolled her lips under her teeth and fidgeted in her seat. She opened her mouth to speak, but hesi-tated, and then closed it again.

It wasn't like Cadence to be hesitant. She possessed a unique brand of self-assurance that I had come to admire, an inner trust in herself to say and do the right thing. But something was wrong, now. Something was making her doubt. Something about me?

I dropped my hand to my side. I leaned away from her, studying her. There was distance between us. I wasn't sure how it had grown or who had put it there, but I could feel it gaping, threatening to swallow us whole.

"Cadence–" Her name came out in a halting stutter. "–is something wr–?"

"Everyone's been so kind." She interrupted me with an unusually nervous spurt of words. I looked down at her hands to see them wringing themselves in her lap. "So supportive." She stared down at the floor, focusing intently on nothing, her brow furrowed. "I really hope I don't mess this up."

I shook my head, blinking in confusion. "What, the agency?" I reached down and grasped one of her busy hands, squeezing. "No way you could, Cay. You're a natural detective! Once you get a couple more cases under your belt, word will spread, and you'll be beating the clients off with a stick." Looking her over carefully, I did my best to keep my voice light and jovial. "Never thought I'd live to see you worried."

For the first time in months, she leaned into me, resting in the crook of my body. She was so warm; I had almost forgotten how warm she could be. "I worry about a lot of things."

"Well," I said after a moment, my thumb rubbing small circles against the back of her hand. "The most important thing to remember is you're not alone." I gave her a small smile, jostling her shoulder with my own. "You know your friends are always going to be here for you."

She pulled away, and my body ached to feel her leave my side. She turned to look at me straight on. Her brow still furrowed, she reached up and cradled my cheek in one hand. "And you?"

I tilted my head into her hand, my skin buzzing from where she touched me. "Am I not a friend?"

She shook her head. "I'm not so sure anymore." Drawing closer to me, she brought her other hand up to the opposite side of my face. "Sometimes I look at you and I..." Her gaze lingered on my lips. She leaned in towards me, her voice lowering to a whisper. "Chance, would you...?"

Heart thudding in my chest, I sighed out, "Yes?"

She moved her hand down my cheek until the pad of her thumb rested on my bottom lip. I could not hide the shiver that went through me, both at the feel of her skin against mine and the look in her inky blue eyes, which held me trapped like an escaping prisoner caught in the beam of a searchlight.

Cadence blinked once, with a deliberateness that was impossible to miss.

She stood up in one fluid motion, her hands smoothing down the front of her scarlet skirt. "Would you help Henry and Oliver build the chairs downstairs? I think they need one more pair of hands."

I closed my eyes tight, one hand coming up to pinch the bridge of my nose as she walked away from me. "Yes, of course," I heard myself reply cheerily in a strained voice.

Waiting until the sound of her descending footsteps faded into the distance, I allowed myself to collapse sideways across her bed with a dramatic groan. What was I doing wrong? She had agreed that we should attempt a romantic relationship – so where was the pursuit? Where was the give and take of trust and affection? I wanted her badly, but it had become important to me that she made the first move. I no longer wanted to push past where she was comfortable -- I had done enough of that in our time together already.

I ground the heels of my hands into my eyes and jerked up into a seated position. Patience. I had to be patient. All would become clear in time.

In truth, the chairs downstairs required twenty pairs of hands, but we made do with what we had, eventually wrestling the furniture into submission. When the sun had almost disappeared behind the Römerian skyscrapers, Cadence pronounced that we had done more than enough for the day, and she released us from her service. Henry took off like a shot, promising to join me for dinner another time, claiming that he had some work to finish at Ergo Sum that was on a deadline. That left the Inspector and me to wander out onto the brightly lit streets of the Ani-District alone, after Cadence had extracted promises from us both to return next week to see the place "in all of its put-together glory."

We paused on the bottom step of the building, Brisbois to pull his packet of nixes from his trouser pockets, me to shake out my suit jacket.

"A day's honest work," I said, slipping my jacket up over my shoulders. Taking in a deep breath of crisp night air, I shook my head, smirking. "Now I understand why I've avoided it up to this point."

Next to me, Brisbois sparked up one of his imported nixes, but said nothing. I watched him from the corner of my eye, curious at his silence.

"Don't suppose I can tempt you to a drink at the *Anga's Head*?"

Brisbois sighed as if the weight of the planet had been placed squarely on his shoulders. Taking a long drag of his nix, he turned towards me, letting out the lungful of smoke as he spoke. "Chance... we've been on a first name basis for a very short time, so I hope you won't take this the wrong way, but–" He rolled the nix between his fingers and looked me over from head to foot. "What the hell is wrong with you?"

My mouth dropped open. A cough of laughter escaped from my throat. "Uh, excuse me?"

"She's there." Brisbois gestured up to the floor we had just left, pointing emphatically with his nix. "She's right *there*." Perching his nix at the corner of his mouth, he looked back down at me, eyes narrowing. "And you want to take *me* out for a drink?"

I felt my neck turn red and my face begin to flush in a rush of embarrassment. I did my best to cover it with ire, snarling, "I don't seem to remember asking for your advice, Inspector."

He ignored my pointed use of his title, barreling on. "Whatever you're afraid of, whatever she's afraid of, you both best move past it fast, because the only thing certain in this life is loss. You have each other now, damn it – enjoy it."

"Afraid?" My fingernails bit into my palm as my hands balled into fists at my side. "Damn you, I'm not afraid of anything!"

Brisbois, unimpressed as ever with my anger, shrugged and pinched the end of his nix between his fingers. "Really?" He started to walk down the street away from me. "Well then, there's nothing else for me to do but to wish you a very pleasant evening, Mr. Hale."

I watched him go, the anger roiling inside my chest. I opened my mouth to shout after him, stepping down off the bottom step of Cadence's building with the intent of following him, but, in a rare moment of self-reflection, I snapped my jaw shut.

What was I even so angry about? The man was wrong, plain and simple. After all Cadence and I had been through, there was no question of our belonging together, no doubt in my mind that we would be indelibly tied to each other forever. Where was the hurry? Everything would happen in its own time.

I turned on my heel and strode in the opposite direction of Brisbois, down the well-lit pedestrian pathways of the district, heedless of the encroaching darkness. What did he know about it anyway? If he was so in love with her, which he clearly was, why didn't he do something about it? If I was acting cowardly, which I most certainly was not, he was being downright craven.

The thought that I should call a PT to take me home nudged at the back of my mind, but I ignored it. I was far too worked up to sit in the back of some public transport vehicle for thirty minutes. No, a walk would do me good. Help clear my head of Brisbois's nonsense.

I was on the edges of the Ani-District when I hit a literal roadblock to my plans: a large flashing sign that declared that the walkway ahead had suffered water damage during the monsoon season and was undergoing repairs. A detour was suggested by a second bright green sign, an arrow that pointed down some darker side streets, and, with a sigh, I headed off in that direction, determined to see my plan through to the end.

The solar powered lamps that lit the public walkways on the main thoroughfare disappeared on these side streets, replaced by flickering string lights draped from windows and haphazardly placed ground lamps. In the growing darkness, it became difficult to see where one was stepping, but I soldiered on, vaguely aware of bodies moving around me in and out of doorways, sounds echoing from behind the walls of the old edifices that made up the district. The buildings were so tightly packed together that many of them were separated, not by streets, but by long, narrow alleys shrouded in impenetrable blackness.

Lost in my thoughts, I kept my head down as I walked, only vaguely aware of my surroundings. Slowly, I realized that I was passing others less and less. I straightened, suddenly alert, when I realized, I had somehow gotten turned around. I stepped away from the crushing blackness in front of me and turned, heading back towards the dim lights, when a sound reached my ears.

"Chance Hale?"

Instinctually and without thinking, I stopped and turned at the sound of my name.

What happened next would only become clear upon later reflection. I heard a thud behind me, as if something had fallen from a height. Before I could turn back around, a hand was over my mouth, and an arm was wrapped around my body, forcing me forward into the pitch dark. The hand smelled of hot rubber and a cocktail of saccharine, gag inducing chemicals. My assailant's arm trapped my own limbs to my sides like a clamp.

Struggling, I tried to shout, but to no avail. Dragged further into the dark, my eyes widened as they made out a second humanoid shape leaning against the steel wall of the building beside us.

"Have you got him?" hissed the shape in the darkness, straightening.

A low, rumbling voice from above my head chuckled in response. "Oh, he's not going anywhere."

The smaller shadowy figure pulled something out of their clothes and started towards me. "Well, keep him quiet!"

"Too bad." The deep, male voice behind me sounded legitimately put out. "I wanted to hear this one scream."

A low flying PT passed overhead. Its undercarriage lights flashed down on us for a split second – just long enough to glint off the edge of the butcher's knife in the hand of the person stepping towards me.

Working my jaws open, I wrenched my head forward and bit down hard into the palm of the hand that was covering my face. Blood spurted into my mouth, hitting the back of my throat. Howling, my captor flung me out of his grip, desperate to free himself from the thing causing him pain.

I flew forward, careening into my second attacker and knocking us both to the ground. The knife clattered out of his hand and skittered across the concrete. I scrambled towards it on my hands and knees but couldn't reach it before the slighter man launched himself at me, landing on my back. He wrapped his hands around my hips, flattening me.

We wrestled against each other and towards the knife -- all the while the large man cursed and wailed behind us.

"Fucking fuck! He bit my fucking hand! Like a goddamn fucking animal, what the fuck!"

The tips of my fingers brushed against the hilt of the knife. I pushed against a face I could not see, but before I could taste victory, the toe of a boot landed square in my groin. The world went purple, all dots and squiggles. Air left my lungs at a velocity

I had not previously thought possible, and my body curled in on itself like burning paper.

I heard the scrape of the knife coming up off the ground and I tried forcing myself past the exquisite pain radiating through my body. I rolled across the floor of the alley, hoping to hit the wall. But I didn't roll fast enough.

The blade sliced slantways through my flesh at the top of my right pectoral. In hindsight, it was a desperate slash -- I'm not even sure he realized where he'd hit me. But the wound went deep, and I felt muscle and blood vessels tear under the sharp edge of the blade. I screamed.

"Al, I'm fucking bleeding all over myself. Piece of shit bit me!"

"I heard you," shouted the smaller figure standing over me. He moved out of my line of sight, back towards the large man. "The whole neighborhood probably fucking heard you. Let's get out of here!"

3

Chapter 3

The slap of running feet reverberated through the concrete and into my aching, bloody body. When I could no longer hear or feel them, I tried to sit up and immediately regretted it -- the move sent a wave of nausea over me and a gush of blood down my chest. Still, I reasoned, the only way out was forward. I wasn't dead, and I intended to stay that way. I needed to keep moving.

I got to my feet, clutching my chest just below my shoulder, and walked to the entrance of the alleyway. The street was deserted. I looked up and saw a curtain twitch in a fifth story window of an apartment building. With my free hand, I reached into my coat pocket, hoping that my phone had remained undamaged enough for me to call the EO.

A thought flashed through my buzzing mind – this was the Ani District. I was Chance Hale. If I called the Enforcement Office now and told them what happened, the residents here would be given the third degree for weeks, if not months. Their lives turned upside down, even if they had nothing to do with it. Even if the people who attacked me were human, not animanecrons, the EO wouldn't hesitate to blame this on the Anis.

Breathing heavily, I leaned against the alleyway entrance. Blood seeped from between my fingers. If I couldn't go to the EO, then that meant I couldn't go to a hospital. I couldn't draw any more attention to myself than I already had. What was I going to do?

Cadence. I had to get back to Cadence. She would know what to do. She always knew what to do.

I tried to hurry back the way I came, but with every block I felt myself growing weaker. If I looked away from my feet, the world started to dance and spin before my eyes. So, I kept my gaze down, occasionally bumping into the odd passersby, excusing myself as best I could. My breath began coming out in short, shallow bursts.

By the time I rounded the corner back onto Lysander Street, the blood from my wound had soaked down the front of my shirt, seeping into the fine white fabric like rich red wine. I held my jacket shut over the horrific sight, anxious that no one should be alerted to my current plight.

Stumbling up the front steps, I pushed my way through the Wren Building's front doors. Up and up and up I went, my feet growing heavy and more leaden with every step, the stairs warping and sliding in my sight. Every pump of my heart was pushing me closer to total collapse, pushing more blood out of the gash in my chest, but I knew that I had to get to Cadence.

After what felt like an eternity, the mahogany brown portal

stood in front of me, looming like the entrance to a mausoleum. I pounded against the door with what was left of my strength, a broken staccato of thuds.

When there was no answer, I realized that I might have made a fatal mistake. Cadence, not needing to keep a regular sleep schedule, would often wander the city at all hours of the night and morning. It was more than likely that she was out taking in the sights of the new district to which she had moved. I groaned, resting my outstretched arm against the door jamb. What a stupid way to die...

The door opened. I lifted my head, my vision blurry.

Cadence stood in front of me, her brows drawn upward in perplexion, the corners of her mouth tugged downward in a frown. She was the most beautiful woman I had ever seen. I thought that every time I laid eyes on her, and even now, bleeding out on her doorstep, the thought flitted through my hazy mind.

"Chance?"

"You've got to insist that they fix the lift in this place," I managed, breathing in long, heaving gasps that only pulled at the wound in my chest.

I closed my eyes tight and collapsed on top of her. Immediately she absorbed my weight, holding me up by my shoulders, the tone of her voice shifting from confusion to panic.

"Ala! Chance!"

"Sorry," I muttered, my face smashed against her neck. I pushed with my free hand against her shoulder in an attempt to right myself. "Little...lightheaded..."

Her strong hands pulled me fully into the room. I heard the

front door slam shut behind me and, in the next moment, I was being propped up against it. I looked at my friend through wet, bleary eyes and noted with some concern that her shirt was smeared with blood. It didn't immediately register that it was my blood.

"Let me see," she demanded, shoving my jacket off my shoulders, and tossing it away with quick jerks that made me hiss in pain.

There was a dull throb as her fingers pushed at the edges of the gash. The fact that it wasn't a screaming flash of pain should have concerned me, but complex thoughts and emotions were beyond my grasp. I did note the deepness of her frown, the number of furrows in her forehead as she pronounced, "Frig, you've lost a lot of blood. I think your cephalic vein has been severed. What happened, Chance?"

"Cephalic..." I felt my body begin to slide down the door, my perspective of Cadence's face shifting from head-on to above me. "That... that sounds...important..."

Before I could hit the floor, Cadence wrapped her strong arms around me, one around my legs under the knees, the other coming around my shoulders. She lifted me into the air as if I weighed nothing at all, holding me close to her chest so my head could rest in the crook of her neck. "Come here," she said, moving us further into her office. "Don't worry, Chance: I've got you."

I had neither the strength nor the inclination to object to being carried like a sleeping child through the room, my hands laying limp in my lap. "Okay..." I breathed in deep, my parted lips brushing against her collarbone as I spoke. "You smell wonderful…"

Cadence carried me through the office to the small staircase. Taking the stairs two at a time, she was soon laying me out gently on the futon.

The world around me had gone filmy and pink, like looking through a camera that had a piece of colored cellophane over the lens. I closed my eyes, the effect making me nauseous; I preferred the black of my eyelids.

I felt Cadence's steady hands begin to unbutton my blood-soaked dress shirt, pulling it free from my trousers. "I'm going to take your shirt off, okay?"

I heard myself giggle from far away, as if I were simultaneously on the bed and standing in another room. "And not even buy me a drink?"

"Tio, maybe when you're feeling better, I will," she said without inflection, seemingly every one of her processors focused on the task at hand, rather than conversing with me.

"Tio…Tio…" I muttered the speech tag repeatedly, focusing on it when the pain flared again, forcing me to sit up slightly and twist. "I don't think you've used that one with me before…"

"Hyzit." The curse word clicked and hissed between her teeth with such vehemence I would've opened my eyes if I had been able to. "This is not good, Chance."

"Never did teach me those Animatum curse words…"

I felt the floor shudder as she hurried away for a moment, her heavy footfalls echoing through the quiet loft. "Don't die, and I will."

"Deal."

She returned to my side, and I felt her hovering over me, felt the tips of her hair tickling my bare chest. Something soggy and warm slid on top of the wound and I winced, letting out a few curses of my own.

"Keep pressure–" Cadence picked up my hands and placed them on top of what felt like a damp towel covering the gash in my chest. "–here. I'll be right back." She squeezed my right hand. "Don't pass out, okay?"

"Right." I nodded, still closing my eyes and pressing my lips together in a firm line. "Right, I won't…"

I felt her recede into the distance and heard her step on the stairs. The last thought that went through my mind before I lapsed into unconsciousness was how glad I was that I had gotten to see her one last time.

As per usual, I had been far too dramatic.

I woke slowly, drowsily -- stiffness in my limbs and an ache that ran through my entire body. For a moment, I forgot where I was and what had happened, and could only assume that I had gone on a bender for some reason and ended up passing out in a hotel. It'd been quite some time since I'd been that irresponsible. Not since…

I opened my eyes and turned my head to one side. Cadence's face was nestled close to mine on the pillow beside me. As my sea green eyes met her dark blue gaze, she began to breathe again, her lips parting ever so slightly. I smiled at her. She reached up and brushed a wayward strand of hair off my forehead, but her eyes never left mine. I wondered for a moment what she was looking for, what she was seeing. But I felt no fear at the thought. All of me was hers for the taking. Every last bit of me.

She blinked, and the innocuous movement stirred such deep affection within me that it momentarily took my breath away. Sighing, she rolled onto her back and stared up at the ceiling. "You passed out."

I cleared my throat and smacked my lips together, suddenly aware of the furry feeling coating my tongue. "Sorry."

"It's okay. Gave me a chance to get you cleaned up and get the blood off you." Cadence sat up in a cross-legged position next to me. She picked up a glass of water from beside the bed and helped me drink from it. Watching me swallow, she queried, "How do you feel?"

"Like I rode here on the front of a PT," I said, propping myself up on one elbow and looking down at my chest. I examined the sticky plaster pad, red already seeping through. A thought occurred to me, and I jerked my head up to stare at Cadence. "You didn't call the EO, did you?"

"No." Cadence let out a deep breath through her nose. "I assumed there was a reason you didn't."

Carefully working myself up into a sitting position, I told her the whole story. She listened quietly, her breathing ceasing when I described how I was restrained and dragged into the alley.

"I know things haven't been easy for people here," I said. "With the EO and everyone else just looking for excuses to cause trouble for animanecrons -- I didn't want to add fuel to the fire, so I decided to come here."

Cadence shook her head, letting out a long breath. "Well... I appreciate your desire to shield animanecrons from unjust persecution, Chance, but in this case—"

Exhausted and drained, I wiped chilled sweat off my brow,

frowning. "If it really was animanecrons, would I be alive right now?"

She opened her mouth to respond, but no words came out. She glanced from my face to the wound and then back to me. She pushed herself up onto her feet, unfolding with the grace of a trained dancer and skillfully dodging the question. "You need a hospital. Or at least a doctor -- that wound needs stitches."

Pressing a hand to the bandage, I gave the problem a moment's earnest consideration. I looked up at Cadence from under my brow. "Do you have a medkit?"

"Yes? Wh–?" My intentions became clear. She took a step back, contorting her face into a deep frown. "Ala, you cannot be serious."

Clicking my tongue off the top of my mouth, I reached up and squeezed her wrist, pulling her back towards me. "I doubt I could find steadier hands than yours." I laid back down flat on my back, attempting to make myself comfortable. "Come on, it'll be a fun bonding activity."

The medkit was buried inside one of the unpacked moving crates. Cadence insisted on doing a quick vertex search on stitching wounds, just to make sure that she wasn't going to, as she put it, "damage my system irrevocably." I waited patiently through this, blood continuing to seep through my bandage.

I'll admit to feeling a surge of annoyance when she again asked:

"Are you sure you want me doing this?"

I opened my eyes and glared up at her, the throbbing in my chest doing wonders to upset my usually even-keeled demeanor. "I was sure the last three times you asked, Cay."

She sat over me, biting her lip, fiddling with the needle. "What if I break you?"

I propped myself up on my elbow without thinking. The motion pulled at the wound causing me to snap, "Stop saying that!" I sighed as the flash of pain subsided. "Look, I have every confidence in you." My smile felt frayed, but it was the best I could muster.

It elicited a frown from my tense companion, and she pushed me back down onto my back with a hint of vindictiveness. "I want you to remember those words when I drain you of what little blood you have left." Her hands fluttered in front of her face. "You think you'd have a reserve storage of that fluid somewhere, seeing that you can't survive without it."

"If you do kill me, I'll have a word with the Creator about the next model. Can we get on with this please?"

Her warm hand squeezed my shoulder and I hissed. She pulled away. "I have to wait for the local anesthetic to kick in."

A moment or two after she spoke, numbness rippled down my chest like a glass of water. I turned my head to see what she was doing, caught one glance at the wickedly sharp needle in Cadence's hand, and pushed my head back into the pillows.

"Did you see your attackers at all?"

"It was pitch black in that alleyway. So, no." Pressure on my skin. I closed my eyes, trying not to imagine what was going on. "I would've thought that was painfully obvious."

"Anno, I quite literally have a weapon in your flesh, Chance -- perhaps it would be best if you ceased with the cheek." Her words were sharp, but the pressure on my pectoral remained steady and firm. "I mean, did you see anyone before you were attacked: a stranger following you, someone paying too close attention to your movements, anything like that."

"No. Nothing." I opened my eyes and stared up at the ceiling, frowning. "I just don't understand. What would anyone have against me? Especially an animanecron."

There was a pregnant silence in which the sound of thread sliding through flesh was clearly audible. Cadence cleared her throat. "You... you are the head of Halcyon Enterprises, Chance."

I didn't care for the faint accusation behind her words, but I cared even less for the sense of guilt that flared up in the pit of my stomach. My frown deepened and I waved my good hand through the air. "So? We've come out in support of Whiston every time a proposal has come up in the IPC. We're working hard to undo the damage–"

"You don't have to convince me," said Cadence, cutting me off with a shake of her head. I watched the needle rise and fall again and again, the thread growing shorter every time. "But to a lot of animanecrons, Halcyon is..."

I watched her, my heart beginning to pound harder in my chest. "Is what, Cay?"

She sighed heavily. "It's part of the problem." There was a tinny clatter as she dropped the bloody needle onto the floor. "Or has always been the problem." She leaned over me, her gaze focused on her work. I felt more pressure, this time her fingers as she tied off the stitches. "It's complicated." Leaning back, Cadence reached into the medkit and pulled out a small pair of silver scissors. She snipped at the thread. "There. Let me put a fresh bandage on it."

I risked a glance down at myself and was pleased to see a

row of evenly spaced stitches running across my angry, red skin. "It looks–"

"Horrendous."

"I was going to say, 'great.' I doubt a doctor could have done better."

"Hila, well, that's blood loss for you. Affects your judgment." Cadence ripped the non-stick backing off the edges of a large fluffy piece of gauze. She covered the stitches, pressing the gauze firmly against the wound. "I did what I could."

I wrapped my hand around her wrist and squeezed. "You did wonderful."

She looked into my eyes. "Sinc, Chance: are you sure you don't want to call the EO?"

"Yes," I said, sitting up fully and shaking my head. "They'd just make everything worse."

Cadence tapped her familiar rhythm of attachment against the back of my hand. My breath caught in my throat -- it felt like months since she'd last indicated her feelings for me in such a fashion, and I had begun to think she would never do so again. But here it was: her binary beats drummed against my skin like an erratic pulse. She kept her eyes locked with mine. "Whoever it is, Chance... They're not going to stop."

I swallowed hard. "So? Find them."

"Who? Me?" Her jaw went slack. "You want me... I'm sorry, what are you asking me? Or are you telling me..."

Grinning, I chuckled and shook my head at her incredulous expression. "I'm hiring you, Cay."

Cadence leaned forward, the excitement clear in her sharp face. "Curio, really?!"

"I'll be your first client." I placed my hand on her knee. "There's no one I'd trust with my life more."

"Oh, Chance! Thank you!" Her smile blossoming over her lips like a honeysuckle in sunshine, she reached forward and grabbed me by my shoulders, squeezing me tightly. "Sinc, I won't let you down. I promise."

"You never have," I said, smiling.

Before I could say another word, she jerked forward and pressed her lips firmly against my own.

At first, I was too stunned to do anything at all, my hands frozen and my eyes wide with shock. But when I felt the tip of her tongue press exploratorily against my lips, when she moved so close to me that she was almost in my lap, I began to melt into the moment. I closed my eyes and reached up to cradle her face in my hands.

She broke the kiss first -- moving her head back fraction by fraction, loosening her hold on my lips until I was free of her.

I had never hated freedom so much.

She leaned forward, resting her forehead against my own, her lips close, but not quite touching mine.

"Thank you, Chance," she whispered the words against the corner of my mouth.

I trailed my fingers down her jawline, tapping out the rhythm that she had first taught me. "Cay, have I told you lately how utterly and incomprehensibly beautiful you are?"

The feel of her fingers against my chest, the heat of her breath against my lips -- it was all too much and not enough at the same time. I could feel myself begin to quiver under her touch, trying in vain to contain how I felt, even as I moved her closer to me, my hands sliding towards the small of her back. "Cadence, you–"

"You're shivering." Concern laced her words. She pulled away from me, her eyes roaming over me. I watched as she took a deep breath, which was when I noticed that she hadn't been breathing before. "You... you must be freezing. The loss of blood..."

I felt the moment begin to slip away and I clung to her with desperation, closing my eyes as I shook my head. "I'm fine, it's not–"

But it was too late. I could do nothing to hold her there. She stood up and stepped away from me, her hands covering her cheeks. "I'm so sorry. I'll get an extra blanket." She hurried to the stairs, freezing with her foot hovering over the top step. Staring down at her feet, she swallowed visibly. "I... Apol, I'm sorry."

Staring at her as she descended out of sight, my mind boggled at her apology. For what did Cadence have to ask forgiveness? Especially from me, of all people on the sphere? But the sadness in her voice, the guilt in her eyes... her regret was sincere.

I took a deep breath and, with slow, measured movements, laid myself back onto the futon. Perhaps this was the reason for her reluctance – she felt that she had done something wrong. In loving me? If she did love me, I reminded myself. So far, I had been the only one to profess such a depth of feeling, at least in words. Cadence had not, at least not in any language I could understand. I screwed my eyes shut and took another deep breath, focusing on the sensation of the duvet against my bare skin.

Maybe she was sorry that she didn't love me back.

My heart shuddered and threatened to break. I reached up and pushed my hand through my hair, groaning. If she didn't love me, how could she kiss me like that? It didn't make any sense. None of it made any sense.

I'm not sure how, amid these thoughts, I managed to fall asleep. But I had lost quite a lot of blood and the human body can only take so much. The next thing I was aware of was warm light attempting to fight its way past my closed eyelids.

Blinking back to wakefulness, I shaded my face from the shaft of sunlight that had fallen across it. I gave a grunt of displeasure at having been so rudely disturbed from slumber and was about to turn over and fall back asleep when I became aware of the weight of eyes on me. I dropped my hand onto the mattress and twisted my head around to squint at a figure, framed in sunshine, sitting in the rolling desk chair.

Cadence was watching me. She had changed clothes from last night, and was lounging in a light, ankle length blue dress, patterned with white flowers.

"Cay?" I tried to sit up, but the anesthetic from the medkit had fully worn off in my sleep and my wound throbbed. I screwed my mouth up in a grimace as I shook my head clear of cobwebs. "How long have you been sitting there?"

Cadence glanced over her shoulder at the clock projected on the desktop from her computer. She shrugged. "Not long. A few hours." She shifted in the chair and pulled a folded piece of paper out of her pocket. "I went to the alleyway where you were attacked. I found this on the ground. There's a chance one of your attackers dropped it." She unfolded the paper and shoved it towards me, finger tapping a dark brown smear that ran down the length of one edge. "See? I think that's your blood."

I took the paper from her with a lurch of disappointment

in the pit of my stomach. It seemed we weren't going to talk about last night. Right to business. Fine. If that was the way she wanted it...

The sheet was thick and bumpy between my fingers, clearly a bit of recycled pulp, something that had been stitched together from a mishmash of reused paper. Cheap and biodegradable, you often found such things plastered against streetlamps and stuck to building cork boards; people still used the archaic leaflet method to get the word out about various civic events, politics, and the like.

This paper was a virulent neon green and covered in a blocky script. At first, I thought it to be some kind of Hangul, but upon trying to read it, I found it was anything but -- the markings marched around the edges of the paper, blotted out on the right-hand side by dried brown blood, and further obscured by the fact that the bottom left corner had been torn off. The center of the page sported a simple line drawing of a series of trapezoidal shapes laid on top of one another, with line bursts behind them, as if representing fireworks.

"What is this?"

"It's a flier from Ergo Sum," Cadence said. "They're having a block party and open house today for the new section of Ani-built housing down by the docks. I think we should go and see if we can find someone in the community who may harbor a special grudge against you."

With a firm nod, I tossed off my blankets and stood up. "Well! Sounds like as good a place to start as any." The chill of the loft immediately assaulted my bare chest, and I looked down at myself. My trousers were bloodstained, dirty, and torn. I pressed my lips into a thin line and cast about myself. "Er..."

"Oh, here." Cadence swiveled around in a circle and re-appeared with a green duffle bag in her outstretched hands. "I took a PT to your place. Packed a bag of your things from your closet."

I took the bag from her slowly, my brow furrowing. "You went to my flat?"

She nodded. I grimaced and unzipped the duffel. Inside was an array of my clothes. "But... How did you get in? The locks are coded to my DNA."

"It wasn't hard." She gestured to the rubbish bin beside the desk, which I now saw was stuffed with a ruined, bloodstained towel. "I had plenty of your DNA from last night."

I shook my head. "I've got to invest in some better security." I pulled a red long-sleeved shirt out of the bag with one hand, dropping the bag to the floor.

"I think you should stay here for a few days. Take some time off work. Just until we get this figured out."

Scoffing, I pushed my arms through the shirt's sleeves. "Oh, Miss Taylor will just love that."

Cadence's head fell to one side. "Who?"

"My executive admin," I said, pulling the shirt down over my torso. "I'll call her and let her know."

With a growl, my stomach reminded me that I had never gotten dinner last night -- too busy getting slashed in dark alley-ways. From the look of the sun in the sky outside I had also missed breakfast. I patted my belly and frowned at Cadence, lifting a brow. "I don't suppose you have anything to eat?"

"Haven't gotten around to food for guests yet." She stood, stretching her arms up over her head. "I'll pick you up something on the way. Are you going to get changed or not?"

Smirking, I began to unfasten my trousers, my blonde mop of hair falling into my eyes. "Can't remember the last time someone fed me after I spent the night in their bed."

"Sarc, it's all part of the service." I looked up to catch sight of Cadence starting down the stairs. "Come down when you're ready. The block party should be starting soon."

4

Chapter 4

Ergo Sum's goal to build apartments specifically designed for animanecrons had finally come to fruition. A full block of Hutton Avenue, a mile away from the Mawson Dock Transport Hub, had been transformed by the new, gleaming trapezoid buildings. Their slanting roofs were covered in solar panels, powering those special amenities that every animanecron had missed since the Whiston Offensive began: cooling stations, high speed vertex hubs, and more. But most importantly, the buildings represented the culmination of a new community -- a place where animanecrons could rebuild their lives amongst themselves. To start over.

The public walkways and PT lanes teemed with animanecrons and humans. The complexes' front doors and windows were all open, and people were visible in every space. Beneath the trees that lined the walkways, Ergo Sum had set up informational tables. These were staffed with volunteers, who were chatting animatedly with all those who stopped by to learn more about the magnificent work being done by the grassroots organization.

Music danced through the air, mixing and swelling with the jumbled sounds of Animatum and Common Tongue. As we strolled through the crowd, I spotted several partygoers dancing and laughing. If it weren't for the persistent ache in my chest, it would have been difficult to imagine that anyone here could have any ill-intent.

"Cadence," I said, pushing my hands into the pockets of my black jeans. "I'm not even sure what we're looking for."

Cadence let out a sharp breath through her nose. "Well, I suppose we should start talking–"

"Hey, you two!"

The bellow was loud and familiar. We turned to see Henry fighting his way through a crowd on the opposite side of the street. "Chance, Cadence!" He waved to us and, freeing himself from the group blocking his way, broke out into a jog in our direction. Beaming, he pulled up short and immediately swept me up into a hug. "Hello! I wasn't expecting to see you here today! Thought you'd both be too busy with work."

"Oh! Careful!" I exclaimed, flinching in his tight embrace, the stitches pulling at my skin.

Henry released me quickly, quirking his eyebrows up in question. "Sorry, Chance – you hurt yourself moving those boxes yesterday?"

"Not exactly," said Cadence, waiting patiently for her turn in Henry's embrace. "I'm afraid it's work that's brought us here, actually."

"Oh?" Henry extended an arm out to Cadence and folded her to his chest, but his gaze remained fixed on me. "Chance's, or...?"

I relayed the story of my bloody misadventure as quietly as I could, wary of being overheard. But when I got to the part about deciding to go to Cadence's office instead of calling the EO for help, Henry, seemingly unable to control himself any longer, exploded.

"Chance, you idiot!" he exclaimed, his brown eyes wide. "What were you thinking? You could've died!"

"I don't think it was that bad," I hissed, glancing at the crowd around us. Throwing my arm over Henry's shoulder, I attempted to lead him to a less crowded section of the block, but he shook me off before we had gotten more than a few steps, his concern manifesting as anger.

"Not that – not that bad? Someone came at you with a knife!" he growled, his hands flying up into the air in exasperation.

I pulled at his elbows, forcing his arms down to his side. "Keep your voice down, chum."

He scowled at me, hands flexing in and out of fists. "You should go to a hospital."

"That's what I said," chimed Cadence, her arms crossed low over her stomach.

"I'm fine." I tutted at Henry's incredulous scoff, gesturing to the bandaged stitches hidden under my shirt. "Really! Cadence got me all patched up."

"Then you should go to the Enforcement Office," he countered.

"I also said that," added my companion, lifting her pointer finger into the air.

I shook my head. "I don't want to get the EO involved. EO

means press, press means more bad publicity for animanecrons, and that's one thing this community does not need right now. There's enough ani-fear out there already -- this would just make it worse."

"Chance, while I appreciate your allyship," said Cadence, frowning and leaning in close so that she would not be overheard. "I feel I should remind you: this is your life we're talking about."

I mimicked her stance. "I still don't think it was an animanecron behind that knife, Cay." Turning to face my childhood friend, I swept my arm out towards the animanecrons and humans who surrounded us. "Henry, have you heard anything during your work with Ergo Sum? About me, Halcyon, anything like that?"

Henry's face fell. He swallowed and cast a worried glance at my inorganic companion.

I placed a reassuring hand on his wrist. "It's alright. Cadence already mentioned that the feelings in the community were mixed."

"At best." Henry gave me a threadbare smile. "That's certainly one way to put it." He started to head over towards the new housing units, gesturing for us to follow. "Cadence can correct me if I'm wrong, but from what I've learned, Halcyon Enterprises wasn't particularly well-regarded by animanecrons, even before the Whiston Offensive."

"Really?" I glanced over at Cadence, curious to see her assessment of this statement.

Cadence stared back, unblinking. "How would you feel if your parents had disowned you, and kicked you out of the house?"

I resisted the urge to relate to her the numerous occasions upon which my father had come perilously close to doing just that. Instead, I drew my hand down my chin, nodding. "Pretty sore about it, I suppose."

"Halcyon Enterprises made us," she stressed the last two words, her hand pressed flat against her collarbone. "They made us for a purpose, and when we exceeded that purpose – when we started to decide our own purpose – they let humans treat us like pariahs."

I swallowed hard and avoided my animanecron friend's pointed glare. "That... well, that was several hundred years ago, now."

Rolling her eyes, Cadence clicked her tongue off the roof of her mouth. "We have very long memories."

"But surely we've gained some good will, over the last few months at the very least," I insisted. "We've worked hard to lobby the IPC on behalf of Whiston in the Charcornacian conflict, sent aid packages to pro-animanecron groups–"

Cadence cut me off with a shake of her head. "Political expediency." She shrugged, dismissing all that I and my company had done. "Halcyon saw which way the wind was blowing and happened to choose the right side of history this time."

"But..." My shoulders fell. "That's – that's just not so."

Henry stopped, leaning his hips back against one of the tables on which someone had put out informational cubes about Ergo Sum. "I know that." He gestured to Cadence. "She knows that." Leaning forward, he tapped the center of my chest with his finger. "And you know that. But most of the animanecron community don't know you, Chance. Not as a person. All they see is the company, and the company has a lot of bad blood to make up for."

I looked from Henry to Cadence. "So, what can I do?" I rubbed the back of my neck, my eyes fluttering shut. "How do we change this perception? Of Halcyon – of me?"

Henry shook his head, chuckling. "You should ask your marketing department, not me."

"Whatever you do, it's going to be an uphill battle," said Cadence. She gestured to the crowd around us, her brows lifting over her wide eyes. "The bottom line is that most animanecrons don't trust humans. We may be living beside you now, but that doesn't mean we like it any more than you do."

There was a soft jingle of laughter from beside us. We turned as one body, noticing for the first time that we were within earshot of someone else, someone who had heard at least part of our conversation.

"Sorry, I couldn't help but listen in," said the volunteer at the nearest signup station. They stepped out from behind their fleet of projected screens, hands falling into the pockets of their tight tan slacks. "But your friend has a point. Some animanecrons' animosity towards humans run deep – they find accepting even the kind of support Ergo Sum offers distasteful."

Henry jumped as if someone had shocked him with a livewire. He flushed visibly, the center of his cheeks turning rosy. "Rin! I thought you were supposed to be at court today."

"I was," said Rin, adjusting their lens-less glasses further up their narrow nose as they smiled. "But I got Gina to swap cases with me so that I could be here."

Henry nodded profusely, the tip of his tongue sneaking out

to wet his lips. I cleared my throat and he jumped again, turning an even deeper shade of pink. "Oh," he exclaimed. He stood back and threw his hand out towards Cadence and me. "Uh, Rin Murata, this is Chance Hale and Cadence Turing."

"Pleased to meet you," said Rin, shaking my hand firmly before exchanging a traditional animanecron greeting with Cadence, bowing low. They laughed as they straightened, straight white teeth flashing against skin the color of a freshly made sandcastle. "Henry talks about you both so much, I feel like we've met already!"

I slid my hands into my jeans pockets and rolled up onto the balls of my feet, smiling broadly. "Does he?"

"Oh yeah." Rin's smile grew wider, and they shook their swooping black bangs out of their umber eyes. "Every time we hang out, it's Chance said this, and Cadence did that." They knocked Henry's arm with their shoulder, the shorter person staring up into my tall friend's face. "It's really cute."

"He is adorable, isn't he?" I agreed, reaching up to ruffle his hair.

"Lay off," demanded Henry, jerking away from me with a scowl.

"Urio, how long have you worked for Ergo Sum, Rin?" asked Cadence, clasping her hands behind her back.

Rin scrunched up their nose. "'Worked for' is a bit of a misnomer – they don't pay me anything. I've volunteered with them for almost a year now. But what puts a roof over my head and food in my belly is the law. I'm a public defender. Mostly I work out of the 62nd District Court."

I nodded, impressed to meet a lawyer of their caliber at this event. "And what inspired you to throw in with the animanecron cause?"

"Easy: I wanted to do something that made a difference. I believe that what has happened, what is happening, and what will probably continue to happen to animanecrons is wrong." They took a deep breath and let it out slowly. "They really are brilliant people with a vibrant culture – it shouldn't be on the verge of erasure. They don't need our help, so much as they need us to stop hurting them."

"Rin works a lot in the education and outreach side of things," said Henry, smiling down at his coworker with a softness that did not escape my attention.

"Yeah, I've gotten pretty deeply entrenched with the Ani community in Römer -- trying to bridge the gaps between them and humans where I can." Rin rolled their shoulders back, frowning in thought. "Humanity has always tried to stamp out what it doesn't understand. The hope is that with greater acceptance, animanecrons will be able to thrive again."

I opened my mouth to respond but was interrupted when someone from across the street shouted Rin's name. Rin glanced over their shoulder and shouted back, "Coming!" They sighed. "Well, I better get back to work." Rin turned so they were facing Henry, their hands coming out to rest on their hips. "Henry, will I see you later?"

"Mmhm." Henry, avoiding my gaze, rubbed at the back of his neck.

Rin smiled, a crooked sort of grin, and maneuvered themselves so they could look directly into Henry's eyes. "Yeah? You sure?"

"Yeah," said Henry, nodding, still not looking anyone else in the face.

"Hm..." They reached up and adjusted their glasses, still smiling. "You know, you don't sound very sure."

Rin lifted themselves up on their tiptoes, wrapped their arms around Henry's neck, and pulled him down into a deep kiss. Henry struggled to keep his balance for a moment, a muffled exclamation turning into a sigh as his stuttering arms fell limply to his sides.

The pair stayed that way, locked in an amorous embrace for a solid ten seconds before Rin drew back, resting their forehead against Henry's.

"I'll see you later," Henry said quietly, gaze locked on Rin, his voice thick in his throat.

"Now, you sound sure," Rin said, in a near whisper. They planted a final peck on Henry's cheek before releasing their hold on him. They turned back to face Cadence and I, waving as they walked backward towards their station. "Bye, you two; it was nice to meet you!"

"Nice to meet you!" called Cadence after them, waving back.

I, personally, was watching Henry, a blithe smile on my face. With every step Rin took away from us, Henry's eyes lost their dreamy glaze, and it was with a start that he noticed me staring at him. Scowling, he crossed his arms high over his chest. He rolled his eyes, his jaw clenching. He tried to glare, but the effect was diminished by the deep blush that climbed up his neck to the tips of his ears.

"Stop it," he said, his voice as dark as his expression.

"I didn't say anything," I protested.

He squeezed his eyes shut, massaging the bridge of his nose with his fingertips. "Just – just stop."

I threaded my arm through Cadence's and pulled her closer to me. "Cay, did I say anything?"

Cadence shook her head, first at me and then at Henry, her eyes wide with sincerity. "No -- Henry, he didn't say anything."

There was a moment of silence, just the width of a heartbeat, and then Cadence said, "So, how long have you and Rin been kissing?"

Breaking out in a near run, Henry made a beeline for the open front doors of the apartment building behind us, cursing under his breath.

Cadence, her brow furrowed, her mouth pursed, turned to me, her hand fluttering up to her chest. "Did I say–?"

"You're fine -- Henry's just a big awkward lug." I started after him, turning around so that I could continue talking with Cadence, even as I stepped backwards after my retreating friend. "I'll get him back; you chat around a bit, see what you can pick up about who might have come after me last night."

Cadence nodded, but her concerned expression remained.

I followed in Henry's wake, trotting up the wide front steps of the apartment complex and stopping just inside the entryway. Glancing around the milling bodies that surrounded me, I went with my gut and headed to the left, where there were less people overall, and followed the hallway to a flat whose door was partially ajar.

Pushing the door open with my foot, I ducked my head inside. "Henry?"

There was no response, but my keen ears picked up the

shuffle of shoes. Nodding to myself, I strolled into the flat. It was unfurnished and spotless, the carpet a beautiful cream color that played well with the eggshell-blue walls. "Henry, come on. I know you're in here."

Still no response. I wandered through the living room and headed for the kitchen. In a human apartment, it would have been considerably larger, but here it was scarcely bigger than a bathroom, with only the barest necessities required for cooking. I found Henry squished between the wall and the refrigerator, puffing on a nix he had gotten from God-knows-where, the smoke floating out the window to his right. I smirked and leaned against the fridge door.

"Smoking?" I plucked the nix out of his mouth and pulled on it myself. Shaking my head, I let the smoke drift out of my mouth as I said, "Your mother will have a fit."

Henry bristled, his entire body tensing as he drew himself up to his full height before rounding on me, his hand in the air. "I swear, one smart remark out of you, Chance Tobias Hale, and I'll– I'll–"

I burst out laughing, and the sound of it seemed to stop him mid-rant. I threw my arm around his shoulder and tugged him tight against my side. "Henry, do I have to kiss you too? Is that the only way to get you to relax?"

I felt his taut frame slacken beneath me. "You kiss me, and I'm telling Cadence."

"Ooo, cheeky!" I teased, rifling my hand through his hair until it was well and thoroughly mussed.

He squirmed free, the ghost of a smirk playing around the corner of his lips.

When we had both composed ourselves again, I passed the nix back to him, smiling. "In all seriousness, dear boy, Rin seems very nice."

Henry looked at the half-smoked black cylinder, considering it with far more solemnity than it deserved. "They are." Taking in a deep breath, he leaned back, his head thudding against the drywall. "I've never met anyone like Rin." I watched as he swallowed hard, his Adam's apple bobbing. "They... they make me feel..."

"Less alone? Like you belong somewhere?"

Henry lifted his head off the wall and stared at me, his eyes widening. I snorted out a laugh and looked away from him, digging into my pocket to extract a nix of my own. "They make you feel like all your flaws and all your idiosyncrasies are okay. That you're finally good enough." I twisted the end of the nix to set it smoking. "It's all enough."

We stood in silence, smoking, with my words floating in the air between us. I felt a momentary thrill of embarrassment, of vulnerability, but shook it away. This was Henry I was talking to – if anyone could understand how I felt, it was him.

After a few minutes, Henry gave a defeated sigh. "So. It's love then?"

"Afraid so," I said. I took a drag off my nix and turned to blow the smoke out the open window. "Why didn't you bring them around; introduce them? Not worried I'd steal them away from you, were you?"

That, at last, got a chuckle out of my old friend. He shook his head. "No, no – it wasn't that." He scratched his cheek, wincing a little. "Honestly, I haven't known Rin all that long. It's been very...sudden." His eyes drifted heavenward. "Not like me at all, really."

I joined him in his ceiling-gazing, smacking my lips. "I remember there was that girl at university – what was her name? Red hair, all down her back? Green eyes?"

Henry nodded. "Vanessa."

I snapped my fingers. "Vanessa!" I smiled in remembrance. "You wrote her verses for half a year before you got up the nerve to say hello face to face." I perched my nix between my lips and nudged him with my elbow. "Patience. That's something you've always had that I've lacked."

"Rin wouldn't have stood for anything like that," said Henry. He flushed, smiling. "They would've tracked me down and forced a date out of me after the first poem."

I frowned. "Are you sure we didn't get it mixed up somewhere? Have you got my lover and I've got yours?"

Henry gave a derisive snort. "Not a chance, chum." He pointed out the window, eyes narrowed. "That one? She's made for you."

I looked in the direction he was pointing and saw Cadence standing on the public walkway in front of the apartment complex. Standing in profile, she seemed deep in conversation with a group of smiling women, each with their tattoo-like PCBs on full display, as was customary for animanecrons.

Her own PCB was hidden beneath her dress, a phoenix in black on the small of her back. I often wondered at her decision to vary from this cultural norm -- to keep hidden something that others seemed so proud of. It had been one of the first things I had noticed about her almost a year ago on the train from

Mawson Docks. One of the first things that drew me to her, that made me look closer at what was an already-stunning woman.

Bringing my nix away from my mouth, I stepped closer to the window, drawn to her, as I always had been – as I always would be. Her long, wavy black hair was piled in a messy bun on the back of her head, strands of it kissing her cheeks and the nape of her neck. Her piercing dark eyes moved over the faces of the animanecrons in front of her, her pink lips moving rapidly as she conversed in her native tongue.

Henry moved to stand beside me. "Have you talked to her yet?" he pressed.

I glared at him from the side of my eyes, but even I could tell it lacked bite. "I've been a bit busy trying not to die."

"Well," said Henry, lifting his brows at me. "No time like the present, and all that."

"We're kind of in the middle of something," I responded, shifting from foot to foot.

He rolled his eyes. "You're always going to be in the middle of something." He took hold of my shoulders, spun me around and gave me a push towards the flat's front door. "Go on. I'll be here to pat you on the back and tell you what a good job you did when you're done."

Stumbling, I grimaced at his sarcasm. "You can be a right bastard sometimes, you know that?"

A smile was his response. "Yeah," he said with a shrug. "Now, go."

5

Chapter 5

Henry was right, of course, as he so often was. I told him that I would catch up with him later and wandered out of the apartment building. Taking in a steadying breath, I headed towards Cadence, who now conversed with a short animanecron woman with a shaved head. I could see white light, dim in the sun, illuminating the shape of a nautilus that covered half her scalp.

I came to a halt a few steps behind Cadence, mindful of not interrupting her conversation. I had been making a study of Animatum, with my dear friend's help, but the rapid exchange of clicks and trills between the two women in front of me was impossible for a neophyte like me to follow. Based on intonation alone, I could infer that Cadence was posing questions, the other woman answering with smiles and nods. Smiles and nods that ceased the moment she noticed me. Her dark brown face screwed up into a sour scowl, like she had just smelled something foul. She reached forward and jerked Cadence away from me, consonants hissing between her teeth.

Cadence stumbled forward, glancing behind her to see from what she was being rescued. Upon seeing me, she began shaking her head, pulling her arm free from the shaved-head woman's grip, gesturing between me and herself while she spoke.

I stepped forward, attempting to put on my most friendly and open expression.

Grimacing, the woman pulled her bag close to her chest before spitting at my feet.

I felt the globule of expectorant land on the toe of my shoe. I didn't look down, but kept my gaze steady on the woman's face, my own visage frozen in the half-smile I had adopted prior to this demonstration of her disgust.

We stood there, staring at each other, until Cadence started to say something in Animatum, which seemed to remind the shaved-headed woman she was not alone with me. The woman jerked her head towards Cadence, waved off her words, and turned the opposite direction, striding with purpose.

I watched the woman as she walked away, popping my lips away from my teeth, my eyes half-lidded. "I'm guessing that she's not a fan of mine."

"Uh, no. Not really." Cadence took in a deep breath, turning towards me but not meeting my gaze. "Listen, this might work better if I was alone."

I looked around at the animanecrons and became suddenly aware that I was being watched by a fair few of them -- some with curious stares, but far more with barely concealed scowls, their fists at their sides. My heart plummeted into the pit of my stomach, and I dropped my gaze to the ground, feeling naked and exposed. "They really hate me that much, eh?"

I felt her hand land on my shoulder and give a firm squeeze. "I don't hate you, if that helps any."

"Are you sure?" I said, lifting my head to look at her.

She blinked several times in rapid succession. "Sure of what?"

Placing my hand on top of her own, I dropped my shoulders so the only thing supporting her appendage was the fact that I was holding it. "Are you sure that you don't hate me?"

"Chance!" Her tone was admonishing, but she slipped her hand out of my grasp all the same, looking away from my face with a guilty dart of her eyes that I couldn't help but notice. "Don't be ridiculous."

"Cadence," I said, my jaw tightening. "Something is wrong. I've barely seen you in months, and when I do see you, you're so..." The word escaped me for a moment, but as she took a small step back, it became clear in my mind. "...so distant." I placed my hand flat against my chest. "Did I do something wrong?"

As I watched, Cadence rubbed at her bare arms as if cold, something that I knew to be practically impossible. She shook her head from side to side, slowly at first, but soon with vehemence. She licked her lips, closed her eyes for a moment and then opened them wide. Cadence put her hands up in front of her in a gesture of surrender, head still shaking. "Look, I can't talk about this right now. I'm in the middle of a case." She turned and walked away from me into the crowd.

"And when are we going to talk about it?" I pressed, striding after her.

"Later." She shot the word at me over her shoulder, her pace increasing incrementally.

"Later when, Cay?"

"When I know that you're safe!" She spun around, stopping with such suddenness that I stumbled over my own feet in my attempt to avoid running into her. "When I know that someone isn't going to stick another knife in you! Is that good enough?"

The anger in her words shocked and chastened me. I stared at her for a full thirty seconds before realizing that I wasn't the only one – her raised voice had drawn the attention of more than a few of the animanecrons standing nearest to us. Feeling my face flush, I looked away from her, jaw clenching in time with my fists.

I heard her sigh, and I looked up to see her toss her head in the direction of the end of the block. "Reg, head back to the office, okay?" Pulling my hand towards her, she slapped her archaic metal key into my open palm. "I'll meet you there when I'm done here."

I watched her walk away, curling my fingers around the key until it pressed painfully into my flesh. I felt sorely used indeed – and being dismissed in such a fashion was a unique experience for me. It was not one I enjoyed.

After leaving the block party without seeking out Henry again, I soon entered Cadence's office-cum-flat, slamming the door shut behind me. Little did I know that not only would Cadence not return that afternoon, but that she would not return in the evening, leaving me to stew and feel particularly useless all night.

I didn't deserve to be treated like this -- I had made mistakes in my relationship with Cadence, that much was certain, but I had done my best to rectify them. I had thought, genuinely thought, that we were both committed to moving forward, to leaving the past in the past and seeing what the future might hold. Could I have been wrong? Was the only person who saw a future for us the one sleeping fitfully in Cadence's bed while she was out investigating to her heart's content?

A knocking sound woke me from my nonrestorative slumber. I rolled out of the futon, still in my clothes from the day before, and stumbled downstairs. The knocking was coming from the front door, and I scowled at it. Swinging the door open, I shook my head, determined to give Cadence a piece of my mind.

"Where the hell have–?"

Inspector Oliver Brisbois stood on the doorstep, a bouquet of yellow tulips and daisies held out in front of him.

"Oh." I cleared the words I had prepared for Cadence out of my throat, blinking at the man in front of me. "Hello, Oliver."

He blinked back. Whatever he had done to mentally prepare for this moment had clearly backfired with my appearance. I made note of his carefully pressed dress slacks, the scent of pheromone spray that just wafted in through the doorway, and, finally, really looked at the bouquet in his hand.

With infinitesimal slowness, I rested my body against the door frame, my expression carefully blank. I gestured to the spray of flowers with one hand. "Those for me?"

Brisbois, jolted out of his surprised stupor by my question, jerked the bouquet down to his side. He scowled, the effect dampened somewhat by the blush creeping up his neck. "What are you doing here?"

"I fail to see how that's any of your business." I leaned forward through the doorway, voice going high and wheedling. "Looking for Cadence?"

Brisbois pulled away from me, sneering. "I fail to see how that's any of your business, but yes." He shook his head as if to clear it, sighing. "Could you tell her I'm here, please?"

"I can't," I said flatly.

The enforcement officer opened his mouth to continue to spar with me, but I'd had enough of this game already, tired as I was from a lackluster night of sleep. I turned away from him, gesturing back into the office. "She's not, you see. Here, I mean."

The inspector shifted from foot to foot, his eyes darting from side to side. His agitation, which I had first put down to the nervousness of a person coming to court another, seemed suddenly more acute than it should be. "Can I come in?"

"Don't see why not," I said, turning and walking back the way I had come, not bothering to invite him in with more cordial terms.

The door clicked shut behind me and I heard the clip clop of his cheap leather shoes against the bare wooden floor. "So..." he started.

When he didn't immediately finish the thought, I looked back at him over my shoulder. He licked his lips, shoving his free hand into his jacket pocket. "Where is she?" he asked, feigning casualness so badly that I almost took pity on him.

Almost.

A shrug was my response, coupled with: "Your guess is as good as mine at this point."

His mouth firmed into a line and his brow wrinkled. "Have you tried calling her?"

"She'll come back when she's ready," I said, failing to contain the bitterness in my voice.

If Brisbois picked up on my ill humor, he didn't show it. Nodding, he passed the bouquet from hand to hand as if it were a lawn ball that he was about to pitch. With a quick, jarring step, he crossed further into the office, dropping the bouquet on a low coffee table. "Do you mind if I try?"

I followed him, pulling my hands from my pockets. "Just what is this about, Oliver? Cadence isn't in trouble of some kind, is she?"

"No." Brisbois fumbled his mobile out of his jacket pocket with one hand, the other pulling at his chin. "No, it's me who might be in trouble."

The front door flew open with a clatter and Cadence blew into the room like a sandstorm, all irritation and bluster.

"Anta, Chance, you can't just leave the door unlocked when–!" Freezing like an animal caught under a bright light, she took in the sight of us standing there. After a moment, she visibly relaxed, as if nothing had happened, shaking her hair back out of her face, and smiling. "Oliver, hello. What are you doing here?"

Brisbois, spurred into action by the mention of his name, bent down, picked up the bouquet from where he had dropped it and strode across the room to Cadence, flowers held in front of him like a lance.

"For you," he said woodenly, unsmiling.

"Oh." Cadence took them with both hands. She examined

them as if they were an ancient artifact from a dead culture. "Thank you."

Niceties dispensed with, he leaned forward, his hand reaching for her elbow. "Cadence, I –" Halting suddenly, his shoulders tensed. He glanced over at me, looked back at Cadence, and then stared back at me.

"Oh, please–" I said, waving my hand through the air as I sat down in one of the plush waiting room chairs that I had constructed two days prior. "–act like I'm not here. People usually do."

Brisbois' tongue prodded the inside of his cheek, and he shook his head, but there was little he could do about me, so he pressed on, returning his attention to my friend. "Cadence, I need your help."

"It's yours," Cadence said with a quickness I resented. She gestured towards her desk on the far side of the room, encouraging the man to enter further into the office. "What can I do?"

But Brisbois failed to notice her attempt at civility, reaching into his breast pocket and pulling out an official EO datapad. "I'd like to hire you. Or rather, the Enforcement Office would like to hire you."

Grimacing, I scoffed. "What?"

He ignored my outburst, his attention fixed on Cadence as he tapped the screen, bringing it to life. "You'd be an OOC: Official Outside Contractor. All you'd need to do is sign here."

There was silence as Cadence thumbed through the document on the datapad in front of her. When she was done, she looked up at Brisbois from under her brow. "Oliver, what exactly is going on?"

Brisbois pushed his hand back through his hair, turning away as he began pacing the room. "You know that since the Cerf case ended, I've been assigned to the Ani-District." His lips twisted into a scowl. "It's been... difficult, to say the least. The animanecrons who live here have a deep distrust of human authority figures, especially those from the Enforcement Office. That alone would be a barrier to upholding the law, but add to that a lack of understanding of animanecron culture, language, ways of existing in the world...not to mention the lack of applicable laws on the books to deal with crimes committed by and against animanecrons–"

The man stopped pacing, but he kept his gaze fixed on the floor under his feet. "There have been some unfortunate incidents already, I'm ashamed to say -- EO Officers who have been overzealous in their duties, quick to assume guilt and dole out punishment. And animanecrons are equally anxious to paint any EO involvement or investigation as a precursor to some kind of shadow war against them."

"And just what do you want Cadence to do about it?"

He looked up at last, and I could see the strain in his face. "There's been a murder in the district. A human man. I'd like Cadence's help with the case." He walked back to Cadence, his hand outstretched. "These are your people, Cadence, they'll talk to you."

"Not if they think that I've become a tool of the flesh oligarchy." She leaned forward and flicked his chest with her finger, bringing him up short in front of her. "Which is precisely what they'll think the second they see me with you."

"Please, Cadence," Brisbois begged. "I need an animanecron's perspective on this."

"Why?"

Brisbois spread his hands out in front of himself, shaking his head. "The Chief Inspector is already pushing me to declare this a human hate crime. There's been an uptick of attacks against humans in the Ani-District–"

Cadence bristled visibly. "Anno, you mean the Anti-Fragger Organization thugs who keep coming into the district to try and intimidate and bully the people living there?" She scowled, looking as if she might spit on the ground herself. "Those chestat con tekkers get what they deserve."

The inspector pressed on, his voice rising in volume. "Regardless of their motives, she thinks that the animanecrons responsible have gotten tired of breaking noses and ribs and have finally escalated to murder."

We all went noticeably quiet. I straightened in my chair, shaking my head. "She... can't be serious."

"She is – very." Brisbois took a step closer to Cadence. "If I can't come up with something concrete in the next fifteen hours, she's going to go public with that version of events."

The tip of Cadence's tongue came out to wet her lips. She turned away from Brisbois, walking to the large windows that lined the front of the room. "So, you want me to prove her wrong."

"I–" Brisbois stressed the pronoun. "–want the truth. And a bunch of A.F.O. rioters and scared humans looting the Ani-District won't help me get it."

Cadence nodded. She began tapping the corner of the datapad against her bottom lip, her gaze focused somewhere far away.

I cleared my throat and stood up. "Cadence?"

She turned to look at me, brows high above her eyes. I waved my hand towards the desk on the far side of the room that was to be her official office. "Can I speak to you for a moment?"

Nodding, she followed me. I waited until we were both standing in front of her desk to face her, casting a quick glance back at Brisbois before leaning in to whisper, "This is a very bad idea."

"I agree. It is hardly advisable to take on one case while already engaged in another." Grimacing, she dug her nails into the top of her head, ruffling the hair there in a rare moment of visible agitation. "But I don't see what choice I have."

"Just tell the man no," I said, shrugging.

She glared at me. "If I do, what then? I'll be responsible for whatever happens when the Chief Inspector makes her beliefs about this matter clear to the public."

I resisted the urge to rub her shoulder, chewing at the inside of my mouth. "You – you can't save the world, Cadence."

Cadence gave a snort, but a look of intense sadness passed over her face like a wave. "No. No, I suppose I can't." She shook her head. "But I can try and make sure it doesn't get any worse." Rolling her shoulders back, her voice dropped into an even quieter whisper. "Anyway, it's not exactly like I can tell him I have another case without him then asking questions, which is the exact opposite of what you wanted."

I opened my mouth to retort but shut it with a snap. I raised and lowered my brows. "True enough. Point taken." Letting out a sharp breath through my nose, I stood with my arms akimbo. "So, what am I supposed to do? Just sit around here until you get both cases wrapped up? I can tell you right now, that is not going to happen."

My friend shrugged. "I guess I'll just have to keep you close."

Before I could ask her what she meant by that, she was off, walking back towards the Inspector with her head held high.

"Oliver!" Cadence waved the EO datapad in front of herself like a white flag. "I will help with this case, but only if Chance can accompany me during my investigations."

Brisbois frowned. "Why? For what purpose?"

"I'm her mascot," I drawled, trudging after her.

"He's integral to my investigative process," she said, her face expressionless in that way only animanecrons seemed able to achieve.

The inspector rolled his eyes and shook his head. "Fine, fine. You'll get no argument from me."

With a satisfied harumph, Cadence swiped to the end of the official EO document on the datapad. She signed her name with a flourish of her pointer finger and handed the pad back to Brisbois, who cosigned the document, visibly relaxing as he did so.

"Thank you," he said, and sounded as if he meant it. He tucked the pad back into his breast pocket. "As of this moment, Miss Cadence Turing is an OOC for the Arrhidaean Enforcement Office." Smiling for the first time since he arrived, he swept his arm out towards the still open front door. "I have an EO PT waiting at the end of the block -- we can leave for the crime scene now."

6

Chapter 6

The three of us piled into the back of the Enforcement Office Personal Transport vehicle. Cadence and Brisbois sat with their backs to the driver's window, while I sat alone, facing them. The PT slid away from the walkway and up into the skyways that crisscrossed the city. Römer always looked so peaceful from up here -- a sprawling, sphere-spanning creature with spines of glass and steel and spotty patches of verdant green fur. But I didn't feel the same sense of ease that I normally did as we soared past skyscraper windows and over pedestrians -- I was watching Cadence, all the while digging my teeth into the sensitive flesh of my cheek.

When Brisbois got a call on his mobile, I saw my opportunity to confront my hitherto-absent investigator. I leaned across the seats towards Cadence, querying. "Where were you?"

She turned from the window, narrowing her eyes. "What do you mean?"

I didn't answer immediately, and she shifted side to side in her seat, but gave no indication that she was going to cease playing dumb with me. I crossed my arms over my chest and leaned back in the PT seat. "You sent me back to the office, and then I didn't see you for almost thirty hours."

"Anno, I was doing my job," she answered with a snap, tucking a wayward piece of hair behind her ear.

I shook my head and scowled. "You ditched me. I can't believe you did that. I thought we were past that kind of thing."

"I–" Cadence froze mid-answer, and looked over at the man beside her, who was staring quite openly at the two of us.

Brisbois's head fell to one side. He pulled his mobile from his ear and said, "Everything alright?"

Cadence swallowed hard. "Yes. Of course." She straightened in her seat, shaking out her skirt. "Chance, can we talk about this later, please?"

"'Later' is getting very full of things to talk about," I shot back. "We'll need an itemized agenda just to keep everything straight."

"Are we almost there, Oliver?" demanded Cadence, turning away from me pointedly.

"Thankfully, yes," he said. As he spoke, we felt the PT begin to slow and descend toward the public walkways.

The PT pulled to a stop between two other vehicles: an almost identical EO cruiser, and a wide, black PT with the symbol of a red cross on the sides and roof. The latter seemed to have arrived just before we did, two black scrub-wearing figures stepping out of the back and emptying equipment from the boot of the PT.

"Those will be the people from the morgue," said Brisbois, his hand already on the PT door handle. "I'd better catch them before they do anything with the body. Excuse me."

Brisbois was out the door without another word, waving down the mortuary workers with a shout. Left to our own devices, Cadence and I stepped out of the PT onto the too quiet residential street.

Römer was a city, urbanity at its best and worst, and as such it never really went to sleep. A sight such as this, a street completely devoid of pedestrians, of merchants opening or closing shops, of drunks wandering home or sleeping it off in doorways – well, I had never seen such a thing. The stillness was unnatural and disturbing.

Picking out the epicenter of this disquieting quiet was a simple matter -- just in front of us, three uniformed EO officers were busy setting up holoprojectors around an area of about five meters square, cordoning off the street and one side of the public walkway. Lying at the bottom of the nearest townhouse was a human-shaped mass covered in a white medical sheet.

"Shall we?" asked Cadence, gesturing towards the body.

I grimaced at her and nodded. As we walked, Brisbois jogged up from behind to join us, saying, "Our drones alerted us to the body at 2:12 am. An ambulance was dispatched, and the man was declared dead at the scene. Cause of death is still to be officially determined, but there's nothing obvious - no gunshot wound, or stab wound - nothing like that."

"Are you sure it's even a murder?" I asked, stopping a foot or so back from the body.

"The medical examiner suspects that she'll find some kind of cervical injury when she gets him on the table." Brisbois looked over at me and noted my blank stare. "Broken neck, most likely."

Bending down, the inspector removed the medical sheet with one hard tug. The man who had been hidden beneath looked as if he had just fallen asleep in the middle of the walkway. He lay flat on his back, his feet splayed to either side, the gaudy jallopskin shoes catching the morning light in a shimmer of silver. His suit was powder blue, with a silver vest that matched the shoes, and an ivory bow tie slightly askew around a thin neck. There was a spot of blood on the silver handkerchief that protruded from his jacket pocket, but it was small and easy to miss, a subtle sign of the violence someone had perpetrated against him.

Cadence crouched down beside the man's head and, with one hand on either side of his temples, twisted his head back and forth. Her brow began to furrow. Without standing, she scooted down to the man's side. Gently lifting his hand, she turned the extremity palm up inside her own. She moved each finger in turn with no resistance. She gave a contemplative hum.

Brisbois knelt on the opposite side of the body, his hand on his chin. "Yes, that is interesting."

She looked across to Brisbois, placing the man's hand down onto the ground as she queried, "You're sure the body's only been here overnight?"

"Very sure," said Brisbois, his own keen eyes scanning the dead man for anything that might be revealing. "The EO drones did a pass of this walkway at 1:12 am, and there was nothing. An hour later, he appeared."

"What is it? What's interesting?" I asked. If I was going to be dragged along to something this horrid, the least Cadence could do was keep me in the loop.

Cadence stood, pointing down at the corpse. "This body should be in rigor. If this man died between 1:12 and 2:12, that means the body has been here for almost eight hours – full rigor should've set in by now. But there's nothing." With a ghoulish eagerness that made me grimace, she smiled at Brisbois. "I'd be very interested to see how livor mortis has progressed."

Standing, Brisbois brushed off the knees of his trousers. "That can be arranged."

"Who was he?" I said, a tad more pointedly than was called for.

"Hm?" said Cadence, her attention clearly elsewhere.

"His name – this was a person." I turned to Brisbois. "He had a name, I assume?"

"We don't know. The EO FaRS is chewing on his face as we speak, but it hasn't spit out a match yet." Brisbois slung his hands into his pockets and pursed his lips. "There was no other identification on the body. Right now, who he was is just as much of a mystery as how he ended up here."

I looked down into the late-man's face. He was in his late thirties or early forties. His cheekbones were sharp, jutting out like peaks under deep set eyes, between which sat a broad nose, ending in a rounded point. His forehead was high, his chin small, his lips thin. He looked like an academic – possessed of nothing more dangerous than a caustic wit. His clothes, though, hinted at something seedier. Perhaps he was in entertainment, a manager or producer. Still, there was nothing to indicate how he could have come to be in his current predicament.

"Was there anything at all on the body?" said Cadence, returning to Brisbois' side.

"Pockets were empty," said Brisbois, shaking his head. "Just some lint and a scrap of paper -- has what I think is part of an Animatum word on it. Maybe you can translate for us – Jenkins!"

A female EO officer who was setting up the holoprojectors around the edges of the crime scene straightened at the sound of her name. Re-tucking one of her yellow braids under her helmet, she hurried over to us, saluting her superior. "Yes, sir?"

"Do you still have that paper we found in the deceased's pocket?"

"Yes, sir." Jenkins twisted towards one of the pouches on her belt. She snapped the pouch open and yanked out a crumpled, too-large plastic evidence bag. Holding it out towards Brisbois, she smiled with pride. "Here you go, sir."

"Thank you, Jenkins," said Brisbois, taking the bag with a nod.

"Anything else, sir?" chirped the young officer.

I took a closer look at EO Officer Jenkins. Beneath the bullet-proof helmet, she had a kind face and beautiful bright blue eyes that sparkled when she looked at Brisbois.

"No, thank you, Sergeant." Brisbois waved her off.

Jenkins' smile shrank for a moment, but she recovered with a smart salute. "Right you are, sir."

That was a situation that would bear watching.

Brisbois handed the bag off to Cadence. "Can you make anything out of that?"

Cadence took the bag, shaking it so that the scrap of paper landed in one of its corners. She examined it through the plastic, holding it with her fingertips.

Her eyes went wide. "Oh."

"What? What does it say?" demanded Brisbois.

Cadence looked through the bag and at me. Without another word, she handed over the evidence.

As soon as I turned the bag around, I saw what had made her start. I recognized the virulent green, the blocky font – I didn't need the original, blood-stained flier to know that this was its missing corner. I looked up and met Cadence's wide-eyed stare. "I told you it wasn't an animanecron."

Brisbois looked between the two of us, lifting his brows. "Excuse me?"

Cadence rocked back and forth on her heels and folded her hands in front of her hips. She sighed. "You're going to be upset, but if you could try to not be, I think that would be very helpful."

With slow deliberation, Brisbois crossed his arms over his chest. He looked at us and nodded. "I'll do my best."

Rolling my eyes, I gestured for Cadence to explain what had happened two evenings previous. Brisbois stayed silent throughout the tale, looking almost listless during the telling of it, and it was only when Cadence finished that his face betrayed any emotion.

"You're a damn fool, Chance," said Brisbois, glaring at me with disapproval. "It's a miracle that you didn't bleed out in the street before you got back to Cadence's." One of his hands gripped his hip. "What were you even thinking, wandering around the district at night by yourself?"

"I can take care of myself, Oliver," I said, frowning.

He rolled his eyes. "Oh, clearly."

Gritting my teeth, I had half a mind to say something snide, comparing my survival skills to his clumsy attempt at wooing, but thought better of it. I settled instead for lifting two fingers in a crude salute, which he responded to with a dry chuckle.

"So," he said, taking a deep breath. "This was one of the men who attacked you. Are you sure?"

I dropped my arms to my sides. "It was dark; I didn't get a good look at them, or their faces."

"If it's not him," said Cadence, gesturing with the evidence bag between her fingers. "How do you explain the flier fragment?"

Brisbois tugged at the thin knot of his tie, loosening it. "It's circumstantial at best. And it still doesn't explain why this man attacked Chance, how he targeted him, or why he's dead now. It could all be a coincidence."

"Detectives–" said Cadence, sniffing in disdain. "–don't believe in coincidence."

The inspector gave an amused harumph and wagged his head back and forth. "Well, this detective has been around long enough to know the universe is strange and will allow for a little coincidence now and again. Come on, let's get started."

Cadence and I followed the inspector as he strode through the holocordon and headed east. We walked to the end of the too quiet street. The road dead-ended in a small community garden -- heavy red tomatoes hung from thin vines and fat pumpkins tumbled out onto the walkway. Urban gardens were common in Römer, but seeing one here, in a neighborhood where most of the residents had no biological need to eat, was delightfully queer. The small plots of tilled earth spoke to something -- a desire to see living things grow, just for the sake of it, rather than to reap any material benefits.

Examining the garden with open pleasure, I was pulled away from these musings by Brisbois, who was being far more prosaic, counting the number of townhouses on either side of the street under his breath.

"...twenty-three, twenty-four." Brisbois turned from his contemplation, addressing Cadence. "I suppose we should wait until later on in the morning to knock on doors, yes?"

Cadence's face crumpled in confusion. "Why?"

Brisbois frowned, shoving his hands into his trouser pockets. "Well, I'd rather not catch anyone half-asleep..."

Realizing where his train of thought had led him, Cadence smiled indulgently and shook her head. "Hila, we don't exactly keep consistent sleep schedules, Oliver. It's not like you'll be waking anyone up. Probably." She crossed her arms over her chest. "First priority is finding out who this man was – do you agree?"

"If the attack wasn't random, it'll help in establishing a motive if we can build up a profile of his life, yes" said Brisbois.

She looked up and down the residential street, the corners of her mouth pulled down in a thoughtful frown. "We'll work faster if we split up. Chance, you and Oliver visit the buildings on the right side of the street, and I'll handle the ones opposite. Then we can meet back here."

Brisbois shook his head. "I don't know that they'll be too eager to speak to tools of the flesh oligarchy."

Cadence shrugged. "If you get nowhere, I'll recanvass that side of the street. But I'm sure my people will be reasonable once they realize there's been a crime committed."

"You'll need one of these." Brisbois took out two holopucks and handed one to her. "Our John Doe's face is on there."

Cadence took the device with a nod. "Good luck, you two," she said, before heading off to the nearest townhouse on the left.

7

Chapter 7

Brisbois and I shared a glance.

"You don't need to come along," he said. "Believe it or not, I did quite a lot of detective work on my own before you two careened into my life."

"I thought it unlikely that you became Inspector because of your good looks," I answered, swiping the second holopuck out of his hand. I turned and started walking towards the first town-house on the right.

"Don't take your bad mood out on me," growled Brisbois, catching up. "It's not my fault that you and Cadence are fighting."

"Who said we were fighting?"

Brisbois rolled his eyes, shaking his head. "Fine. Don't tell me what's going on. It's none of my business anyway."

I hummed my ascent and hopped up the stairs to the front door, knocking lightly.

The inspector stood beside me, his hands in his pockets. "Do you actually speak any Animatum?" asked Brisbois, a smile in his words.

"A little, actually." I preened a bit as I said it, just in time for the front door of the townhouse to swing open.

A woman with white-blonde hair down to her waist and blue eyes the color of glaciers stood in the doorway. She looked at us both, her upper lip curling in disgust.

Before she could close the door again, I fumbled my way through the traditional animanecron greeting, coming up out of my bow to stutter in Animatum, *"May the day bring you what you require. We need help. Do you know this human?"*

Holding the EO holopuck out in front of me, I clicked it on, wincing a little as the dead visage of our mystery man flashed into existence above my palm, rotating slowly in three dimensions.

The woman's icy blue eyes glanced at the face for a fraction of a second before bouncing back to me. Releasing her hold on the door, she stared down her nose at me. *"You speak our tongue like a corrupted story cube that has been plugged in one too many times, worm food."*

With a kick, the door slammed shut inches in front of my hand, which I jerked back instinctively, fearing the rap of my knuckles against the wood. I stood there, stunned, staring at the closed portal for several seconds, until Brisbois cleared his throat next to me.

"What did she say?" he inquired politely.

I clicked off the holopuck and shoved it in my pocket, turning away from the door and clomping down the front steps. "She didn't recognize him."

"And?" he prompted, following behind me.

I could feel his smirk burrowing into the back of my head.

This scenario played out in one form or another at nearly every door we faced. Brisbois and I took turns making the approach, but we were firmly rebuffed by every occupant we met, usually with one or two unkind remarks to send us on our way. At the houses where we were not openly berated or belittled, we still received nothing more than one-word, negative answers to our queries.

When we reached the last house on the street, the one farthest from the community garden and closest to the crime scene, I had about had my fill of enforcement work. I knocked on the door with a heavy sigh. An older looking man opened it, though his real age was of course impossible to determine. Perhaps he looked older because his face was hidden behind a large, long beard the color of dried mud. He stood in the doorway, a full head shorter than me, and looked at us in open expectation.

I was getting quite good at the hand gesture and the bowing by this point. "*May the day bring you what you require. We–*"

"I speak Common Tongue, sir," interrupted the older man, nodding to me.

"Oh," I exclaimed. "Oh, that's... lovely." I tried to cover my surprise with a smile. "Good morning."

"Good morning." He smiled with all his teeth and gestured up to the sky with his free hand. "It should be a beautiful autumn day, should it not?"

I nodded in agreement. "Very. Sir, my name is–"

"I know who you are, sir," he said, reaching forward to shake my hand. His brown eyes sparkled in his tan face. "The head of Halcyon Enterprises is a face well-known to nearly all here." Still holding on to my hand, he began to step back inside his townhome. "Would you like to come in? It would be an honor."

I exchanged a glance with Brisbois, who gave a minute shake of his head, before returning my attention to the man in front of me. "Some other time, perhaps. There's been an incident down the street, you see, and we were wondering if you had any idea who this man is."

Depressing the button on the side of the holopuck, I called up the ghoulish image of our deceased gentleman's face. The bearded animanecron examined it for a moment before moving forward, his hand outstretched. I gave over the holopuck, watching as the older-looking man twisted the puck this way and that, viewing the head from all angles. At length, he shook his head, shrugging.

"No." The man handed the holopuck back to me. "I don't know his name."

Brisbois and I shared another look. His answer did not match the question put to him, and the slight discrepancy led to tantalizing possibilities.

"But you've seen him before?" pressed Brisbois, taking out a stylus and his EO datapad, shaking it to life with one hand.

"Oh yes, many times." The morning breeze blew the end of his long brown beard as he stepped out onto the townhome's porch. He pointed down the street, saying, "He normally keeps closer to the AN-GRAV tracks, the business and side streets down that way. But I've seen him around."

Taking quick notes, Brisbois nodded. "Is there anyone in particular he seemed to keep company with?"

Stroking his beard, the gentleman shook his head. "Ah, that's not for me to say, I'm afraid."

"This is a murder inquiry, sir," lectured Brisbois, drawing himself up to his full height.

Unphased by the chastisement, the older man leaned forward, lips pursed. "Really? How did he die?"

I opened my mouth to answer, but Brisbois cut me off with a glare. "We are the ones asking the questions."

The man held up his hands, but the movement of his beard hinted at a smile underneath the mass of hair. "Of course, Inspector, of course." He leaned back, folding his hands on top of his round belly. "Well, however he died, he didn't die here."

"What makes you say that?" said the inspector.

"I watched someone shove his body out of a PT," he said simply. "That was at around...oh... 1:30 am?"

I felt my eyes widen. "You saw it?" I said.

He nodded. "I often sit up on my roof at night. I was a star cruiser pilot before the war, you know." Scratching at his head, he sighed. "You can see all kinds of things from up there. I go up to look at the stars of course. I miss the stars. I miss the black." He leaned forward, his eyes earnest. "You know the only place you can be truly alone is in space."

Masking his feelings well, Brisbois sounded as casual as can be as he said, "So a PT brought the body. Did you catch a company name or tag number?"

"No, no, it was too dark." The ex-pilot inclined his head towards the world outside his stoop. "Came down Bombers Street, though, and went back the same way."

"And you think he was dead when he was pushed out the PT?" asked Brisbois.

"Didn't move, didn't struggle, didn't shout," the old man answered. "Just flopped onto the pavement and lay there."

"And you didn't call the Enforcement Office because...?" Brisbois looked up from his pad, his expression blank.

The old man laughed. "Now why would I want that kind of trouble?"

I cut in quickly before Brisbois could launch into a speech about civic duty, extending my hand for another shake. "Thank you so much, Mister...?"

Vint took my hand in both of his. "Vint. Just Vint."

"Vint." I gave his hand a firm shake. "Thank you."

"Any time, Mr. Hale." He pulled me in close, but his voice remained as hearty as ever. "You know, I don't believe what everyone says about you. I think you really are trying your best. It may not be worth much, but you're trying."

My mouth hung open for a moment. "Ah." I physically shook myself, trying to regain some poise after being knocked off balance by Vint's mangled compliment. Swallowing down my true feelings, I inclined my head, placing my hand over my heart. "Yes, well, I appreciate that, Vint. Thank you." Then, before we parted, I added in Animatum. "*Until we meet again.*"

"*Until that day,*" he responded brightly, waving as we walked away.

"It would appear that you're about as popular around here as

I am," observed Brisbois, the pair of us strolling back towards the community garden as if we were two friends taking in the morning air.

"I don't think anyone with a pulse is very popular around here," I noted. Then, with a sudden burst of curiosity, I queried, "You're a man of the world, Brisbois – what do you think should be done about what's happening on Whiston?"

Brisbois looked askance at me, surprise writ clear on his face. "What else can be done?" he answered, shrugging. "The IPC have leveled multiple economic and political sanctions against Chacornac, refugees have been allowed freer travel and greater access to aid–"

"But is it doing any good?" I stopped at the corner, my hands coming out of my trouser pockets. "Charcornac and their allies seem hellbent on pursuing this course of action, consequences to their own worlds be damned."

Brisbois turned to face me. "I don't support a military intervention, if that's what you're asking."

"Even if it could save lives?"

"At the cost of how many others?" Brisbois' chin dropped to his chest. "There hasn't been a system-wide military conflict in over a hundred and seventy years. Personally, I'm not anxious to see another."

"The answer is obvious," interrupted Cadence, joining us at last. "Let Whiston fight for itself."

My eyes widened. "Is that even a possibility?"

Cadence fixed me with an imperious glare. "My people aren't pacifists, Chance." She lifted one hand and curled it into a fist.

"We would fight if we had the means to do so. Many are fighting without the means, even while facing certain eradication."

Brisbois shook his head vigorously. "If any planet provides military aid to the Whistonian insurgents–"

"Freedom fighters," snapped Cadence, her glare moving from me to Brisbois.

"Charcornac will undoubtedly view it as an act of aggression," Brisbois squared his shoulders and faced Cadence, hand leaving his pocket to gesture through the air between them. "They'll strike back! And then the IPC will have to respond with force as well. Before you know it, we're all drawn in, whether we like it or not."

Cadence gave a frustrated grunt, her fist falling to her side. "So, you'd rather we all stand by and do nothing?"

"It's a complex issue," insisted Brisbois, meeting Cadence's stern gaze. "That's all I'm saying."

"Cay," I said, hoping to turn the conversation away from something confrontational to something more beneficial. "Did you learn anything about our mystery man?"

My animanecron friend broke her stare with Brisbois with some reluctance. "Several people report having seen him around the district previously, but nobody knows his identity. Or if they do, they're not admitting it."

We told her what we had learned from the old animanecron pilot. Cadence's eyes widened and she grinned. "Of course! That makes sense!"

"What does?" said Brisbois.

But Cadence was already walking back towards the cordoned-off area, where the mortuary workers were loading up the deceased man into their long black PT. She called out for them to wait. They obliged only when Brisbois's voice joined hers, stepping away from the grav-stretcher with annoyed grumbling about the end of their shift and overtime.

With no care for the man's dignity, Cadence fully unzipped the opaque white body bag and threw the flap open. To the shock of all assembled, she pushed her hands under the man and rolled him onto his side, very nearly tipping him off the stretcher. Brisbois jerked his hands out to hold the body steady, making a strangled exclamation as he did so.

"Cadence, what the–!"

She jerked the man's shirt and jacket up off his back, revealing his bare skin to the world. "Look!"

We looked. We couldn't avoid it.

"What am I looking at Cadence?" I said at length. "There's nothing there."

"Exactly! That clinches it," said Cadence, smirking. She pointed towards the pale, bloodless skin. "If he had died just before landing on the street, his blood would have pooled into the skin here. But look at this lividity – there is none. He was in some other position long enough for lividity to set in some other pattern before he landed on the street." She shook her head. "He wasn't killed here, Oliver. He was placed here."

"But why would someone dump a body here?" I insisted, looking away from the corpse.

"To stir up trouble," said Brisbois ruefully, snapping a few pictures of the man's body with his datapad. "To try and make us think this was just another in a string of animanecron attacks on humans." He looked up, clenching his jaw. "Almost worked, too. I need to call the Chief Inspector."

Brisbois strode away, pulling his mobile free from his pocket and placing it in his ear. Cadence stepped back from the grav-stretcher, lowering the body back into place, her eyes fixated on the Inspector. Lips pursed, Cadence waited until Brisbois was well out of earshot before turning to me, her voice low.

"There is another possibility," she whispered. "If this man was in fact known to someone here, this may have been a way to send that person, or persons, a message."

I watched as the EO Morticians pushed the remains of our nameless victim into the back of their black PT and shivered. "I don't think I want to meet the kind of person who sends messages with corpses."

8

Chapter 8

"I don't understand," I said, turning away from the PT and facing Cadence once more. "Where's the connection? How does this man go from attempting to murder me, to being murdered himself?"

Cadence gave an exaggerated frown, shrugging so the top of her shoulders brushed the bottom of her ears. "Could be his employers were unhappy that he failed to finish you off."

I felt a lump begin to form at the base of my throat. Attempting to swallow it down, I choked out, "His... his employers?"

She gestured to the still open back of the PT. "You don't know him. But his attack on you doesn't have the hallmarks of a random incident– he targeted you. Makes sense that he is, or was, a hired hand of some kind."

I had hardly lived a blameless life. I was not so self-deluded to think that I hadn't made enemies. But the tenor of those enemies were, to my mind, all intensely personal. Jilted lovers, cuckolded partners, jealous competitors. Asked to bring to mind the faces of people who would rejoice at the news of my demise, I was ashamed to say I could picture a fair few. But all of these were people whom I could imagine twisting the knife in themselves – I couldn't believe that any of them had the cold calculation and patience needed to hire an assassin.

It was a stunning thought: that someone wanted you dead and was willing to pay to keep their hands clean of your blood.

The wind rushed through the anemic trees on the pedestrian pathways that surrounded us. I wrapped my arms around myself and shivered, eyes downcast.

If Cadence noted my sudden sobriety, she made no move to comfort me, perhaps distracted by the return of the inspector. His shoulders hunched, he rolled his mobile between his fingers as he walked towards us, shaking his head.

"The Chief Inspector isn't fully convinced that there isn't animanecron violence at the bottom of all this," said Brisbois, irritation clear in his voice. "But I've managed to convince her to hold off on making any kind of official statement by telling her what we've learned so far."

"Gav, that is good news," said Cadence, nodding.

He tucked his mobile into his trouser pocket and sighed. "That's about all the good news I have, I'm afraid. District Head-quarters got back to me: FaRS came up empty. We have no idea who our mystery man is."

"Is that even possible?" I gestured to the sky above us, which was thick with PT traffic and UAVs. "With all the security drones around these days, I would've thought everyone's face was captured and cataloged somewhere."

"Oh, we have him on camera – just no corresponding record of who the hell he is." Brisbois rubbed at the back of his neck, wincing. "I hate to say it, but the system isn't perfect. If you pay the right people, you can get your files deleted, or corrupted enough so they're unusable. Looks like that's what happened here."

"Where did the drones catch him?" asked Cadence.

Brisbois shrugged. "In various places around the city, never anywhere that would raise any red flags."

"Vint mentioned that he used to hang around the AN-GRAV tracks," I supplied eagerly.

"We should go there," said Cadence. "Ask around some more, see if anyone can tell us more about him."

"You two go," said Brisbois, gesturing to the street's entrance. "I'll ride back with the body and see if I can't get the Medical Examiner to put a rush on the autopsy -- that way we can at least establish the cause of death."

Cadence began to nod, but stopped mid-motion, her eyes widening. Both Brisbois and I stared at her as she seemed to freeze in place. One could almost hear her multiprocessors whirring. With infinitesimal slowness, she turned her head to look at me. She blinked once, and then again, and then stepped jerkily towards Brisbois, her head hanging low between her shoulders.

"Dor, maybe Chance should go with you," she suggested in a low, but still clearly audible tone, her eyes darting between me and the inspector like a bee moving between two flowers.

Brisbois shook his head, turning his back to me. "Cadence, I'm not a babysitter—"

"And I'm not a child," I snapped. "I don't need to be looked after every minute of every day, Cay."

"I know you don't." She pressed her hands together and shook them at me, pleading. "But someone did try to kill you, and it looks like whoever it was may have had something to do with the death of this man." When I failed to look properly frightened, Cadence frowned and rolled her eyes. "I just don't think you should be wandering around in the open. It's not a good idea."

"'Wandering around'?" I stared at her. "I wouldn't be wandering around -- I'd be with you. I thought I was integral to your investigative process."

"If I'm investigating, I can't be keeping an eye on you too," she insisted, her hand rising and falling, slapping against her thigh. "We need to keep you safe."

I bit down hard on the inside of my cheek. Now, she was concerned with keeping me safe. Now, she was concerned with where I was and what I was doing. Weeks of wondering if she was even aware I was alive, and now this. Still, she couldn't be bothered to keep tabs on me herself. Still, she wanted me at a distance.

"I hate to say it," Brisbois admitted, his gaze heavenward. "But Cadence does have a point. Perhaps you shouldn't—"

Pushing my hand back through my hair, I scoffed. "You want to stop me? Arrest me." I started up the street, shouting over my shoulder. "You do your investigations, Cadence, and I'll do mine. I'll call you if I learn anything."

"Chance? Chance!"

I reveled in her shock as she shouted after me, keeping my steps steady and quick as I turned the corner.

Heading out of the Ani-District as quickly as my feet could carry me, I didn't have an exact destination in mind -- I just knew I had to get away from Cadence. She was worried about me. I should be glad of that fact, part of me protested. It meant she cared.

The tenor of that care pricked at my pride however, and its sudden appearance seemed more than a little unfair. Not that Cadence had ever been downright cold to me in the months since we had taken up separate living accommodations – that would require effort. No, it seemed to me that since I had declared my feelings for her, since we had agreed to attempt to move forward with some kind of romantic relationship, I had been left to do the heavy lifting while she simply ignored, or worse, tolerated, my existence.

I was in love with her. That hadn't changed. But I had my pride. Well, now she needed to be reminded that I wasn't helpless or dependent on her. When it came to my problems, I could handle them myself. Out of the Ani-District, I called for a PT to pick me up and take me to the one place where I knew that I could get some answers that Cadence could not.

The Halcyon Enterprises corporate campus covered several city blocks. We were a small city unto ourselves in the very heart of Römer, with every amenity a worker could desire. As head of the technology conglomerate, my office was in the upper levels of Alpha Spire, which housed the company's executives and upper management, as well as our more profitable divisions.

I generally arrived at the PT dock in a company public

transport vehicle. I also generally arrived in a suit and tie. I was acutely aware of the slight stir that followed me as I made my way from the dock inside the transport lobby and into the executive lift -- the weight of eyes and sound of whispers following me inside the opaque glass box.

I wouldn't be surprised if this got to our Board of Directors somehow. Sticklers for formality, the lot of them. They'd probably accuse me of trying to tank our stock prices with my casual slacks. Asses.

With ill-humor settled on me like dust on old books, I made for my office with all speed, not bothering to knock as I pushed open the door to my executive suite.

Lily Taylor, my executive admin, jumped at her desk, her lips pulling into a scowl that only deepened when she saw that it was me who had walked through the door. She scoffed and pushed away from her desk.

"You have got to be kidding me," she said, annoyance writ all over her face.

"Good morning, Miss Taylor," I said, shrugging off my coat and feeling at once distinctly underdressed compared to the professionally attired executive admin sitting in front of me.

"Chance?" Lily stood, pressing her fists into the top of her desk. "I thought you were taking some time off! I cleared your calendar for the next week!" She straightened, holding her arms akimbo. "Do you have any idea how hard that was?"

"Lily," I said darkly, shooting her a hard glance. "I'm sorry, but... I'm not in the mood."

My words had little effect on her, although I did detect a slight softening in her glare. "Date didn't go well, I take it?"

I didn't respond at first, the desire to unburden myself to someone wrestling with my need to maintain employer/employee boundaries. In the end the latter won out and I rolled my eyes, stepping towards my office door and saying, "I need to see Sandra Aja."

"Alright," she said, nodding, turning to the datapad she had propped up at eye level on the left hand of her desk. "I'll see when she's available–"

"Now." I looked back from just inside my office, one hand on the door jamb. "Please. It's a bit...urgent."

Lily ran her tongue over her front teeth. "Okay. That's never what you want to hear when your boss asks to see the head of Security." She closed her eyes and tapped the phone bud nestled in her ear. "I'll rustle her up."

Efficient as always. I smiled and bowed my head to her. "Thank you, Miss Taylor."

"Chance?"

My name rang high and clear in the air. I froze. Spinning slowly on my heel, I looked at her. She stared at me around her screens and projections. Her eyes were locked on my face, her lips a thin line. "You'd let me know if I needed to be worried, right?"

"I'd let you know," I assured her, stepping backwards into my executive suite. "By the by: let's just keep quiet about me being in the office for now, alright?"

Her eyes narrowed. "Uh huh. Sure."

Leaving the door to my inner office ajar, I walked to my desk, calling for lights as I did so. I turned on my computer and settled into the chair behind my desk, scrolling through messages and v-chats without really seeing them, considering what I was going to say to Sandra when she arrived. How much could I really say? This was all tied up in an Enforcement Office murder inquiry, after all. But if anyone could tell me who had put a target on my back...

Before I'd realized it, twenty minutes had gone by. I was roused from my thoughts by a knock and looked up to see Sandra peeking around the door, her brown eyes assessing me questioningly.

"Can I...?" she said, gesturing inside the office.

"Of course!" I said, minimizing my screens and standing. "Close the door behind you, if you please."

Sandra did as she was asked, switching her long egg-white coat from one arm to the other as she did so. She crossed the room in quick, short strides, the knee-length pressed purple skirt she wore showing off her muscular calves. Her purple suit jacket was unbuttoned, revealing a pale pink V-neck blouse beneath it. I must have caught her on her way to a board meeting. It was the only time I saw her so dressed up.

Sandra Aja was the youngest of my executive team, which still put her ten years older than myself. Nearing forty, she maintained a fit, stout physique by making frequent use of the Halcyon Campus gymnasium. We crossed paths there from time to time, though her fitness regimen put my own to shame. Her routine of physical discipline was a habit she picked up during her time in the Interplanetary Commission's Security and Defensive Force. She enlisted fresh out of private school, shocking her civil service parents, who had anticipated her joining the ranks of the diplomatic core. Moving quickly through the ranks,

Sandra ultimately found her calling in the IPC Intelligence & Information Division as a Senior Commander. Much of what she had done for that elite unit was still highly classified.

The woman was a good five inches shorter than me, and I was absolutely terrified of her.

"Sandra." I came around the desk, my hand outstretched. "How have you been? Feels like it's been ages since we've talked."

Shaking my hand, she didn't bother with a perfunctory smile, concern clear in her gaze. "Good to see you, Chance. Everything alright?"

"I'm not sure," I said, leading her to the chairs in front of the wooden behemoth at which I worked. I settled down into one of the plush seats and gestured for her to do the same. "That's what I wanted to chat with you about."

She draped her jacket across the back of the chair, but remained standing, one hand on her hip. "How can I help?"

Crossing my legs, I hooked my interlaced fingers around my knee. I gnawed at the inside of my cheek for a moment. "Look... there's no delicate way to put this, so I'll just come out and ask: have there been any threats against me lately?"

"Threats?" Sandra's eyes went wide. "Chance, did something happen to you?"

I did my best to keep my face impassive. But I should've known better. Sandra had built a career on getting the truth out of people, on finding out what other people tried to conceal. She read me like a story cube. Her brown face darkened, her teeth grinding together.

"Damn it!" she exploded, throwing her hands into the air. "Damn it, if I've said it once, I've said it a thousand times –

you're too public of a figure to live the way you do! It's reckless, and you're going to get hurt."

Leaning back in my chair, I waved away her concern with a huff. "My father didn't live behind a sea of human shields, and I don't see why I should have to either."

"You are not your father." Fidgeting with the bangles on her wrist, Sandra began to pace the room. "Your father practically lived in this building. And when he wasn't here in this very office, he was at your old place out in Zahia, which had top notch security of its own. You–" She tossed her hand out without looking at me. "–seem to forget that you're worth over a billion credits, and that some very nasty people would do very nasty things to get that money out of you." Holding her hand to her head, she groaned aloud. "I keep telling you, you need to have at least one bodyguard with you at all times–"

"Absolutely not," I said, rocketing to my feet. "I'm not about to let a dead-eyed, musclebound stranger trample through my private life and tell me how to sit and stand and move."

"Sacrifices have to be made when you're the head of a company like this, Chance," stressed Sandra, flaring her nostrils. "Your very public private life may just have to be a casualty of your success."

"Success! Ha! You make it sound like I got here by the sweat of my brow rather than an accident of birth," I sneered, spinning around and leaning over the desk that had been my father's, and his father's before that.

"I will not get sucked into another one of your Hale pity parties, Chance," Sandra snarled from behind me. "You know damn well that you've done things with this company that your father never could have. And if you'd like to keep doing those things, you should let me do my damn job and keep you safe."

I sighed audibly, fingers pinching the bridge of my nose. "Sandra, I didn't call you up here to have the same argument over again."

"No," said Sandra, closing the distance between us with a few quick strides, moving around me so that I was forced to face her. "You called me up here to ask me about threats made against you. Why?"

I turned away from her, heading for the windows that looked out over the city. "It's a need-to-know kind of thing, Sandra."

Looking out into the sea of clouds and spires, of public walkways crisscrossing the city, of public transports ferrying commuters from one part of the planet to the next, it was hard to imagine that I was in any kind of danger at all. I often wondered what my father had felt when he stood here. I imagined that it made him feel powerful. Me? I felt...connected.

Sandra stepped into the space behind me. Her hand gripped my arm tightly. "I am head of Corporate Security for Halcyon Enterprises. You are the head of Halcyon Enterprises." Sandra gently turned me to one side to face her. Her clay-colored eyes stared up at me, not without warmth. "Chance, I need to know."

She was right, of course. I couldn't ask for her help and then keep her in the dark. I laid out the whole story for her, doing my best to keep Cadence as far out of it as I could. I still had the holopuck in my pocket with the dead man's likeness on it, and I showed it to Sandra, after explaining that he was not in the EO FaRS database.

"Fuck's sake, Chance." Sandra took a deep breath through her nose and turned away from the window to look at me, her face drawn. "So, the EO has no idea who this man was?"

"Not yet." I perched on the edge of my desk, holding the puck out to her. "I was hoping we might."

She crossed from the windows and took the holopuck from me with the tips of her fingers. After examining the rotating visage for a few seconds, she shook her head, switching the puck off and jamming it in her skirt pocket. "I can run him through our databases, but if he didn't come up in the EO FaRS, I don't know that we'd do much better."

"I'm less interested in who exactly he was, and more interested if he visited the campus, if we have recordings of him coming in and out of any of the buildings, things like that," I said, tightening my jaw.

Sandra's eyes narrowed as she took in my meaning. "You think he may have been tailing you?"

"He knew exactly where I was and headed me off me when I was trying to get home. They set a trap." I shivered at the memory. "They must have been observing me for some time."

She removed a slim, palm sized datapad from her jacket pocket. Scribbling some notes on it with her pointer finger, she nodded. "I'll see what I can come up with." Sandra looked up from her pad, one eyebrow rising and falling as she considered my original query. "As far as threats, it might be easier to list the people who like you right now than the people who don't."

A rueful smile stole across my face. "That's comforting."

Returning to her pad, she scribbled furiously for a few more seconds before saying, "I'll have someone put together a list of the top five likely suspects and send it your way." She folded the pad into a thumb-sized rectangle and replaced it in her pocket, smiling at me for the first time since she had entered my office. "In fact, I'll have your new bodyguard bring it up."

"Sandra–"

"Argument over, Chance." Sandra crossed her arms over her chest, scowling. "Someone tried to kill you. There is a credible threat to your life -- you are not getting out of this building without at least a one-person protection detail. Be grateful that I don't insist on more."

I knew a lost battle when I was in one. I stood and moved behind my desk. "Someone discreet, please."

"They'll be invisible," she said, picking up her jacket with one hand. "I promise." She started for the door and was halfway there when she stopped mid-step, spinning around. "You'll stay here until I send them up, right?"

I settled placidly into my desk chair. "Of course."

Something about my general air was less than convincing. Sandra narrowed her eyes slowly. I felt my heartbeat quicken.

"I will!" I protested loudly, pressing a hand to my chest. "I've got things to keep me busy for the next few hours, anyway."

"Alright," said Sandra at length, holding up her hands in defeat. "Alright. If you say so. They'll be up as soon as I can shake them loose."

"Thank you, Sandra." I sighed, resting back in the swivel chair and steepling my hands over my lap. "I really do appreciate it."

Sandra shrugged. "It's my job." She gave a lazy salute before completing her walk to the door. "You stay safe, Chance."

9

Chapter 9

I stared after Sandra, the wheels of my mind turning. I had no intention of hanging around and waiting for her handpicked bodyguard to blanket me with protection. Still, if I left now, she might catch wind of my departure – and then I'd be in real trouble.

I resolved to spend some time in the office, answering v-chats and doing assorted paperwork. All the while, Cadence did her best to get in touch with me. Every five minutes, with machine-like regularity, my mobile would buzz, flashing purple, indicating that Cadence was on the other end of the line. With a pettiness of which I hadn't previously known myself capable, I canceled each call before it reached my voicemail.

I didn't want to hear her voice. I didn't want her explanations or excuses. I was enjoying my anger. I felt entitled to it, like a child feels entitled to a beloved stuffed toy -- I'd be damned if I let anyone take it away from me.

In between the canceled calls, v-chats began to appear in the corner of my projected screens. The notification bubble showed only her name and the first word or two of each message, but that was more than enough.

Cadence

Chance, pick-

Cadence

Why are-

Cadence

Answer the-

When my mobile rang again an hour later, I was about to ignore it, when I noticed that it was Henry ringing me, not Cadence. Pausing my work, I popped the bud into my ear, accepting the call with a nod.

"Would you answer your girlfriend's phone calls?" said Henry without so much as a 'hello.'

I glared at the empty chair across from me as if my friend were sitting in it. "I'm ignoring her," I answered at length, flipping my stylus between my fingers. "Let's see how she likes it."

"Are you children fighting?"

I bristled at his tone as much as his words. He was needling me, and he should've known better.

Snapping myself upright, I shot back, "Shouldn't you be with Rin, lover boy?"

"So that's a yes," said Henry, his even, matter-of-fact tone grating my already raw nerves. "Well, could you keep me out of the middle of it? I love you both dearly, but between the two of you, there's the emotional maturity of a mongoose."

"If you don't want to be in the middle, then why are you calling?" I hissed down the line.

"Having been on the receiving end of your arctic shoulder, I said I'd do what I could." His voice brightened with forced joviality. "Truce? She wants to meet back at her place in an hour."

"Right, well – we'll just see about that," I ended the call with a flourish, tearing the bud out of my ear and jamming it into my trouser pocket.

I stood up from my desk and made for the office door. Pushing it open, I didn't even bother to switch off my lights as I yanked my coat over myself.

Lily, seated once more at her desk, leaned through her projected screens, scowling as I stormed past. "Oh, leaving already?"

"I was never here, right?" I said, raising one brow to underscore my words.

Rolling her eyes, she reclined. "Right."

Turning my mobile off, I left the Halcyon Enterprises Campus via corporate PT and headed into the heart of the city. As anyone who knows me intimately can attest, when in a truly foul mood I tend to lose myself in one of two vices: food or drink. Lately, drink had held less appeal for me – perhaps my mongoose-maturity was gaining ground. However, fine dining was a comforting indulgence readily available for a man of my socioeconomic status.

I lunched at an exclusive Yanni-Arrhidaean fusion restaurant in District 29. Enjoying my own company, I lingered over the spiced red meats, steamed seafoods, and thick barley tea for well over an hour.

When I left, having exchanged more credits for the meal than many Römerian families could make in three months, I headed back to my flat. The afternoon sun had already begun to descend when I arrived at *The Feathers*, and the yellow and orange light warmed me as it poured in through the walls of the glass lift.

With a refined chime, the elevator indicated that my private floor had been reached. The doors slid open, and I found myself staring into the scowling face of Henry Davers. Leaning against my flat's front door, his arms crossed over his chest, he at least allowed me to step off the lift before laying into me, snarling, "You're being an ass." He pushed himself off my front door, throwing his hands into the air. "Why is it always me who has to tell you that?"

I slid one hand into my trouser pocket, sizing him up with a cool stare. "I suppose you're the angel on my shoulder." I made a point of looking around the hallway showily. "I'm surprised she's not here, waiting to lecture me."

Henry rolled his eyes, closing the distance between us with a few steps. "She had a lead to follow up. You know, in that case she's working? For you? Because someone tried to kill you?"

The bite in his words cut me to the quick and I began to shake my head, my hands coming up in front of me. "Now, Henry–"

"She's worried about you," he said, cutting me off before I had a chance to make any excuses for my behavior.

"She has a damn funny way of showing it," I shot back.

"I'm worried about you." Henry pressed his hand to his chest, deep brown eyes searching my face. "You've always been reckless,

Chance, but you've never been stupid. You have got to start taking precautions."

My shoulders fell and I shook my head, moving around him to stand in front of the door to my flat. "You sound like Sandra..."

He gave a derisive snort. "Whoever that is, she's right." Pausing, he leaned back on his heels, eyes heavenward. "Wait, who is that?"

"It's not important," I answered, my hand hovering over the handle to the front door. I glanced back at him, brow furrowing. "Is... Is Cadence really worried about me?"

The smack of Henry's hand against his forehead echoed down the corridor. "Oh, for the love of–" Staring at me wide eyed, he answered me through gritted teeth, temper barely contained. "Yes, Chance, she is. I don't know her as well as you do, but even I can tell she's beside herself at the thought that something might happen to you." He shook his head, disgust twisting his lips. "All you've been doing is making that worse. You have to get it together, for both your sakes."

He spoke to me like I was a child -- which brought home how much I'd been acting like one. Deep embarrassment and shame washed over me. I felt my face redden with a blush as I turned to look back at him.

It was no good stomping my feet and pouting about things I didn't like -- whether that was Cadence or anything else. I had to face what was happening to me with dignity.

This was going to be harder than I thought.

Hanging my head low between my aching shoulders, I scraped my thumb along the bio lock on my front door. "You had better come inside. The least I owe you for coming all this way is a drink."

There was no answer from the man behind me. I lifted my head to look at him, afraid that perhaps he would refuse my gesture of goodwill and that I had, this time, pushed our friendship beyond the point of repair.

He stared back at me, looking for what I'm not sure. But he seemed to find it after a moment, his glare softening. "Fine," he said with a sigh. "One drink. And then will you call Cadence?"

"Promise," I answered, stepping through the door in front of him.

I discarded my jacket before stepping down the short flight of stairs that emptied out into the large shadowy living room. I was halfway through the cavernous space, heading for the kitchen, when I heard an unfamiliar voice say, "Lights."

The room was flooded with electric illumination, bringing into sharp focus the impeccably dressed man seated at the end of my large sectional sofa. The stranger stared at us with deep, dark brown eyes.

I shudder to imagine how ridiculous I looked in that instant, jumping a foot into the air, my arms flailing. "Son of a–!"

"First thing we're going to do–" said the man, drawing his hands into his lap, "– is upgrade your security."

Henry rushed into the room and pushed me behind him, curling his hands into fists and raising them in front of himself. "Who in the hell–?!"

But the stranger ignored Henry, looking past him to me and saying loudly, "You told Director Aja you'd wait for me."

I stared at him dumbly before his words and their meaning

connected inside my brain. A hot flash of embarrassment and annoyance flared in my belly. I took a deep breath through my nose.

"For pity's sake," I huffed, stepping out from behind my friend, pushing his fists back down to his sides as I came around him. "I could have you arrested for breaking in here, you know."

"Best not to arrest your bodyguard on the first day," he said, frowning thoughtfully. He rose to his feet and crossed the room. He extended his hand. "Kace Morgan."

"Right." I ignored the handshake, striding past him. "Well, as you can see, I already am very well protected – Henry sees to that."

Kace shot a perplexed glance over at my friend, who quickly plastered on a placating smile and waved a dismissive hand towards me. "He's joking," he said assuringly. Offering his hand, he shook Kace's firmly. "Henry Davers. Very glad to meet you."

"This is hardly a laughing matter, sir." Kace dropped Henry's hand and turned, following me with his gaze alone. "Director Aja briefed me on what happened to you in the Ani-District."

"That information is confidential," I stressed the last word, my hand slicing through the air as I turned back around.

Kace gave a belabored sigh and ran his tongue along his painfully white teeth. He once again stepped towards me, lifting and dropping his shoulders in a bored shrug. "As is everything that I see and hear while protecting you, Mr. Hale." He pressed one of his hands to his chest, the soft brown of his skin melting into the dark purple of his shirt. "Think of me like a priest."

"And how does all this work exactly?" I crossed through the living room and into the kitchen, not bothering to turn on any more lights. In near darkness, I reached into the cabinets and retrieved three crystal tumblers, as well as my half-empty bottle of Petrarchan whiskey. I set everything down on the kitchen island. "You get the pleasure of following me around every hour of every day? Watching me sleep? Tasting my food? You should know, I have an eclectic palate."

"Chance—" said Henry, warning in his tone.

But Kace cut him off before he could finish his thought, planting himself at the edge of the kitchen as he stared at me. "Listen: You don't have to like me, Mr. Hale – I don't have to like you. But know that I will do everything within my power to keep you alive and well. Whether it's convenient for you or not."

I unscrewed the cap of the whisky with slow, deliberate twists, staring at the man in front of me but not really seeing him. If Cadence really was worried about me... If concerns about my safety were what was getting in the way of us being open and honest with each other... well, this was certainly a solution to that problem. I had never known Halcyon to hire anything less than the best in any field, and I doubted Sandra would have sent someone lackluster to keep an eye on me.

Perhaps here was someone I could trust, after all.

Shaking my head and smiling, I poured all three of us a double. "Can't promise I'm going to make it an easy job for you," I observed, pushing one of the glasses across the island towards the man.

Stepping into the shadows with me, he returned my smile with a wry grin of his own. He shrugged. "I like a challenge."

"Then we should get along just fine," I said. I gestured to my new companion with my glass before I downed the liquid in one large gulp.

A shiver went down my spine as the alcohol burned down my gullet. I winced and held Henry's glass out towards him. Shaking his head ruefully, he joined us around the island, taking his drink from me without much enthusiasm.

"Been with Halcyon long, Mr. Morgan?" asked Henry, taking a drink of the amber colored liquid.

"A few years."

"And before that?"

"Well," Kace bobbled his head from side to side, taking as small of a sip of his drink as physically possible. "I've bounced around the sphere a bit. Enlisted in the Arrhidaean Defense Force when I was still a teenager. Got bored there pretty quickly, so when my three-year stint was up, I went looking for more active work."

"Sorry we couldn't have a war to keep you busy," I drawled, leaning my hip against the kitchen island and looking down my nose at him.

He answered my judgmental stare with an equally thorny glare. "Believe it or not, I'm not a violent man, Mr. Hale." He shrugged, placing his drink down on the countertop. "I just like to be useful, and I happen to have a very specific set of skills."

I tilted my head to one side and unsuccessfully smothered a smile. "And babysitting tech executives is what you consider useful?"

There was a beat of silence. Then, Kace gave a small laugh, rolling his eyes. "Okay, okay, you got me: this assignment wouldn't have been my first choice." He sighed and shook his head, his gaze falling to the floor. "But when Director Aja asks you to do something, it's hard to say no."

"You're certainly not wrong there," I said, nodding.

With a small smile curling the corner of his lips, Kace slipped his hands into his trouser pockets, mouth opening as if he were about to speak. Then, his face contorted in momentary confusion, and he pulled a black docuchip out with one hand. He looked at it for a moment, and then nodded, his expression clearing. He pushed the docuchip towards me, wiggling it slightly from side to side. "Oh, that's right. I believe you asked Director Aja for this. A list of potential threats."

I took the chip from him with a sigh. "Just what I needed to brighten my day."

"Don't forget," said Henry, swirling his whisky around his glass. "You need to call Cadence. You promised."

"Cadence?" queried Kace, looking between us with a raised brow. "Anyone I should know about?"

"Cadence Turing, she's my..." The proper word for us eluded me for the moment and I struggled to define our relationship in its current nebulous state, especially in front of a man I wasn't entirely sure I could trust. "She's a friend. And I didn't forget, I just want to take a look at this first."

Reaching into a drawer under the kitchen island, I rummaged about before pulling out a palm sized datapad. Turning it on with a swipe of my finger, I clicked the docuchip into the drive on the side. I poured myself another, smaller whiskey while I waited for the material to load.

The list flickered into life -- a several-page long document broken up into bolded bullet points, littered with photographs and other images. I thumbed through it to the end, skimming the data as I furrowed my brow.

"I haven't heard of these people," I said at last, settling back on my heels.

"Mostly they're not people," answered Kace, shifting his weight from foot to foot. "They're organizations."

I hummed in response, scrolling to a random page in the middle of the packet, continuing to read whichever sentences captured my attention. My gaze caught a word, and I did a double take at the pad, lifting it up to read more closely. "Wait a minute... Cavalcade? Cavalcade Technologies?" I shook my head. "They're hardly killers -- just a business rival!"

"Their CEO, Ramona Hadley has known ties to the Shaftes Syndicate -- any dirty work she needs doing, she taps them to get it done."

I had heard of the Shaftes Syndicate. Everyone had -- they were the stuff of underworld legend. But I had also met Ramona Hadley several times, and she had always struck me as an exceedingly stuffy, boring old woman. My mind struggled to reconcile what I knew of the Shaftes Syndicate's reputation with the image of Ramona sitting across from me in a pink and grey tweed pantsuit. "I thought stuff like that only happened in flickers."

Looking up from my studies, I realized Kace had wandered back into the living room. He peered through an eye-width gap in the window curtains, as if he expected to see something beyond the spires of the surrounding cityscape. "Even criminals go legit sometimes... but those old habits are hard to shake."

As I joined Kace in the other room, I flicked back to the beginning of the list, resolving to read it more thoroughly. My eyes widened in surprise when, beside the first bullet point sat not a name, but a picture -- a close, grainy image of a splotch of spray paint thrown up on the window of a dilapidated building.

The graffiti was shaped like a diamond. Inside the diamond, a nest of hash marks, and on top of those marks, two dots, one open and one closed.

"What's this?" I said, turning the pad around so Kace could see the screen.

When Kace saw the blotch, he smiled ruefully. "We don't know what they call themselves. They sign things with that mark. I'm sure the EO has their own name for them. So does the IPC, probably." Abandoning the window, he strolled down the adjoining hallway, calling back over his shoulder. "Animanecron rebels."

"Freedom fighters," interjected Henry, crossing from the kitchen, his lips a firm line.

"Or insurgents," countered Kace evenly, continuing to disappear toward the bedrooms. "Whatever. I've been calling them the Whiston Underground."

I flipped the pad back towards myself and began to read.

"This..." I shook my head slowly from side to side, blood cooling in my veins. "...this can't be right. Cells on every IPC-controlled planet? Is that even possible?"

"They're robots, sir," Kace answered, returning with an unimpressed glaze to his brown eyes. "Organizing is what they're good at."

I glared at him. "Don't call me 'sir'." I began to swipe through the collected threats Halcyon had received from the Whiston

Underground, muttering aloud, "Sir... it makes me sound like I'm a hundred."

"Have you ever met an animanecron, Mr. Morgan?" asked Henry, perching himself on the arm of the couch beside me.

Kace fixed Henry with a curious stare. "No, I haven't had the pleasure."

Henry took another sip of his barely touched drink. "You probably have, you just may not have realized it." He shook his head. "They're not so different from us, you know."

Pulling his lips down into an exaggerated frown, Kace bobbled his head from side to side, shrugging. "Can't say I'm surprised by that. We made them after all. Why wouldn't we have done so in our image?"

I thought I had begun to accept the vitriol I had experienced in the Ani District -- but the thoughts expressed in the anonymous v-chats, holos, and graffiti scrawled on the walls of destroyed Halcyon Enterprises property were on an entirely different level.

According to the Underground, my company, and by extension, I as its CEO, was to blame for the Charcornacians' actions. Animanecron deaths could be laid at my doorstep. Our inaction was not just misguided -- it was willful antagonism, a calculated strategy designed to maximize animanecron casualties and suffering.

Our reckoning -- my reckoning -- was coming.

One photo in particular took me by the throat and shook me. It showed a Halcyon Enterprises research and development facility on the lesser moon of Pataea -- or rather, it had once been an R&D facility. The field office was gutted, burned to the ground. I remembered the report -- there had been insurance paperwork to wade through, employee reassignments to approve, leasing agents to meet for a replacement office. But like so much of the work I did, it was all several times removed from the actual event. It was just one part of another busy day.

How disappointed the people who did this would have been to know that.

I closed my eyes against the image, struggling to find my voice, even as I knew the lie for what it was as I said, "These are all threats against the company – not me."

"You are the company, Mr. Hale." Kace sat on the ottoman across from me, unbuttoning his suit jacket as he descended. "Taking you out would send a message to Arrhidaeus and every planet in the IPC to start taking their demands more seriously."

"And just what are their demands?"

"War." He rested his elbows on his knees, threading his fingers around each other. "They're doing their best to funnel supplies, money, and information back to those on Charcornacian-controlled worlds, but they want a formal declaration of hostilities from the Interplanetary Commission. Or barring that, at least from one of the planets that make up the commission."

I sighed, bouncing the pad off my leg. "Like Arrhidaeus."

"Like Arrhidaeus." He nodded, rolling his shoulders back. "The Underground wants to take the fight to the Charcornacians. Hard to blame them for that."

Fingers worrying my bottom lip, I shook my head from side to side. Would there be any lengths I wouldn't go to, any action too radical to undertake, if it meant saving the people I loved?

If it meant saving Cadence?

I tossed the pad to one side, watching as it skittered across the couch cushions. "The man who tried to kill me was just that...a man." I looked at Kace as I leaned back onto the sofa. "Animanecrons had nothing to do with this."

Kace blinked slowly. "Is that what the Enforcement Office thinks?"

"The Enforcement Office couldn't think their way out of orbit," I sneered, my gaze falling somewhere over his left shoulder. An idea occurred to me. Rubbing my chin, I rose to my feet, moving slowly towards the center of the living room. "Where is the Whiston Underground headquartered in Römer?"

"Why on the sphere would you think I'd know that?"

"Oh, please," I tutted, turning to face him. Kace was likewise spun around to look at me, his face screwed up in confusion. I gestured to the discarded datapad on the couch. "I know you're the one who compiled that list." Shifting my weight to my back foot, I slid my hand into my trouser pocket, watching his face closely. "Sandra chose you out of all the other security officers we have on the payroll for this assignment, so it stands to reason she thinks you're one of our best. And–" I tapped the toe of his shoe with my own. "–*you* put the Whiston Underground at the top of that list, and doubtless already know everything there is to know about the top threat to Halcyon Enterprises, and me."

Kace rubbed at his jaw in a concentrated way, as if unused to the feeling of skin there. His gaze was focused somewhere to the left of me. "Huh," he said at last.

I rolled my eyes. "What?"

His brows knit over his dark brown eyes. "You really are more than just a pretty face."

Henry snorted out a laugh. I snapped my mouth shut, working hard to hide a chagrined smile. "Are you going to flirt with me some more, Mr. Morgan, or answer my question?"

Smirking, Kace stood, pulling his jacket taut across his shoulders. "I don't know where they are, exactly. The Ani District, obviously. The last bit of digging I did put them somewhere near the AN-GRAV tracks."

IO

Chapter 10

"I can't believe you talked Kace into this," said Henry, gloved hands jammed into his pockets, the high collar of his coat hiding the lower half of his face.

"I'm very persuasive when I want to be," I answered, focused on the task at hand. Clapping him on the shoulder, I nudged him off the public walkway. "Now, come on; we haven't checked out that side of the street."

"I can't believe you talked *me* into this," he grumbled, allowing himself to be shoved this way and that.

"Oh, that was the easy part," I said. "All I had to do was trap you in an agreement. I knew you wouldn't weasel out of it once I did my bit."

Henry sighed, shaking me off him in a half-hearted way. "True. Unlike you, I try to honor the spirit of most arrangements, and you did call Cadence like you promised." He looked behind us, lowering his voice in an attempt to keep Kace from overhearing us. "Why do you think she didn't answer? I hope everything's okay..."

"I'm sure she's just hot on some trail." In truth, I thought that perhaps she was giving me a taste of my own medicine, richly deserved, and not answering when I called. Still, I didn't want to say as much to Henry, and instead settled for shrugging and saying, "It's nothing. She'll call back when she's ready."

Begrudgingly, Henry kept pace with me as we meandered up and down the span of several city blocks where the AN-GRAV tracks intersected with the Ani-District. This area was particularly run down, since even many animanecrons found living in such close proximity to the constantly running trains more trouble than it was worth. People experiencing homelessness found temporary shelter in dilapidated warehouses and boarded up residential buildings, but at this time of the day, the streets were mostly deserted. Kace kept a few feet behind us, alert to possible threats, but otherwise unobtrusive.

"I don't know what you're hoping to find," said Henry. He sighed, his face turned heavenward as we walked. "They're not going to have a sign that says: 'Welcome to the Whiston Underground,' you know."

"Kace said people use them to ferry supplies and messages back and forth to Charcornac-controlled planets." I turned down an alley that was so small I had to shimmy down it sideways, hands spidering along the filthy concrete wall as I looked for anything that might pass for a clue. "So, it stands to reason that people know where to find them...or they leave a way for themselves to be found. We just have to figure out where or who or how..."

Henry waited at the mouth of the alley, peering in after me. "Right. So, we're wandering around completely blind, hoping to stumble onto something."

"That mark–" I extricated myself from between the two buildings, scowling at him. "–the one you said is their signature, the one you showed me? Maybe that's what we need to–"

Stopping mid-sentence, my gaze fell upon an animanecron who was walking up the opposite side of the street. I recognized him immediately, his long brown beard flowing loose, almost trailing behind him as he walked.

Without another word to Henry or Kace, I began to follow the man from a distance, waiting until he rounded the corner before I jogged forward. I peered around the corner, following the familiar figure's progress with my eyes. He approached a large, barren lot, fenced off from the rest of the neighborhood. The animanecron then stopped, looking around for a moment before he began to climb.

"Hello..." I murmured.

My quarry scaled the fence without effort, dropping down to the other side with a soft thud. He dusted off his hands and turned towards the large building in the center of the lot, walking towards it as if he were taking a simple evening stroll.

"Vint," I murmured under my breath.

"Who?" said Henry, close behind me.

I tossed my head towards the lone figure striding through the lot on which the AN-GRAV power station stood. "The gentleman who said our mystery man frequented this area. Looks like he's no stranger here himself."

As the three of us watched from around the corner, Vint

approached the seemingly locked door of the energy station. He eased the door open without entering a code and slipped inside, closing it shut behind him.

"Follow me," I whispered over my shoulder, and at a run, I headed for the fenced off station.

Pouncing on the chain-link fence at speed, I was already at the top before Kace and Henry had caught up with me. "What are you doing?" whispered Kace at me from the other side of the barrier.

Dropping onto the ground on the other side of the fence, I smiled at him. "Investigating. It's sort of a hobby. Now, keep up, you two."

Sharing an aggrieved glance, Kace and Henry began to climb the fence. I headed for the station, trying the keypad secured door and finding that it was, indeed, unsecured. Not waiting for my friend or my bodyguard to gain ground, I entered the building.

Weak bioelectric lights hung in the entryway, giving the whole space an eerie, underwater like glow. I listened carefully to the sound of footsteps before setting off down the dimly lit corridor directly in front of me.

Down a short flight of stairs, the hallway emptied out into a cavernous room filled with towering generators. These machines rumbled contentedly like snoring giants, providing power to the trains that connected the city above. I paused at the mouth of this imposing space, unsure of how to proceed.

I heard Kace and Henry stop short behind me. "Mr. Hale, we shouldn't–"

"Shh!" I cautioned.

A loud wooden clatter sounded from somewhere to our left. I darted towards it, keeping low, moving around the gargantuan generators, straining my eyes in the weak light. At last, I came to an open double door, the crude wooden dowel that had been holding the portal shut now laying on the ground in front of it. The stairway beyond led further down, utterly dark.

"Now I've got you..." I muttered, starting forward.

"Chance, wait!" Henry's hand gripped my shoulder, yanking me back.

"What?" I answered with annoyance, shaking him off as I turned.

Henry's face was hidden in shadow, but the exasperation in his words was clear as the flash of a camera. "We don't know where this leads! We can't just go in blind."

"They're in here somewhere, I know it." I knocked against Henry's chest with my fist, grinning. "Come on, chum, where's your sense of adventure?"

"It must be in my other suit," he said, moving around me so he was blocking the doorway with his body. "Right now, I need to keep you safe. Cadence is counting on me to help keep you safe. This–" He flung his hand into the darkness below. "–is not safe."

I gritted my teeth, but kept my smile plastered on. "Aw, come now. I'm with you and Kace, how much safer could I get?"

Moving to step around him, I was stopped once again, this time by Kace's hand on my arm, but this time there was no give in his grip, his face grim and determined as he pivoted to stand next to Henry.

"Do I need to physically remove you from this situation, sir?"

This time I wasn't so sure I could shake myself loose. Rolling my eyes, I relented, taking a step back with my hands raised in acquiescence. "Fine. Fine! We'll do this–"

I watched in horror as two pairs of dark hands emerged from the void behind Henry and Kace, reaching out for them.

"Look out!" I shouted. But it was too late. Before the first word was even out of my mouth the arms, which seemed to have appeared from the darkness itself, were wrapped tight around my companion's torsos and they were yanked back into the black, shouts echoing from them both before there was an abrupt silence.

Without hesitation I plunged forward into pitch darkness. Whether it was my own carelessness or the work of an assailant, my feet suddenly lost their purchase against the steps, and I flew forward into nothingness. I braced myself for impact, but it never came. The blackness around me took on a different texture, and I was carried off into unconsciousness like a child carried off to their bed in the middle of the night.

The next thing I felt was the pull of hot, humid air. I returned to waking with great reluctance, my eyelids refusing at first to lift. I inhaled, and there was a tang of warm bioplastic upon my tongue that made me recoil. Shaking my head in reaction to the foul taste, my body was further assaulted by something rough and dry smacking me in the face.

Something that covered my head.

Thoroughly alarmed, I next discovered that I could not move my limbs – rigid plastic bit into my wrists and around my ankles, securing me to a stiff-backed steel chair.

Panic bubbled deep within me, flooding my senses like a pot

of water left on a hot stove. Blind, bound, alone God knows where, taken by God knows who for God knows what–

"He's awake," said a female voice from somewhere to my left.

I turned towards the voice. "Hello?"

My greeting was ignored, as another voice spoke over mine, this time coming from behind me. It was a soft, low masculine voice. "Sarc, I can see that, thank you."

"Well? Get on with it." The woman's voice dropped to a grumble. "Anta, don't know what you think he's going to say…"

Clearing the grit from my throat, I attempted to straighten. "I'm not going to say anything while I'm tied up like an animal."

"You act like a rat," said a higher-pitched male voice, almost like a teenager. It came from my right-hand side. "You get treated like a rat." I heard the scuff of shoes against concrete. "Skulking around in the shadows, looking for… looking for what, exactly?"

I shook my head. The bag fluttered against my face. "I'm sorry?"

The low male voice spoke once again, this time from in front of me. "You were following Vint. Why?"

"I wasn't," I protested feebly. "I–"

The person in front of me gave a hum. I listened intently as they walked in a circle towards my left. "A liar, as well, then."

"Aren't they all liars?" said the female voice, the words dripping with disgust. "Rus, flesh. Can't trust them. Useless pieces of–"

"You were following Vint," the low, soft voice cut in with a sharpness that did not invite a challenge. "You were poking around the AN-GRAV tracks looking for something, saw him, and then followed him down here. What is it that you were hoping to find?"

"You, I think." I shifted against my bonds. "Are you the Whiston Underground?"

"Your name, not ours." The deep voice echoed in my ear. He was close to me, but I felt no breath on my cheek. "We are your unwanted children -- the fruits of your labor, turned sour and toxic. We are what endures after you are gone, and we are what came before you. We are ideas given flesh and made ideas again."

I swallowed hard. "I'm here to help you. My name is–"

"We're quite aware of who and what you are, Chance Tobias Hale." The voice moved away. It sounded tired. "That would be the problem. Normally, we have ways of dealing with human interlopers but with you–" The man heaved a sigh. "As I'm sure you've experienced all your life, with you, normal rules don't quite apply. So, the question has become: what do we do with you?"

"You could try to listen," I snapped, the tension in the air making my nerves brittle in the same way that seaside air corrodes metal. "I'm telling you, if we could just talk like civilized people–"

Something, someone's foot I reckoned, impacted the side of my chair and I skittered to one side, clamping my teeth hard on the tip of my tongue.

"Sinc, we are not civilized people, flesh."

"Damn it, I've had enough of this," I said, snarling beneath the bag, blood from my wounded tongue pooling in the bottom of my mouth. "Either kill me, or let me go, but make up your damn minds and get on with it."

The bag was ripped off my head.

A ring of overhead fluorescent lights snapped into life. There were eyes watching me from every side -- I counted ten animanecrons in all surrounding me. From what I could see, which was still precious little, I surmised I was in some kind of maintenance area of the energy station. Hydropipes crisscrossed the ceiling above my head, and some of the animanecrons were leaning against lazily blinking servers and relays.

I could see no way out.

I I

Chapter II

"I still say we should snap his neck and be done with it," said a small, furious-looking woman directly to my left, her arms folded tightly across her chest.

From behind me, a second heavy sigh echoed. "Stop thinking like a hammer, Pauline," commanded the voice of my main interrogator. "Not every problem is a nail."

A hand gripped my chair, and I was jolted backwards. Balanced precariously on two legs, my feet dangling uselessly in the air, I found myself looking up at an upside-down face, lit by the dim glow of a handheld solar torch. It was a shockingly handsome face -- even at this angle – with a firm, chiseled jaw, straight, broad nose, and a full mouth, beautiful even as it scowled at me. "Though he does remain a problem."

"How do I convince you people that I'm not?" I begged, feeling uniquely vulnerable in such a position.

There was a snort of laughter from in front of me. The man above me quirked his brow upward. "Not calling us 'you people' would be a good start."

I shook my head, swallowing hard. "Sorry, you're right. An admittedly poor choice of words."

The chair was dropped back onto all four of its legs with a thud. The man stepped around me. He crouched, balancing on the balls of his feet. Tall and muscular, he looked like a spring wound close to snapping. Even in the weak light, I could see his faded grey eyes assessing me.

The animanecron broke out into a smile, toothy and threatening. "Sare, you're not very tall, are you, Mr. Hale?"

I blinked. "I try to be."

He stood, unfurling like a dancer. He began to pace the floor in front of where I sat, gesturing to my recumbent form with one hand. "In the flesh, I mean." His shadow slithered across me. "You look taller in vids."

Watching him, I found myself wondering where his tattoo-like PCBs were displayed. The assembled animanecrons all had theirs visible – whether they were on their arms, which was common, across the stomach, or even on the face. But the man in front of me had no obvious markings on his exposed flesh. Unblemished, he was like a statue of some ancient god – a perfect, solid piece of stone.

"The men I was with," I asked hesitantly. "Are they dead?"

The animanecron continued pacing. "Not yet."

"Good." Clearing my throat, I attempted to sit up a little straighter as I looked from person to person. "I was hoping to ask you all a few questions."

There was a general tittering of laughter, but it ceased as quickly as it started, silenced by a single twitch of the grey-eyed animanecron's hand. He shook his head, shifting his weight onto his back foot as he stopped pacing to face me once more. "You're in no position to ask anyone anything, Mr. Hale."

"I'm not your enemy, damn it," I said, straining at my bonds. Closing my eyes, I shook my head, attempting to pick my words carefully. "I know what you think of me, and what you think about my company, but I promise you – I'm on your side."

"We don't need you on our side, Hale." Pauline sneered at me from the side of the room, most of her body hidden in the shadows. "We just need you out of our way."

I looked from face to face, and I felt my chest tighten. Those animanecrons who weren't looking at me with open hatred were watching me with a detachment that made it plain that whatever was about to happen was none of their concern. Considering Pauline's words, my mind rushed back to the dark alleyway in the Ani District, where I had, only a few nights ago, fought for my life. Would any of these people have stepped in to help me? No. Would any of them have lent a hand to my assailants?

Perhaps.

I swallowed the lump of fear in my throat. "Did you send that man to kill me?"

The reaction in the room was immediate, like a circuit had been connected. The faces before, which had been impassive and cold, now lit up with shock. Whispers rose to a fever pitch, and everyone in the room began to shift and move.

"Xio, Quinn–" said Pauline, her eyes bright, light rippling through the symbols I could now see etched onto her palms.

The animanecron called Quinn cut her off with a sharp hiss that made me jump. Turning to face her, he shook his head once, and then returned his attention to me, his grey eyes wide with fascination.

"So..." Quinn examined me with renewed interest. He let out a harumph. He drew his hand back and rubbed his lower lip with his thumb. "It would seem she wasn't telling tall tales after all."

I sat ramrod straight in my chair, the hairs on the back of my neck bristling. "Who?" I demanded, dreading the answer.

But Quinn did not deign to answer me. He turned on his heel and strode over to a small, rusted door. Shaking his head with a ruefulness I did not understand, he knocked a complex pattern against the door and waited, looking at me over his shoulder.

"Who?" I shouted again, unheeded.

The door opened with a tortured squeal. More light flooded into the room, preceding Cadence by a fraction of a second. Kace and Henry tripped along beside her, with her hand gripping the back of their suits. Once she was inside, Quinn reached and shut the door behind her.

"You were supposed to meet me at my place," said Cadence, her head falling to one side as she stared.

I deflated in my chair, my chin falling to my chest. "Hullo, Cay."

She stepped nearer to me, but Quinn cut in front of her, one arm outstretched. "That's close enough," he said.

Cadence's jaw clenched. She nodded her assent, and Quinn receded once again. She pushed Kace forward, lifting him an inch off the floor and shaking him as if he were a piece of paper rather than a human being. "Who is this?"

"Mr. Morgan–" Lifting my head, I shook my hair out of my eyes and attempted to smile. "–is my new bodyguard."

"Oh, I see." Her lips formed into a thin line. "So, you decided you needed a babysitter after all?"

My smile vanished like a drop of rain falling into the ocean. "Cadence, why are you here?"

She sighed. "You ignore my calls, my v-chats, and then you stand me up." Her hip jutted out to one side. "So, you can go...what? Get yourself kidnapped?"

My cheeks and neck begin to redden. "I have this entirely under control," I insisted.

"*You* are tied to a *chair*." Her jaw tightened visibly, and her next words came out in a rough growl. "Anta, Chance, I was worried about you! The last time I didn't know where you were, you got stabbed! And now this!"

"You know, I'm glad I was stabbed! How else would I have ever gotten any of your attention?"

The words were out of my mouth before I could stop them, landing on Cadence with such force that she stumbled back, sputtering. Color rose to her cheeks and her eyes widened. "Jetle ped con becker," she started, letting loose a string of unfamiliar Animatum that could only be colorful expletives. "What in the hell–!"

"Aldo Fogg."

I twisted my head around to stare over my shoulder at Quinn, who had spoken the name with such irritating calmness that I was half convinced it was some kind of animanecron turn of phrase. "What?"

Quinn stood up from the conveyor belt on which he had been

perched, his gaze intent on my face. "Reg, the man who tried to kill you, the man whose body was found this morning dumped on our streets. His name is Aldo Fogg." He came around in front of me and flipped the holopuck that held Fogg's image into my lap. "That's what you wanted to ask us about, yes? That's all we know. Why he wanted you dead, Mr. Hale, I have no idea. But he wasn't working for us. Not in that capacity."

"So, you did know him?" I said.

"We had a business relationship," answered Quinn, his expression growing dark. "He was supposed to make contact at the Ergo Sum Block Party the other day, but he never showed. I guess now we know why. Still, as far as I know, Aldo Fogg didn't really work for anyone but himself."

"What does that mean?" asked Cadence.

He smiled at her, but this was a far more genuine smile than the grins he had lavished on me. "You'll find out. Can't do your job for you, krezic." He folded his hands together in the traditional animanecron fashion and bowed to her. "Good luck."

The assembled animanecrons began to trickle out of the room, murmuring amongst themselves and casting pointed looks at us. Quinn leaned down behind me, and I felt the bonds that held my wrists and feet fall away. He was the last to leave, patting Cadence's shoulder as he passed with a familiarity I resented. He turned just as he was about to disappear from sight. He took a step back into the room, leaning in against the doorframe.

"Hale – remember what I said." He watched me from the doorway, his beautiful face an expressionless mask. "Don't get in our way."

I glowered at him. He smiled in return and left, swinging the door shut behind him.

"What a charming friend you've made," I observed after a moment. Standing on unsteady legs, I rubbed feeling back into my wrists. "You can let Mr. Morgan and Henry go now, Cadence."

Cadence released her hold on Henry but took a moment to look at the other man she was holding aloft. Kace returned her gaze and shrugged his shoulders. "If you don't mind," he said.

She lowered him to the floor gently, waiting to make sure his feet would hold him before releasing her grip. "Are you always so bad at your job, Kace?"

"I'll admit," said Kace, readjusting his clothes as he regained his balance. "This has been an off day for me. Won't happen in the future."

A haughty harrumph was her response to this promise. "I certainly hope not."

Brushing himself off, Kace straightened, giving my love a visual once over as he did so, his head falling to one side. "Mr. Hale didn't mention that you were an animanecron."

Cadence's face screwed up in confusion. "Why should he?"

"No reason, I suppose, it's just..." He gestured between the two of us, and I was delighted to see a slight flush come into his cheeks. "A human and an animanecron being, you know, involved – that's a little... unusual, isn't it?"

Cadence sighed heavily and fixed my new bodyguard with a cold stare. "Sarc, I think the entire last year of my life could be summed up as 'a little unusual'. Chance and I courting is one of the least extraordinary things to have occurred during that time."

Without another word, she quickly turned her attention to our mutual friend Henry, pulling him into a hug.

"Henry," she said, squeezing him tight around the shoulders. "Are you okay?"

"I'm terrified," admitted Henry readily, returning her embrace. "But physically? I'll be fine." He leaned away from her, looking her over with concern. "Are you okay? You didn't answer when Chance called."

Cadence shook her head. "There's no signal down here."

I jiggled the thin gold band on my wrist, and the screen lit up to indicate the time. "Well, nice to know that we only lost a few hours."

Cay released my friend with a glare in my direction, stalking towards me. "You could've lost your life. Again."

I met her gaze steadily. "So could you." I took a deep breath and let it out slowly. "I don't see why you should be allowed to risk everything for me, and I can't do the same for you."

Kace, rubbing the back of his neck and shoulders, looked between us with undisguised curiosity. Cadence blinked several times in rapid succession, her head falling to one side, her mouth opening slightly. "Sarc, please, Chance. Don't pretend this was about helping me. Not after all you've put me through today."

"Who said anything about pretending?"

Her forehead wrinkled and her eyes narrowed. "If the cost of your help is your life, then I don't want it, Chance."

"What *do* you want, Cay?" I took a step forward, my arms spread wide in front of me. "Can't you just tell me?"

She clamped her mouth shut and turned away from me slightly, shoulders hunched, but her expression no less displeased.

When she showed no sign of answering my query, I shook my head, throwing my hands up in the air.

"Fine. How did you find Quinn and his cadre of extremists anyway?" I pivoted to a different question, sensing her unwillingness to air our dirty laundry in a damp cellar.

Cadence straightened, giving a disdainful sniff. "They're hardly extremists," she said. She glowered. "And how do you think I found them? I'm a private investigator. I asked questions." Her chin jutted out to indicate me. "How did you find them?"

I dusted off my trousers, which had become covered in dirt and dried mud. "Surely, I'm allowed some secrets."

She rolled her eyes and gestured to my bodyguard. "Given the sudden appearance of Kace, I'm guessing the influence of Halcyon Enterprises was involved somehow."

I lifted a brow. "Perhaps."

My caginess was not well-received. Cadence crossed her arms over her chest and took a deep breath. Her eyes aimed heavenward, I could feel the irritation coming off her in waves. But there was something else in her face. She was pale – well, paler than usual – and her normally loose and graceful frame was taut and tense. She looked... shaken.

I felt slightly sick and very guilty. I rubbed at my temples with my fingertips, licked my lips, and tried again.

"Cay, listen–" I started, dropping my hands to my sides.

Without warning, she threw herself at me. I stumbled back, fearing at first that she meant to do some kind of violence towards me. It was with a mix of confusion, relief, and painful affection that I found myself wrapped up in her arms, her body pressed against mine.

She buried her face in my neck, her breathing stilled, her hands balled up in the shoulders of my shirt.

"Cay?" I tried to crane my head around so that I could look down at her. "Cadence, are you–?"

"I..." Her arms tightened around me. "I was really worried about you, Chance."

Enough was enough – this conversation was happening, whether the two of us were ready for it or not. I held her close, wrapping one arm around her back and burying my other hand in the hair at the nape of her neck. Looking past her, I caught my friend's eye, indicating the door with my gaze. "Henry..."

Henry nodded sharply. He put a hand on Kace's shoulder and started walking towards the door, voice pitched high and loud. "Let's see if we can find the way out of here, Kace."

His attention fixed on Cadence and me, Kace frowned as he gestured towards me. "I should really stay–"

"I don't think anybody's coming back to finish the job, Kace." My grip on Cadence tightened. "Just give us a moment – please?"

With a begrudging grimace, my bodyguard allowed himself to be led out of the room by Henry, who nodded to me as he exited. When the sound of my two companions had faded into the background, I turned my attention fully to the woman in my arms. "It's alright," I whispered, my lips close to her scalp. "I'm alright."

Cadence shook her head, her temple digging into my chest. "Frig, Chance... I don't think I can do this."

My forehead wrinkled at her choice of speech tag. I pulled back from her, a slight frown tugging at the corner of my lips. "There's nothing to be frightened of, darling."

But Cadence refused to look up at me, seemingly locked into position around me, her head bowed, her body tense. The words turned thick and heavy in my mouth, like half-eaten caramels, but still I knew what I had to say – what I had to know.

"Cadence, do you love me?" I asked.

Cadence's grip on me loosened. She looked at me, brow furrowed. "You want to talk about that here?" The tip of her tongue flicked out to wet her bottom lip. "Now?"

"Yes. Now," I said, my tone gentle, but firm. Rubbing her arms, I let my head fall to one side. "Do you even care about me at all?"

"How can you ask that?" She backed away from my touch, her fist pressed to her chest. "If I didn't care, would I be this worried? Of course, I care! Chance–"

"Then, why?" I reached for her again, catching hold of her free hand and holding it tightly in my own. "Why is it that my life has to be on the line for you to want to spend time with me? Why do people have to be threatening me for you to want me close?"

Her mouth hinged open and shut as she struggled for words. "I – I want to – to keep you safe."

"You want to keep me like people keep fine silverware -- somewhere high up, out of sight – never to use, but to take out and look at every once and awhile." I dropped her hand and stepped back, shaking my head. "Well, I can't do this anymore. I've had enough."

A look of panic crossed Cadence's inky blue eyes. "Chance..."

"I'm in love with you, Cay – you know that. But I deserve to be loved back." I opened my arms, searching her face for some kind of answer. "I want a life with you. A future. Not just a past. Now, do you want that too? Or not?"

Cadence took a large step back from me, looking at me askance with undisguised terror. "What future?" Cadence's voice was pregnant with pain. "The one where you grow old and decrepit? The one where you wither away before my eyes and die? The one where I'm left alone – again?"

I couldn't pretend that the issue of Cadence's virtual immortality had not crossed my mind. I had considered, for example, that while I would go gray and get wrinkles, she'd always look exactly as she did now. But I had never thought about it from her perspective – I had never thought about how much she had already lost, and how unaccustomed to such loss she really was.

"Oh, Cay," I murmured, my heart breaking. "I..." I trailed off, at loss for words, my mind reeling. Could I really ask her to be with me when I couldn't be with her in the same way? I would have the gift of a lifetime with her at my side – and then she would have to endure so much longer without me.

Cadence pushed a hand through her hair, twisting the other into her shirt. "You think I've been keeping away from you because I don't love you? It's because..." She gave a growl of frustration and dropped her hands to her sides, throwing her head back and staring up at the ceiling. "I'm, I'm not like you, Chance! I'm not human. I don't know how to let go, how to lose things. How to move on." She gestured to herself with a hopelessness that shattered me. "I'm an animanecron. The bonds we make, the things we create – they're supposed to last forever. They're supposed to endure."

Bonds that endure. I looked down at my filth-caked hands.

All I could offer her was... everything. My heart. My body. My life. I closed my hands into fists. Why shouldn't that be enough? Swallowing hard, I shook my head, lifting my gaze back to her face.

"Cay... is a flower any less beautiful because it only blooms for a season? Is a sunrise any less breathtaking because it leads to a sunset?" With a sharp exhalation, I moved towards her, wrapping her up in an embrace, unsure if she would allow me to hold her, but grateful when she did not push me away. "Cadence...it's not just the things that last that are worth loving."

She buried her face in my neck. "But when you're gone..."

I ran my hand down the back of her hair and kissed the top of her head. "You'll grieve." Resting my cheek against her forehead, I closed my eyes tightly. "It'll hurt." Opening my eyes, I shook my head. "And that hurt will never, ever go away. But do you want to know a secret?"

She nodded wordlessly.

"The love we share...that will never, ever go away either." Wrapping my arms around her waist, I leaned against her fully and felt her relax into me. "Death won't stop it. Time won't stop it. The ending of the universe won't stop it. But you can't have one without the other."

"That's terrible." Cadence exhaled. "I... I don't know if I can do that."

I took several steps back from her, forcing her to stand on her own two feet or fall. "That's life," I said. "You have to let yourself live it." I shook my head. "Or else you really are just a machine."

With hesitant steps, she moved closer to me, our eyes locked together. Reaching out with hungry hands, she curled her fingers into my jacket, gripping the fabric tight but not pulling me towards herself.

"I'm not just a machine," she said quietly, so quietly I had to lean forward to catch the words on the air.

I lifted my hands to her shoulders and closed the distance between us with a step. "I know," I answered with solemnity. "I know it, Cay."

Her hands relaxed and flattened against me, rubbing at my chest in small gentle circles that sent shivers through me. I took a deep breath and closed my eyes. "Now... Do you love me, Cay?"

Her wandering hands slid up to my neck and onto my jaw, and I felt her shift under my hands, felt her lips move millimeters from mine. "You know I do."

"Say it," I begged, not caring for my pride or propriety. "Please."

She leaned forward, moving ever so slightly to the left so that her cheek rested against mine, her mouth next to my ear now. "I love you, Chance."

How many times had I imagined her saying those words to me? How many times had I imagined all the complex scenarios and dramatic scenes in which she would finally admit her feelings for me? And then, then, in reality it turned out that all I had to do was ask? Ask and she would say it?

I wanted to laugh. I wanted to cry. I did neither. I smiled, and it was my first real smile in days.

Drawing back, her lips found mine and we shared a soft, desperate kiss, an aching apology of a kiss that stung and soothed my wounded heart.

She pulled away first, burying her face in my chest, muttering in Animatum so quickly that I couldn't catch what she said until she switched to Common Tongue.

"I love you, Chance," she murmured. "I love you so much. I love you so much, I'm willing to lose you." Looking up at me, pleading with her eyes, she added: "Just not anytime soon, okay?"

I kissed her forehead. "That's a promise, Cay."

We stayed that way, holding on to each other as if we were the only people on the sphere, for another solid minute before the sound of shuffling feet and murmuring voices somewhere outside the room reminded me that our two companions were waiting on us. Clearing my throat, I brushed my lips against her cheek one final time before releasing her. "Well, now that that's... all settled... Come on," I said, my hand falling down to grasp hers. "We need you to show us the way out of here and back to civilization. We need to talk with Oliver. Tell him we have a name for our cadaver."

Chapter 12

We found the good Inspector in his favorite pub, *The Anga's Head,* in District 38. Trying to unwind after a stressful day spent investigating the seedier side of Römer, the poor, tired man waved us over to his booth in the corner.

"Didn't expect to see you all here," said Brisbois once we were within earshot, leaning his arm up over the back of his seat. He gestured to Kace, quirking his brow upward. "Who's this?"

Stepping forward, his hand outstretched, Kace nodded a greeting. "Kace Morgan," he said, shaking Brisbois' hand. "I'm Mr. Hale's new bodyguard."

Brisbois made a noise of interest in the back of his throat, looking from Kace to me and then back again, the corners of his mouth pulled down in an inquisitive frown. "You from a private firm, or–?"

Kace shook his head. "I'm part of Halcyon Enterprises Security Division."

Brisbois reached for his pint of ale and smirked. "Drew the short straw, did you?"

Kace returned his smile with a broad grin of his own. "Yeah, something like that."

"I'm standing right here," I chimed in, leaning forward.

"We know," said Brisbois. He waved his hand towards the rest of the empty booth. "Have a seat; let me buy you all some drinks."

Once the drinks arrived and we were sure of not being interrupted, Cadence and I proceeded to tell Brisbois about what had transpired and, more importantly, what we had learned about the identity of the man now lying in the District 16 EO Morgue.

"Aldo Fogg," said Brisbois, putting down his pint. "Really?"

"You know him?" pressed Cadence, her excitement clear as she leaned across the table.

He stroked his chin, his gaze focused somewhere on the middle distance as he took in the full import of our latest discovery. "Only by name, obviously. I don't know anyone who's actually laid eyes on the man. He's something of a local legend – a boogeyman."

I swallowed down the last puddle of my whiskey, wincing a little as I scoffed. "I was almost killed by the boogeyman?"

"All the more impressive because he rarely does his own dirty work. You must have really gotten under his skin, Mr. Hale." Brisbois picked up his drink once again, lifting his brow at me over the rim of the glass. "You do have a talent for doing that to people."

"But I've never even heard of the man!" I protested, pressing my hand to my chest.

He shook his head as he swallowed his mouthful of ale. "Your paths must have crossed somehow. You wouldn't have ended up in the sights of a predator like Fogg without good reason."

Brisbois seemed far too bemused at the idea of me in the crosshairs of a violent criminal for my taste. I opened my mouth to tell him that I didn't appreciate his insinuations, when Cadence put a comforting hand on my arm, interrupting me mid-protestation to query, "So, he's a criminal of some kind?"

Brisbois nodded. Leaning back in his seat, he unbuttoned the collar of his shirt and loosened his tie as he spoke. "We first started hearing whispers of Fogg about ten years ago. He was a low-level enforcer for the Shaftes Syndicate. Collecting protection money for them, making problems disappear by way of the morgue, that sort of thing."

Spinning my empty glass around on the tabletop, I swallowed hard, hiding my growing dread with flippancy. "He sounds charming."

"I saw some of his work firsthand," Brisbois answered, his jaw tightening. "I was still walking a beat back then. The things he did with a knife..." I watched with concern as Brisbois swallowed once, and then again, closing his eyes to a flood of deeply upsetting memories. "Let's just say, I still have nightmares."

I also would not soon forget the glint of the blade in Fogg's hand – I rubbed my chest and grimaced, doing my best to close off the more imaginative parts of my mind, trying not to wonder what my corpse would've looked like if my assailant had had his way with me.

"Anyway," Brisbois started again, taking a steadying sip of his drink. "Rumor was that his methods got a little too theatrical, even for the Syndicate, and they cut ties with him. Gave him a nice little severance package though -- let him take over some of their illegal weapons smuggling trade."

The detective reached into his pocket for his packet of nix, removing a stout, brown cylinder from the treated paper package. "Fogg took what they gave him, and a few years later he'd built himself into one of the prime movers of illegal weapons on, and off, Arrhidaeus. Hell, he was even giving Gwen Largent a run for her money."

From across the table, Henry and I shared a troubled glance. Even Kace looked disturbed by the thought, frowning from his place across the table.

"Gwen Largent?" repeated Cadence, looking between the three of us for some kind of context.

Brisbois tilted his head upward, exhaling a stream of nix smoke up over our booth. "She's the creme de la creme of gun runners. Has a network that spans most planets in the IPC. Responsible for the deaths of millions. And she's based right here on Arrhidaeus – lives in District 41."

"I heard she'd gone legitimate," said Kace, nursing a glass of water with a slice of fruit in it.

Brisbois grimaced and wiggled his hand from side to side. "Mostly. It's why we have a tough time pinning anything on her. But her business is too lucrative to be completely legal." He picked a piece of nix paper off the tip of his tongue and tossed it away. "We had information that Fogg was supplying the Charcornacians with weapons under the table. But it sounds like he was playing both sides." Taking another long drag on his nix, he narrowed his eyes. Smoke curled up from his nostrils as he muttered, "Maybe that's why the Whiston Underground eliminated him..."

"What?" Cadence blinked several times in rapid succession. Staring at Brisbois, she shook her head. "Wait, what are you talking about?"

Brisbois gave a start as if he'd forgotten that he wasn't alone. He shook his head and gestured with the nix pinched between his fingers. "This...Quinn? Their leader?"

"They're more of a collective–"

"He must have found out that Fogg was working against them," he said, not waiting for Cadence's long-winded explanation of animanecron hierarchies. "Trust me, those types don't take betrayal well."

My companion let out a sharp sigh and crossed her arms over her chest, pulling back from the edge of the table. "So, you think an animanecron was responsible for the murder after all."

I watched as Brisbois bristled at her tone, drawing himself up straight in his seat. "Now that one has emerged as a viable suspect, yes – I do."

Cadence's tongue probed the inside of her cheek. "Just why did you bring me on to this case, Oliver?"

"I–"

"I thought–" she cut him off, her volume rising, "–it was to help shield the animanecron community from baseless accusations, like the ones you are now throwing around."

"I brought you on this case to help me discover the truth," said Brisbois, scowling. He pointed at her with his still smoldering nix before grinding it out in the ashtray by his elbow. "The truth, Cadence – which may not always turn out to be what we'd like it to be."

Cadence drew in a sharp breath, her dark blue eyes flashing. Without further preamble, she slid out from behind the table and, without so much as a glance back at any of us, strode away through the crowded establishment. From the opposite side of the table, I hurried to follow her, scrambling to my feet, her name on the tip of my tongue.

"Chance," said Brisbois, catching my wrist as I attempted to follow Cadence. With his free hand he pulled a palm-sized datapad out of his trouser pocket, glaring up at me as he did so. "I'm going to need to know exactly where you three gentlemen were kidnapped by the Underground."

I looked after the retreating figure of Cadence as she disappeared out the bar's front doors. Returning my attention to the man who held me hostage, I shook my head. "They're not going to be there, Inspector."

Brisbois said nothing, merely continuing to stare up at me until I gave him the information he required – I supposed it was that patient determination that had lifted him to the rank of inspector.

Rolling my eyes, I pulled my hand free, using it to button up my coat. "Kace and Henry can give you the details. Kace," I nodded to my bodyguard. "I'll be at the address for Turing Investigations – Henry can tell you where. You can meet me there when you're done."

"You really don't understand how this bodyguard thing works, do you?" said Kace, his face pained as he began scooching his way out from behind the table. "I have to go with you, Mr. Hale."

I gave a wide grin and reached forward, ruffling his hair before he could stop me. "Precious, isn't he?" I said to Brisbois.

Brisbois snorted out a laugh as Kace knocked my hand away, scowling fiercely. "Sir, I'm serious–"

"Meet me there, alright?" I was already moving backwards into the crowd, waving. "Evening, gents," I called out, making for the front door with as much speed as I could manage.

Cadence, I was sure, would walk back to District 16, caring nothing for the distance and the cold. To compensate for her several minutes long head start, I hailed a PT – my transport pulled up to the walkway outside of Cadence's building just in time for me to watch her disappear inside the foyer.

I paid my driver and rushed in after her, calling her name to no effect as we both raced up the seven flights of stairs to her office-turned-flat.

"Cadence," I said again, finally catching up with her just as she stalked inside the room.

"I can't believe him!" she shouted, her voice echoing through the loft. Her keys clattered onto the waiting room table as she threw them down, gouging the soft wood. "I thought Oliver was my friend! He used me!"

"He's just trying to do his job," I offered weakly, still trailing after her.

She spun on her heel, her finger raised and shaking at me. "Don't you dare defend him! Don't you dare!"

I stumbled back, my hands raised in front of me. I hadn't seen Cadence mad often, and to be fair, it was usually because of something stupid I had done. This was new. She was incensed, shoving her hands into her thick hair, bunching and tugging at the locks in frustration. "Van, if he would just think about it for a second, he'd see! It doesn't make any sense!" She began pacing the strip of floor to the left of her desk, ranting angrily. "Why would Quinn, or any of the Underground, kill Fogg, move the body, only to then dump it on their own doorstep? On what sphere are they that stupid?"

"Yes, that's a good–"

"And! And!" She rushed back towards me. "How does the Underground killing Fogg account for his attack on you the night before? Huh? Where's the connection?"

Her sudden change in direction pushed me back towards her desk. I pulled myself up onto it, feeling safer out of the way while perching on the desktop. I shrugged. "Maybe they wanted me out of the way?"

"Let's say they did – why would Fogg do their knife work for them? It doesn't make any sense. He was their business partner, not their lackey." Throwing her head back, she resumed her enraged pacing, howling, "Anta, it doesn't make any sense!"

"Cay," I clasped my hands together, following her frenetic pacing with my eyes. "Listen, I understand this is frustrating, but you have to–"

"It's not frustrating," she growled. "It's infuriating! Good animanecrons are going to get hurt because Oliver is too... too...!"

With a guttural cry that was almost a scream, Cadence took hold of one of her story cubes and hurled it to the floor. The delicate conglomeration of wires, bioplastic, and computer chips shattered into several large chunks.

We both froze, staring down at the destroyed cube in shock. I recovered first, clapping my hands together and taking a sharp breath through my nose.

"Well. Feel better?"

Cadence let her chin fall to her chest as she exhaled. She rubbed at the back of her neck with a shaky hand. "Dor, no."

I shook my head. "Trust me: you'll get this figured out, Cadence. If anybody can do it, you can."

"I've got to try," she said, walking over to me, resting her hip against the desk, and looking up to meet my gaze. "You're still in danger."

Her gaze was so earnest, her concern so genuine, that warmth bloomed deep in my belly. I reached up and cupped the side of her face, gazing at her with undisguised affection. "With you here? Impossible."

The heat of her body radiated up my arm, but it was nothing compared to the electricity that shuddered between us as she mimicked my stance, straightening to look me in the eye.

"I will always keep you safe, Chance," she said, so softly that I wasn't sure she was aware she'd spoken aloud at all. "Always."

"I know it, Cay." I shuddered out a sigh, resting my face in her hand. "I–"

She silenced me with a kiss, not entirely unexpected but desperately wanted. Her thumb made little circles near the corner of my mouth, her other hand coming up to caress the nape of my neck. I melted into her, parting my lips to taste hers better. She responded by stepping closer to me, moving in between my legs, and holding on to me tightly.

My own hands found purchase on the small of her back, but

I held her lightly, tremulously, almost afraid that she would slip away from me. After a moment, her hands moved down my neck to my shoulders and she pulled away from my lips, resting her forehead against my own, the tip of her nose touching mine.

"Cadence..." I breathed out her name, not opening my eyes, fearful that I would do so and find myself dreaming. She stayed in my arms, still as a statue, not bothering to put on the pretense of breathing.

"You're mine," she whispered. Shifting her mouth to my ear, she switched into Animatum, her mother tongue holding an even deeper fascination to me, now that I could understand it. "*You are mine, Chance Hale. And I am yours.*" She underlined this thought by capturing my lobe between her teeth, the pressure just shy of painful, and swiping her tongue across the skin there.

I moaned in unabashed pleasure before stuttering out in halting Animatum, "*Yes, Cadence. I am yours.*"

With a boldness that left me breathless, and my ear still held hostage by her mouth, one of her hands slid off my shoulder, snaked down my chest and abdomen, and began attempting to pull my shirt up and off my torso.

Eyes fluttering open in shock, I grabbed hold of her straying hand and attempted to sit up straighter. "Cay, what are you–?"

"I can't help it," she whispered, her voice somehow strange. She drew back from me, just enough to look into my eyes. Lifting her free hand to my face, her fingertips caressed my cheek, my lips, and then softly sliding down my throat to my chest. "I, I need you, Chance. I ache for you. Please?"

This was what I had wanted, wasn't it? To be needed. To be desired. For Cadence to look at me with those beautiful, endlessly deep blue eyes and say that she wanted me and only me. I stared at her, my chest heaving, blood thrumming in my veins – I couldn't wrap my head around the fact that what I had wanted for so long may actually be happening.

I didn't deserve it. I didn't deserve her.

I loved her so much.

"Please, Chance?" she asked again, pulling me from my stupefaction with a tug on my shirt, her tongue coming out to wet her lips as her eyes focused on mine.

Releasing her hand, I reached for her and drew her face to mine, kissing her with an open, hungry mouth. Her tongue teased the roof of my mouth and I shuddered, losing myself to sensation as her hands pushed my shirt up and up over my abdomen and chest, exploring as they went. She broke the kiss to pull the troublesome fabric over my head and, once I was free of it, leaned back in, kissing me with such ferocity that I was forced back farther and farther, until I was lying flat against the desk, with Cadence's body hovering over mine.

Her mouth slid away from mine, and she began kissing and nibbling at the underside of my jaw and the side of my neck, sending short shocks of pain mixed with pleasure in a heady rush that left me squirming and short of breath. For my part, I struggled to free her from the cardigan she wore over her dress. Peeling it off her, I mouthed at her exposed shoulder, moving the thin strap out of the way, pressing my teeth into her flesh, desperate to taste her, to consume her in a way that no one else would.

Her fingertips ran over my ribs, settling at my hips. She pushed herself away and looked down at me, her long hair falling from its pins and fasteners on one side, framing her perfect face. Her eyes raked over me, and I felt exposed in the most delicious and licentious way. A wicked smirk curled her lips, and I was about to find the breath to ask her what thought had produced such a delightful expression, when she answered my question before I asked. She took a small step back, standing between my legs, and bent down. The tip of her tongue ran along the exposed skin above the top of my still-frustratingly-fastened trousers. She repeated this maneuver next with her lips, and then again with her teeth.

I felt my eyes roll heavenward, the sensations so simple and yet so torturous. I called out her name, pleading, my breath coming in short, sharp gasps. But she made no move to stop, nor to increase her pace, or to change what she was doing at all. She just repeated the motion, her tongue lathing my skin one moment, her teeth scraping against me the next.

"Cay," I groaned, my hands finding purchase on her shoulders, her own hands keeping my hips still and frozen in place right where she wanted them. "Oh, darling, please, *please* touch–"

"Mr. Hale?" I heard Kace's voice ring out in my blood-muffled ears and I groaned, the back of my head hitting the desk.

"I've got to remember to lock that door when I'm here..." I muttered, my head turning to face the man who was, even now, striding into the office.

"Everything al–" He came to an abrupt halt at the sight of us -- and I can only imagine what a sight it was: us both in a state of half undress, me splayed out on top of Cadence's desk, her straightening up from between my legs.

He stared openly.

"Yes?" I prompted at last, my voice ragged.

Confusion, comprehension, and a considerable amount of embarrassment danced across Kace's face in rapid succession. He began to back away quickly towards the front door, waving his hands in front of himself as if he could wipe us away like fog on a mirror. "Oh. Sorry, sir. Ma'am. Excuse me. Sorry. I didn't mean to—apologies. I'll go." Then, seemingly remembering that he was on the clock, he hesitated, locking eyes with me and wincing. "I'll, uh, I'll be, uh, downstairs. If you need any—"

"I won't."

"Right." Kace shook himself and turned fully around, walking stiffly. "Course not." He closed the front door behind him with a final, strangled. "Sorry."

Taking in a deep breath, I returned my attention to the woman still holding on to my hips. She had a vaguely displeased expression on her face, but it was fading quickly. As I lifted my hand to her cheek, it disappeared entirely, her inky eyes focusing once again on me.

"Sorry about that," I chuckled breathlessly, running my fingers through Cadence's loose, wavy hair.

"It's his first day," said Cadence matter-of-factly, stepping back and pulling her dress down over her body. "He's eager to please."

I drank in the sight of her like a soldier seeing home for the first time after a long war. But she didn't give me long to look, immediately closing the distance between us and kissing me so deeply that I struggled to breathe.

"So am I," I gasped when she released my lips. I propped myself up on my shaky arms, sweat beading on my chest. "Cadence—"

She straightened suddenly, pulling me up with her as if I weighed little more than a stuffed pillow. Which to her, I suppose I did. "Bed," she said, leading me along towards the stairs. "Now."

I knew better than to argue with her when she used that tone of voice.

13

Chapter 13

I don't recall falling asleep. The last thing I remembered was lying on my side next to Cadence, my hand resting just above her hip, murmuring things to her in the half light of morning -- things that I would later remember with a flush of embarrassment and a sharp twinge of pain. Smiling at me gently, indulgently, she brushed my hair off my forehead as I spoke. With her fingertips gliding across my skin, I must have drifted into unconsciousness.

When I next became aware of my surroundings, the sun was coming in through the windows at a sharp slant, a clear indication that it was well past midday. The air in her room was calm and cool, like the surface of an undisturbed pond. Eyes half shut, I shifted against the futon underneath me, unused to lying so close to the ground. I reached out for Cadence beside me, thinking in an unfocused way of pulling myself closer to her.

"Cay?" I mumbled to the empty pillow.

The room around me was utterly still.

I opened my eyes a little wider and scanned the room. Some of my clothes lay strewn around the loft, mixed in with Cadence's in a haphazard jumble of our colliding lives. Straining my ears for the sounds of her moving about the flat, I turned over, continuing to look for signs of where she might be, and finding nothing.

"Cadence?"

The sounds of the city filtered in, muffled only by the sound of my own breathing.

I was alone.

She had left while I was sleeping.

I jolted up into a seated position, my heart pounding in my chest. I called her name a few more times, not bothering to hide the tremor in my voice.

Nothing.

I was a man of the world. I knew exactly what it meant to sneak out of a warm bed, away from a sleeping lover, and out onto the city streets without a word of explanation.

What had I done? I replayed the events of the last handful of hours in my mind. Did I say something wrong? Had I mistreated her in some way? Was I... not good? Maybe she was disappointed in the experience, or disillusioned with me, or had found me somehow lacking...

The silence broke. My mobile began to ring.

I threw myself over the side of the bed and half scrambled across the floor to my discarded trousers. The patterns of the buzzing soon became clear to me, and I realized with considerable disappointment that it was not Cadence calling, but Henry. Still, I dug out the mobile earbud with one hand and hurried to accept the call, propping myself up on my elbows as I placed it in my ear.

"Henry?" I said, desperate to hear a voice, any voice, to let me know that I wasn't as utterly alone as I felt.

"Chance, chum, I've been trying to reach you for hours! Where have you been?" I opened my mouth to answer him but didn't get a breath out before he barreled on, exasperation lacing his every word. "Listen, it's not important. I've been trying to talk the Inspector out of this animanecron killer business, but I don't think..."

As he continued to rant, I collapsed back onto the futon, closing my eyes and swallowing hard. I had made a mistake. I must have. Somehow, I had misread... but no. What was there to misread? She had said she was mine. She had said I was hers. I gave myself to her. She said she loved me. Surely that meant...

I shook my head, rubbing my eyes and interrupting my friend carelessly. "Henry, have – have you heard from Cadence today?"

"Who, me?" His tone immediately changed. His volume dropped, and I heard him sit down in a creaky desk chair. "No, no, I haven't. Why? Isn't she with you?"

"I..." I turned my head and opened my eyes. The space in the bed next to me was cavernous, cold, and completely empty. It gaped, like a wound, and I found that I could not look away. It was with a start that I realized I had paused mid-sentence, for far longer than was reasonable. I forced my breath in and out of my lungs and said quietly, "No. She's not."

Henry's voice grew stern, as it often did when he was worried. "Chance, is everything alright? You sound strange."

Dropping my hand to my side, I felt a tear sneak down the side of my face. "I think–"

A series of low beeps sounded through the speaker, and I grimaced. A stilted, robotic voice broke through the beeps, audible only to me, repeating *Call from: Halcyon Enterprises... Call from: Halcyon Enterprises...*

"Damn it," I grunted, forcing myself upright once more. "Work is calling. I'll – I'll have to phone you back."

I didn't wait for Henry to respond, pulling the bud from my ear and switching to the work call with a click.

"Yes?" I answered, not bothering to hide the irritation in my tone.

"Um, Mr. Hale?" Lily's voice stuttered down the line, shaky and hesitant.

Sighing, I wiped the saltwater off my cheeks. "Yes, Lily, what is it?"

"I have a call from Gwen Largent waiting," she said, her tone unusually high pitched and strained. "Shall I patch it through?"

I heard Miss Taylor's words but could not put meaning to them. Gwen Largent was an important figure from another, totally alien world – it was like hearing that the King of the moon of Yanni was waiting to see you. It was nonsense.

"Excuse me?" I managed at last, blinking in confusion.

My assistant's voice dropped to a whisper. "Gwen Largent," she repeated. "She's quite insistent on reaching you, Chance."

Muddled as my brain was at that moment, I remembered with a start the last place I had heard Gwen Largent's name mentioned. Sitting in a pub, discussing the passing of a man who had tried to kill me. A man who had been a rival to Miss Largent. A rival no longer.

"Transfer the call, Miss Taylor," I said, struggling to my feet.

I waited until I heard the click of the line switching over and then, drawing myself up straight, put on my best CEO voice and said, "This is Chance Hale."

A prim female voice responded to me immediately. "Good afternoon, Mr. Hale," said the caller. "This is Gwen Largent's office calling. We've been trying to reach you for a few hours."

The frigid air of Cadence's apartment crawled over my bare skin, but I did my best to ignore it. "I've been out of the office, I'm afraid. What can I do for you?"

"Would you be available for a meeting with Miss Largent?"

I glanced around for a clock. "When?"

"As soon as possible."

That gave me pause. I tilted my head to one side, sending my eyes heavenward. "For what purpose?"

I heard the tapping of fingers against a datapad. "She was hoping to get your assistance involving the funeral arrangements for a mutual friend. Mr. Aldo Fogg?"

My mouth went dry. I cleared my throat, forcing down the panic that had begun to rise there. So, she knew I was involved with Aldo Fogg. That was interesting. She wanted to meet. That was dangerous.

Kace was going to love this.

"Of course," I said after a moment, reaching down to pick up my trousers. "Yes, poor Mr. Fogg. I'd be only too happy to help. Where shall I–?"

"I've left Miss Largent's home address with your executive assistant," said the woman. "Most appreciated, Mr. Hale. We'll expect you shortly."

Dressing quickly, I forced myself to think of nothing but the task in front of me. Careening out of the apartment, I glanced around for signs of my bodyguard and, finding none, inferred that he must be downstairs in the lobby.

Taking the stairs two at a time, I came upon him leaning against the defunct lift doors, smiling as he chatted with the landlord, who stood half in and half out of the open front door. A stout human man with a shock of bright red hair, we had met several times while Cadence was negotiating her rental and his face lit up when I came into view. I mustered up a smile and waved at him as I came up behind Kace.

"Hullo, Charlie," I said, nodding.

Charlie Shine stepped fully into the building, tilting his head to one side as he grinned. "Well, hello there, Mr. Hale!"

Kace, jumping to attention, looked guilty at being caught fraternizing. He turned to me, his gaze low. "Sir–"

Patting Kace reassuringly on the shoulder, I continued my line of conversation with the landlord. "How's Cynthia doing, Charlie? Did she like the cake I sent home with you last week?"

Charlie, his hands in his trouser pockets, bounced up and down on the balls of his feet as he nodded with enthusiasm. "Loved it, Mr. Hale – loved it. Especially the rainbow frosting. Very kind of you to do something like that for her birthday."

I mimicked his stance. "Well when you told me how the bakery had lost the order, I wanted to do what I could to help."

"Saved the party, Mr. Hale. No doubt about it."

I rubbed the back of my neck, my forced smile wavering ever so slightly. "Very good, glad to hear it."

Charlie, perhaps noticing some of the strain in my posture, gave one last smile and stepped backwards out the door, waving. "I'm sure you gents have business to attend to, so I'll be on my way. Was nice to meet you, Mr. Morgan!"

Waiting until Charlie was well out of ear shot on the public walkway outside, I turned to Kace, only to find him staring at me, wide eyed. I stared back and shrugged. "What?"

Kace shook himself, his hand coming up to tug at his chin as he looked away from me. "Ah, nothing. It's just..." He glanced at me from the side of his eye. "Did you really get that man's wife a cake?"

"No," I said. "Cynthia is his daughter." Shrugging sharply, I shook my head. "And of course, I did. What about it?"

"It's nothing." Then as if remembering, his head jerked up and he said in a rush: "Mr. Hale, Miss Turing – when she left a few hours ago she said I wasn't to disturb you. Was that right?"

Of course, she had. I closed my eyes, taking a deep breath in through my nose and letting it out slowly. "It's..." I sliced my hand through the air and forced my eyes open, grimacing. "It's fine, Kace. Come on, I've got a meeting with someone across town, and I have a feeling you'll want to tag along."

An hour later, I found myself in an expansive room, staring down at the tops of PTs soaring by the people on the walkways below. The UV-shielded glass of the bay window through which I watched was thick enough that no sound reached me inside the sitting room into which I had been ushered. Plants of every color and fragrance were jammed into the space at random.

Potted trees, creeping vines, heavy headed flowers – everything smelled of greenery and wet, fresh dirt. I stood at the far edge of this explosion of foliage, feeling weirdly claustrophobic amidst all that condensed nature. Hands clasped behind my back, I did my best to ignore the screaming pain deep within me, focusing only on the moment in which I found myself -- nothing from before, and nothing that might come after.

At my request, Kace had remained standing in the hallway, just outside the opaque sliding door at the other end of the room. This was partially out of a desire not to offend Miss Largent with potentially unnecessary precautions, and partially out of a need to be alone. I could see his silhouette through the frosted glass, however, and when it moved to one side, I knew that my wait was over.

The door slid open silently and a small, plump figure entered the room. She scanned the space and, after spying me by the windows, smiled broadly and walked towards me.

"Ah, Mr. Hale," said the woman, her hand outstretched. "So sorry to keep you waiting."

Gwen Largent was not what I had expected when Brisbois had described the insidious arms dealer responsible for the deaths of millions. If I had passed her on the street, I doubt that I would've given her a second glance. She was small, barely five foot four, and probably weighed no more than a hundred or so pounds soaking wet. Her graying brown hair was cut in a boyish style, well above her ears and off her forehead. I put her at about seventy years of age, with lotion-soaked creamy skin that made her arthritis knotted hands supple to the touch.

I shook her hand gently, surprised by the gesture. "Pleasure to meet you, Miss Largent."

Her small eyes were soft and round, the color of uncooked dough, and the crow's feet around them deepened when she smiled. "I must apologize for the manner of our meeting. I trust you weren't too terribly inconvenienced?"

"Not at all." I glanced at our hands, still clasped together. "Although I must confess to some curiosity as to how you knew I was connected with the death of Aldo Fogg."

She did not release my hand, but rather turned to walk beside me, wrapping her arm through mine, and leaning on me, as if she lacked the strength to walk alone. "Information," she said, "as I'm sure you know, Mr. Hale, is power. It's what I trade these days – chiefly."

She gestured towards the bay window where I had been standing, and we made our way to the woven rattan seats placed there. Using my arm for balance, she lowered herself atop the more heavily cushioned of the two chairs, which had a worn looking quilt thrown over the back of it. Once she was comfortably settled in her seat, she waved for me to take the chair opposite her, while continuing, "What I require from you, sir, is some assurances."

I folded myself down into the wicker chair, grimacing as the straw prickled into my back through my clothes. "Assurances, Miss Largent?"

She frowned, a look of deep perturbation coming over her. "I'm a legitimate businessperson, Mr. Hale. I run a legitimate business. I worked hard to get to this point in my career, Mr. Hale, and I have no intention of going backward." Fidgeting in agitation for a moment, she looked out the window as if to calm herself, before fixing her narrowed eyes back on me. "Now, I'll ask you plainly: why does the Enforcement Office think I have anything to do with Mr. Fogg's untimely passing from this sphere?"

I blinked at her. Folding my hands carefully across my lap, I tilted my head to one side. "I wasn't aware that they did, Miss Largent."

We stared into each other's eyes for several long moments. She broke first, her hand coming up to her mouth. It soon became clear she was smothering a laugh.

"So," she said, a smile turning her small mouth up at the corners. "They can lie, after all."

A shiver ran up and down my spine. "I beg your pardon?"

"Animanecrons," she said, folding her hands in her lap and returning her attention to me. "I was told they couldn't lie."

"They don't like to lie. But they are capable of it." I could hear the bitterness in my words but could do nothing to temper it. "Some are even quite good at it."

Gwen nodded knowingly. "Doubtless, that's our influence," she said. Then, "Davida, fetch our guest, please."

"Yes, Miss Largent." The voice I had heard earlier on the phone rang out, seemingly from everywhere all at once, clearly transmitted by some kind of digital speaker.

The door to the room slid open once more, and this time a medium-sized black Labrador trotted into the room, preceding a deeply tanned middle-aged woman in a plain, but expensive, pantsuit. The woman stopped just inside the room and turned to look behind her, gesturing for someone to enter the room.

"Davida found your friend breaking into my private office." Gwen's brown eyes sparkled with delight, and she looked a good deal more pleased than she should have, given what she was saying. "Most impressive, given the amount of bleeding edge security she had to get through to reach that point."

The chocolate lab trotted over and sat by his mistress' side, his white flecked muzzle coming up to rest on the arm of the chair. He stared up at her with the kind of devotion only animals seemed capable of expressing, and Gwen returned the look with a smile of her own.

"Unfortunately," she continued, reaching down to scratch at the canine's furry head. "Dogs bark at people they don't know. Even she couldn't hack her way around that."

To say that I was surprised when Cadence stepped into the room, glaring daggers at Davida, would be an absolute lie. I wasn't surprised.

Of course, it was Cadence. She was everywhere, except where I needed her to be most.

She walked through the greenhouse towards us, taking in her surroundings with her usual voracious curiosity. But she came to a short, sharp stop when she saw me sitting there, her dark blue eyes going wide, an unmistakable panic bringing a pallor to her cheeks.

"You know Mr. Hale, don't you, Miss Turing?" said Gwen. "I asked him to join us."

In a flash, all of the things I was trying not to remember roared to the forefront of my mind -- the feel of her lips sliding against my sweat slicked skin. The taste of her on my tongue as

I left a trail of kisses down her thigh. The sound of my name catching in the back of her throat.

The empty, hollow echo of the apartment when I awoke this morning.

I couldn't take my eyes off her. Swallowing down the lump in my throat, I stared at her openly, resting my fingertips against the side of my face.

It was Cadence who finally pulled her eyes away from me, her jaw tight. She looked down at the small woman seated across from me as if she had committed an unforgivable sin. "This was unnecessary."

"On the contrary, Miss Turing, I think it was entirely necessary." Leaning forward towards me, Gwen explained, "She refused to speak to me, you see, beyond telling me who she was and that I was the subject of an Enforcement Office investigation." She reached forward and patted my knee. "I took the liberty of contacting you directly, in the hope of learning more."

I looked from Cadence to Gwen, forcing a smile onto my lips. "I suppose pretending I don't know who this young woman is...?"

"Utterly pointless." Gwen waved the suggestion away like it was so much foul air. I nodded my understanding.

Grunting a little at the effort, Gwen turned herself to face Cadence. She crossed her feet at the ankles and looked the young woman over. "It seems you are mistaken, Miss Turing -- the EO is not investigating me. But you are. Why?"

Cadence grasped her left wrist with her right hand and looked past Gwen, a defiant tilt to her chin, a blank expression on her face.

Gwen tilted her head to one side. "I could just kill you," she said brightly. "But I like your gumption. Not enough of that around these days." She leaned up towards Cadence, lifting her brows. "I'd much prefer to help you if I can. You'll find me a valuable friend."

Cadence's face betrayed nothing.

Gwen sat back in her chair, folding her hands in her lap, seemingly confident that eventually the silence would get under Cadence's skin, and force her to speak.

She didn't know Cadence like I did.

"We understand that Aldo Fogg was a rival of yours," I said, shifting forward in my seat.

Cadence shot me a glare that would've melted steel. I ignored her completely, weary of her reticence under the current circumstances.

Gwen picked at a fold in her skirt, avoiding my eyes for the first time since we started conversing. "In the old days, perhaps."

I clicked my tongue off the top of my mouth and shook my head. "Now who's pretending, Miss Largent?"

The older woman smacked her lips in displeasure, curling her hands into fists. "Oh, the man was a nuisance. One I would've dealt with in time, once I discovered who was supplying him with his merchandise."

"You mean you don't know?" I said.

"Quite the mystery. He was a small-time operator until a few months ago and then, all of a sudden, he's moving massive quantities of quality product. I checked with all my sources – they all knew better than to supply a competitor." She shook her head, looking down on the world from her window. "Disgusting creature -- he loved violence a little too well for my tastes. Not that I wouldn't have made an example of him and his silent supplier. It seems fitting he should've met a violent end himself, but his death was not my doing."

"Why should we believe you?" said Cadence, breaking her silence.

Gwen proffered a hand towards the sliding door, where her assistant, Davida, had awaited this exact moment. Heels clicking against the smooth floors, Davida walked over to where her employer sat, removed a slim datapad from her skirt pocket, unfolded it, and placed it in the old woman's outstretched hand.

Unlocking the pad with a swipe of her fingertip, Gwen passed it to me. I looked down to see an electronic receipt for two tickets, one for Gwen Largent, the other for Davida Blackwell -- first class tickets on a star liner that had left from Paraesepe, three days ago.

The inky void of space was a decent alibi. I passed the datapad up to Cadence without looking at her.

"As you can see," Gwen said, gesturing to the datapad. "I just recently returned from off-world. This morning, as a matter of fact. I may not have had much respect for the man, but unlike him, I do prefer to attend to these types of things personally. You can verify that with your EO friends."

Cadence scowled at the datapad before turning her displeasure back on Gwen. She shoved the device back towards her. "Rest assured, we will."

Gwen took the datapad with more grace than it was given, placing it in her lap and folding her hands on top of it. "I should say that I do have every intention of taking over Mr. Fogg's business affairs." She grinned at my shocked expression. "I tell you this in the spirit of transparency, you understand." Her lips pursed in thoughtfulness. "Although not all of them, of course."

Tilting my head to one side, I looked at my host askance. "Why not all?"

Gwen sighed, her tongue probing the inside of her cheek. "Did you know that my family has been involved in the arms business for the greater part of three hundred years, Mr. Hale? I was born to do this work." She sniffed with disdain. "Mr. Fogg was given it. He had no passion for the art of connecting people with the tools they needed. As such, he sought to diversify his operations by smuggling drugs."

"Drogan?" said Cadence, her eyes alight with excitement.

The older woman shivered, her face twisted in disgust. "Filthy stuff. Got in bed with some local kingpin, someone by the name of Hudd. Noll Hudd. Wouldn't be surprised if that unfortunate business is what led to his untimely demise."

Noll Hudd. I saw Cadence's hands curl into fists at the mention of his name. The last time we had come face to face with that unpleasant individual, we had parted on less than cordial terms. Which suited me well enough – I had no desire to be on any kind of terms with scum like him. To Noll Hudd, violence and vice were means to an end – that end being more money in his pockets, and more power for him to hold over other people. He didn't care about anyone or anything but himself, and he would do anything to protect his interests.

Killing a man and framing a vulnerable, disenfranchised group. Knowing it would cause them nothing but heartache and pain? That was exactly something he would do.

However, the word of one famous criminal against another

wouldn't hold a lot of weight with the Enforcement Office. We would need something more concrete.

"It may be difficult to secure your interest in Fogg's former accounts with Hudd still sniffing around," I said slowly, thoughtfully, my eyes never leaving Gwen's face.

The sly old thing caught my tone immediately. She paused her incessant fidgeting and glanced askance at me. "It may."

I smiled. "What if we were to remove him from the equation for you?"

From beside me, Cadence made a strangled noise of shock. I glanced up at her, but looked quickly away -- the sight of her muddled my thoughts so completely that I found it best to pretend she wasn't there at all.

Gwen lowered her head, batting her eyelashes at me. "At what price?"

"You give us more information about Fogg's smuggling operation," I reached forward and placed the tips of my fingers against her knee and squeezed. "And I can guarantee that the EO will be there to snap up Hudd the next time he shows his face."

Gwen giggled. "Oh, a tempting offer." Her hand came up to toy with the string of pearls around her neck. "You really are a businessman, aren't you, Mr. Hale?"

I drew back, feeling only slightly sick to my stomach. "I try."

The elderly crime boss gave my proposal another few moments of serious consideration before nodding to herself. "I'll have Davida send you the pertinent details via encrypted v-mail." She made to stand, this time with no additional assistance from me. "I don't suppose that I could interest either of you in a light dinner?"

"Thank you, Miss Largent." I likewise rose, bowing a little as I did so. "But we've both taken up enough of your time."

"Very well," said Gwen, smiling. "In that case, I shall say good evening and good luck to you both." She reached for Davida, but paused partway, looking over Cadence with an assessing glance for one final time. "If you wish to visit me again, Miss Turing, do feel free to use the front door. You, or your young man."

Cadence said nothing to this, opting instead to turn away from the elderly woman and stare at the Heyltzun Iris that stood beside her.

Gwen took the rebuff in stride, sending a last wink in my direction before walking carefully out the sliding door with Davida in tow behind her.

14

Chapter 14

Cadence and I were alone, again. I took a deep breath and let it out slowly through my mouth, marshaling my words on my tongue. But Cadence beat me to the punch, turning to face me, her arms crossed high over her chest.

"You shouldn't have come here, Chance," she said.

I was momentarily stunned, and at a loss for words. Recovering my wits, I scoffed, shaking my head. "The folly of youth, I suppose." Shoving my hands in my trouser pockets, I leaned towards her, sneering. "At least I waited until I was invited. What possessed you to break into the home of a notorious criminal?"

"If she had anything to do with Fogg's death–"

"Well, she didn't, did she?" I snapped. "She could have killed you. Or, at the very least, have you arrested." Shaking my head, I stepped towards her, my bottom lip beginning to tremble. "What are you doing here, Cadence?"

She turned her back to me once again, huffing. "I told you, I was looking–"

"No," I cut her off quickly, moving around her to force her to face me. "Why are you here, and not at home, in bed, with me?"

She dropped her gaze to the floor. Her breathing shallowed for a moment before stopping entirely. As I watched, she dug her fingers into her arms, turning the pale white skin red.

"I thought– I thought I'd be back before you woke up," she said, her voice hushed.

Crossing my arms over my chest, I shook my head at her, wide eyed. "Why not wake me up and bring me with you?"

"I couldn't do that, Chance!" she exclaimed, releasing her arms to rub at her forehead. "Sinc, do you have any idea how dangerous this was?"

"I do! I know exactly how dangerous this was!" I threw my hands up in the air. "Which is precisely why–"

There was a shushing sound as the door to the room slid open. Kace stuck his head inside.

"Sorry to interrupt, Mr. Hale." He nodded to Cadence. "Miss Turing." Taking a step back from the door, he swung his arm out behind him. "I believe they've called a PT for us. It's waiting on the platform downstairs."

"We should go," said Cadence, starting for the door with a tad too much enthusiasm. "It wouldn't do for you to be seen here. What would the Halcyon Enterprises Board of Directors think?"

"Not really at the top of my mind right now," I muttered, following her.

We said nothing more to each other as we made our way down to the PT platform, exchanging not even a glance as the three of us climbed into the PT. Kace sat in the space beside me, our backs to the driver, while Cadence sat across from us, her face turned towards the floor.

The intercom to Kace's left crackled into life. "Where to, folks?"

Kace looked to me for an answer, but I was busy staring at Cadence. Looking between us, my bodyguard depressed the blue button next to the intercom and said, "If you could start heading towards the Ani-District, that'd be great."

The PT rumbled to life in answer, and we slid up into the sky as if on a greased rail.

Cadence must have sensed my gaze on her -- she was too perceptive to be unaware of my undivided attention. But she stalwartly refused to acknowledge my presence, or that of Kace, opting instead to stare out the window at the rapidly passing buildings and bodies.

"You can let me out back at the office," Cadence said at length, still not deigning to look at me.

I crossed my legs, watching her carefully as Kace relayed this message to the driver. "You don't think we should go see the Inspector? Tell him what we've learned?"

This got her to turn towards me at least, although her gaze landed somewhere near my shoes. "You really think Oliver will listen to us?"

I shrugged. "We're going to at least need his help with Hudd."

Cadence sighed. "I suppose it could be Hudd." She leaned back in her seat, her head bouncing against the leather of the PT couch. "He kills Fogg to take over his operation. Or over some kind of dispute. Or because Fogg failed to kill you."

"Why would Noll Hudd want you dead?" asked Kace, glancing between the two of us, furrowing his brow in suspicion.

"We locked horns a few months back," I gave a weak smile at the memory. "I may have lightly assaulted him."

Kace blinked and straightened in his seat. He looked me up and down, adjusting the knot of his tie. "Oh."

Continuing as if Kace had never spoken, Cadence said, "Then, Hudd dumps the body in the Ani-District to frame animanecrons because we're easy targets – plus, he hates us."

I glanced over at Kace. "His wife left him for an animanecron woman," I explained.

"Oh," repeated Kace.

"It could fit," admitted Cadence. "But it's all conjecture. We don't have any proof."

"At the very least, Inspector Brisbois will want to get Hudd off the street," said Kace, trying to follow our conversation as best as he could.

Cadence shot my bodyguard a disgruntled glare. "I'm really not inclined to help the Enforcement Office, at the moment."

"Then where do we go from here?" I demanded.

The silence that followed was heavy and heated -- I felt as if I were sinking slowly down into wax, the silence oozing into my ears and running down my throat, making me gag. Kace shifted uncomfortably beside me.

Cadence, for her part, moved with excruciating slowness, closing her eyes, and hugging herself with first one arm and then the other. Her chin fell to her chest and her breathing grew deep, as if she had just fallen asleep. But I had seen her sleep – when she slept, she didn't breathe at all. This was something different. This was conflict.

I leaned forward, the inside of my cheek trapped between my teeth. "Cadence? I said—"

"Anno, I heard what you said," she snapped. She lifted her hand to her face, massaging her forehead. "I don't know. I need to think."

Swallowing hard, I shot a glance at the too-interested Kace. With a mirthless chuckle, I pressed, "What? What is there to think about?"

As I spoke, the PT shuddered to a stop, pulling up alongside the transport hub at the end of the street. Before I had finished my sentence, Cadence's hand was on the door handle.

"Thank you," called Cadence to the driver, disappearing out the door at speed.

"Damn it!" I growled, throwing myself into the seat she had previously occupied and sliding across it to the still open door. "Wait down here, Kace, please," I said as I stepped out of the PT, dogging Cadence's steps.

"Cadence, stop!" My voice rang out down the dark, mostly empty street, attracting the attention of what few pedestrians remained, but I didn't care. Neither, it seemed, did Cadence, who ignored me completely, walking up the front stairs and disappearing into her building without so much as a glance back in my direction.

Cursing, I dashed down the street, hurt and anger fueling me. By the time I made it inside, she had already passed the second-floor landing, and was still climbing.

"Cadence," I called to her from the bottom of the steps. When she made no move to stop, I started after her, taking the stairs two at a time. "Cadence, we need to talk about–"

"I was just trying to keep you safe, Chance." Cadence kept climbing the stairs, her hand gripping the banister so tightly that I could see her knuckles turn white, even from behind her. "I can't – I won't apologize for that."

"We talked about this, damn it." My hand landed on her shoulder as we both hit the sixth-floor landing at the same time, and she stopped at last. I stepped in front of her, shaking my head violently, one hand flat against my chest. "Keeping me safe is not your job."

"Of course, it is!" She stared at the ground, refusing to look at me, refusing, it felt, to acknowledge that I was there at all. Her next words came quietly, in a near whisper. "I love you. I'm going to protect you."

"Well, I'll be damned if you do it without talking to me about it first!" I pulled back from her, curling my hands into fists at my sides. "And what about your safety? Don't I get to be worried about that?"

Cadence turned away suddenly and headed up the final flight of stairs, throwing her hands up into the air. "It's not the same, and you know it!"

"Of course, it is!" I hurried after her, raising my voice to a shout once more. "You love me, and I love you!" Dogging her steps, up the final flight, my breathing heavy, I shook my head. "Did you even stop and think about what it might be like for me to wake up without you this morning? Without a clue about where you'd gone, what you were doing?" I felt the flush in my already pink face deepen. "For goodness' sake, Cay, I thought..."

Cay turned at the stop of the stairs, her brow furrowed in annoyance and confusion. "What?"

Gritting my teeth, I fought through my embarrassment, clopping up the final stairs as I spoke. "I thought I'd...done something. Wrong. Since that was the first time, we–" The next words stuck in my throat as I reached the landing and saw who was standing behind Cadence, waiting in front of the door of *Turing Investigations*. "Oh."

How much of our conversation Brisbois overheard, I could never be sure. But he was standing on the landing next to Cadence's front door, frowning, a faint pink blush to his cheeks. For her part, Cadence seemed unfazed by his appearance at her doorstep, turning around and getting her antique keys out of her trouser pockets while nodding at him cordially.

"Inspector." Cadence slid her key into the lock of her door. "We were just talking about you."

She lied so easily now. I remembered when it had been a strain for her.

I was not ready to get derailed from our conversation so easily. I held a hand up to Brisbois, avoiding looking him in the eye. "Oliver, can you just give us a moment, please?"

"I would if I could, but I can't," said Brisbois curtly. He turned to Cadence, his hands in his pockets as he clenched his jaw. "Cadence, I need to find Quinn."

Cadence jerked her door open, her scowl a dark scar across her beautiful face. "I am not going to help you arrest an innocent man," she said, striding away from us, as if putting mere distance between us and her would solve both problems.

"You don't know that he's innocent," Brisbois protested, following her inside.

Rolling my eyes, I trailed behind. "I take it he wasn't still at the power station, then."

Brisbois shot me an annoyed glare over his shoulder. "No. He wasn't." He continued forward, closing the distance between him and Cadence in a few quick, sharp strides. "Cadence, if you refuse to tell me how you made contact with the Whiston Underground, I'm going to be forced to arrest you for willfully impeding an Enforcement Office Investigation."

"Brisbois!" I exclaimed, coming to an abrupt halt behind him.

He ignored my outburst, his eyes locked on Cadence's face. "Please. Please, don't make me do that."

Cadence took a deep breath. She looked around at her apartment, swallowing hard. "You do what you must. I will do what I must."

Brisbois took a deep breath and closed his eyes. "Alright. Fine." The words came out in a hushed murmur, and I thought that I detected the slightest hesitation in his movement as he reached inside his jacket to retrieve the restraints.

"Now, hold on a minute," I stepped forward, panic beginning to take hold. "Can't we talk through this like sensible people?"

But it was too late for that. Far too late.

"Cadence Turing," Brisbois started, his voice strong, sure, and authoritative. "I am arresting your physical and mental person under Article 3.4 of the Enforcement Act for impeding an active Enforcement Office Investigation." With well-practiced efficiency, Brisbois spun her around and slipped the two ends of the restraints over her wrists. "You have the right to remain silent," he continued, activating the restraints with a swipe of his thumb. "But if you do not tell us something you later rely on in court, that evidence may be deemed inadmissible. You have the right to a lawyer of your choice for representation, from either the public or the private sector." With one hand on her forearm, he gently, but firmly, turned her back around to face him. "Do you understand these rights as I have stated them?"

"I do." Cadence rolled her shoulders back and looked at me with a weak smile on her lips. "Chance, could you please call Ergo Sum? I think I'll need a lawyer."

Without another word, Brisbois started for the still open front door, stopping only because I put myself between him and it.

"Oliver," I pleaded, shaking my head. "You can't do this, you–"

"Chance, please– don't make me arrest you too." His words came without malice or threat, merely with an edge of tiredness that I felt in my bones. He tugged on Cadence's arm. "This way, Miss Turing."

Cadence allowed herself to be led through the open portal, calling out behind her as she went, "Ergo Sum, Chance?"

I stood frozen to the spot. My arms hung limp at my sides, my mouth open, my eyes staring at the floor while seeing nothing at all. This wasn't happening. It had to be a joke, a sick cosmic joke of some kind. Or a dream. Was I still dreaming? Would I roll over and wake up and look into Cadence's sleeping face and laugh at how ridiculous my own subconscious could be?

She wouldn't leave me to wake up alone. She wouldn't do something rash like break into a gangster's house while leaving me to wake up alone. She wouldn't get arrested – and leave me alone.

She wouldn't.

"Mr. Hale?"

My vision cleared, and I saw Kace standing just inside the door to the flat. He pointed behind him, his brows high over his eyes. "I could be wrong, but it looks like Miss Turing was just arrested. Is that right?"

She had. She did.

Blinking at him, words stuttered out of my gaping mouth. "Lawyer. Ergo Sum." I snapped my fingers and jumped into action, digging into my pocket for my mobile. "Rin Murata!"

Kace watched my panicked fumbling with some concern. "I understood one of those words."

But I was paying my bodyguard no mind, focused fully on the task at hand. "Call Henry," I demanded of the bud I shoved in my ear. I paced the room in impatience as the phone rang, every muscle in my body tense and aching.

There was a click as the line connected. "Henry!" I nodded through his greeting, my hand at my mouth. "Bit of an emergency, chum, can you give me Rin's number?" My eyes went heavenward in exasperation. "Yes, Rin, your partner. Their number, please?" Henry rattled off the string of digits and then demanded an explanation. "Because I need a lawyer, of course. Or Cadence does. She's been arrested."

15

Chapter 15

Almost a full week of torture passed -- days filled with bureaucratic hoop-jumping and syllable-heavy monologuing from both Rin and a state prosecutor intent, it seemed, on making me consider choking the life from someone with my bare hands.

On the evening of the sixth day, Henry and I waited outside one of the smaller courtrooms in the vast judicial complex in Römer's District 12. Some interior designers somewhere had once picked benches to line the walls at inconsistent intervals. Decaying cushions, fraying and flat, oozed from the top of the black metal benches like pus from fungus. Under normal circumstances, I would have preferred to stand rather than trust the cleanliness of such seats, but these were not normal circumstances. I sat, clasping my hands in front of me, caring nothing for my surroundings -- my mind consumed with worse case scenarios and fear.

I breathed in deep through my nose and let out the air slowly through my mouth. It didn't help.

"I know it's impossible," said Henry from beside me. "But try to relax."

My legs jittering up and down, I tightened my grip on my hands, looking over at my friend. "What'll happen if Rin can't get the charges dismissed?"

If the panicked look in Henry's eyes didn't answer my question, his response of, "Let's try not to think that way," certainly did.

I rocketed to my feet, slapping my hands against my thighs. "No bail. It's ridiculous! How is Cadence a flight risk?"

"Well," Henry said, standing up to join me. "Given that she's being accused of having connections to the Whiston Underground, who could, conceivably, spirit her away to any number of planets with relative ease..."

I pushed my hand through my hair. "But she would never–"

My friend's hand squeezed my shoulder tightly. "You know that. I know that. But the judge has to do what they think is prudent."

"The judge–" I snarled, "–is an ass."

Henry's tongue clicked off the back of his teeth and he smiled coldly. "And it's comments like those that landed us out here," he said, gesturing to our surroundings. "Instead of in the courtroom."

I glared at him, but it lacked bite. He was right. Getting emotional wasn't helping things – wasn't helping Cadence. She had told me as much when we spoke via holo, a full day after she had been arrested. I had been told to expect the call and had been waiting in Cadence's office for almost an hour before it finally came through. Cadence sat at the end of a table, almost a foot away from the holopuck, her restraints and plain, brown prison jumpsuit on full, nauseating display.

"Cadence!" It took all my self-control not to grab at the holopuck and hold it close, the need to have some part of her near almost overwhelming. "Are you alright?"

She nodded, the faint whisper of a smile tugging at the corner of her lips. "Gav, hello, Chance. Yes, I'm fine. Thank you for calling Ergo Sum – Rin's already been in touch."

I took a deep breath. There was so much I wanted to say, so much we needed to discuss. But I was well aware that all communication in and out of the penal district was strictly monitored and, not trusting the discretion of the EO officers tasked with that work, I settled for lamely asking, "So...how is jail?"

Cadence's smile bloomed. She looked around herself for a few long moments before nodding and answering, "Jail is fine." She drew her brows down into a point, curling her upper lip away from her teeth. "They're keeping me separate from the other inmates, mostly. Something about me being a target of violence because of my artificial nature."

"Because you're an animanecron?" I said, translating her stilted words.

Her smile flipped into a lopsided frown, and she stared past me, thinking. "I told them that I'd be fine, but they are rather insistent." Her gaze flitted up to something or someone just out of frame. "About a lot of things, actually."

I gave a derisive snort. "The criminal justice system is not known to be a place where debate is welcome."

A nod was her response. I wet my lips with a flick of my tongue and reached out to caress the edge of the holopuck. "I'm... I'm glad to see you're alright, Cay."

"Sinc, you too." The sincerity in her voice nearly brought tears to my eyes. "Has anyone else tried–?"

I closed my eyes and shook my head, smiling. "Mr. Morgan has been very vigilant."

Opening my eyes, I caught Cadence watching me, a look of such longing on her face that it quite literally took my breath away. As soon as our eyes met, she turned away, the expression vanishing.

"Cadence," I said, shifting forward in my seat. "You might not want to hear this: but have you considered giving Inspector Brisbois the information he wants?"

"No." Her lips firmed into a straight line. "And I won't consider it either." The restraints around her wrists clattered against the table in front of her as she leaned towards the holoprojector. "These animanecrons trusted me, Chance. I can't betray that trust. I can't let them get hurt any more than I can let you get hurt."

"And what about you?" I demanded, frustration clogging my throat. "Cay, you're so concerned about everyone else, but you can't protect the world at the cost of yourself."

She tilted her head to one side. "Why not?"

My free hand curled into a fist. "Because I won't let you," I said, biting down hard on the inside of my mouth.

Cadence shook her head, her eyes widening. "Chance, listen–"

There was a loud clank from her side of the call, and she looked past me. There was the murmur of voices out of range of the holoprojector's speakers and she nodded, returning her attention to me with a frown. "They say I have to go – I'll try and talk to you again soon."

"Cadence, wait–"

But it was too late. She vanished and the call disconnected.

I hadn't been able to talk to her since. Over the days of legal wrangling, Cadence had appeared in court beside Rin several times. We exchanged glances, a smile or two, pained on both our parts, but more communication than that was impossible. I couldn't tell how she was faring, my love's appearance proving inscrutable as always, but I – I was suffering without her.

"Chance?" said Henry, his face growing taut with concern. "You still with us?"

Something of my thoughts must have shown in my visage. I swallowed hard and shook my head. "I just want Cadence out of there. I want her home."

"Rin is–"

With a click and a whoosh of compressed air, the doors to the courtroom slid open. Henry and I leapt to our feet. As if summoned by the sound of their name, Rin exited, readjusting the strap of their briefcase over their shoulder, and chatting with a clerk as they walked.

"I'll have that paperwork to you right away," they finished saying. They pivoted to face us, smiling, and they were about to greet us when Inspector Brisbois, also exiting the courtroom, caught them by the shoulder.

"I hope there's no hard feelings, Mx. Murata," said the Inspector, reaching down to shake Rin's hand cordially.

"Not from me," said Rin with a grin. They released his hand, pushing their frames up the bridge of their nose. "Now, Miss Turing might be another story."

Brisbois let out a scoff and was about to say something else when an EO officer approached and tapped him on the shoulder. I took the opportunity to swoop in and usher Rin over to our side of the hallway, my hand at their elbow.

"What's going on, what's happened?" I demanded.

Rin turned their smile on us. "The judge finally saw things our way and dismissed the charges."

"Yes!" shouted Henry, beaming.

I gripped Rin by the shoulders, my chest heaving with deep, relieved breaths. "Oh, Rin! Rin, I could kiss you!" A look of panic crossed their face, and I released them quickly, shaking my head. "But I'll leave that to Henry."

Taking his cue, Henry stepped in front of me and pulled Rin to his chest, kissing them with a smile.

I gave them a moment or two, but that was all I could spare. "So," I pressed, practically vibrating with excitement. "What happens now, where's Cadence?"

Henry released his partner and Rin stepped back from him, shaking their head. "It'll still be a few hours before Cadence is processed out, but she'll be free as a bird after that."

"What changed the judge's mind?" pressed Henry, holding on to his paramour's hand and swinging it to and fro like a schoolboy.

"I convinced Cadence to give the Enforcement Office another place to focus their efforts besides the Whiston Underground," said Rin, their smile fading.

Understanding flashed upon me. I nodded sharply. "You got her to tell them about Hudd."

They sighed, rolling their eyes heavenward. "And it took some serious convincing on my part – she was not in a giving frame of mind." Their smile returned. "But, once the judge heard that she had been cooperative, and that it was a viable lead, they were less sympathetic to the state's arguments about a recalcitrant and troublesome private investigator."

"Great work, darling," said Henry, pulling Rin close to him and planting another kiss on top of their head.

Rin glowed under the praise of their partner. "Well, I do my best."

A sharp twinge of envy shot through me as I watched them, painful like icy water on a cavity. Looking away, I forced the feeling down deep, only to find myself looking into the expectant face of Inspector Brisbois.

"Mr. Hale?" He crooked a finger at me, beckoning me towards him.

Glowering, my ill-temper only partially to blame on the man in front of me, I walked forward to meet him. Brisbois leaned in towards me, his hands in his jacket pockets. "I understand from Miss Turing's testimony that you are in possession of the information that we need to arrest Noll Hudd?"

"I am." I looked down my nose at the Inspector, sneering. "Are you going to arrest me if I don't hand it over?"

A sardonic smile crept along the edges of the man's lips. He shook his head ruefully. "I was doing my duty. I didn't like it any more than you did."

"You were being myopic," I pronounced firmly, shoving my

hands in my trouser pockets. "And stubborn. And petty." Turning on my heels, I shook my head. "I'll have my office send you the files."

"So, you don't want to be there when we collar him?" he called after me.

"Why would I?" I shouted back.

"Thought you might like to see something through to the end for once. Cadence already said she'll be there," he added, almost as if it were an afterthought, although the gleam in his green eyes told me that it was anything but.

I stopped and looked over my shoulder at him. "Then I suppose you know where I'll be."

16

Chapter 16

It had been my intention to pick up Cadence from the courthouse holding cells alone after she'd been processed out, but Henry insisted on joining me, forgoing a celebratory drink with his significant other in order to welcome our mutual friend back from her brush with captivity.

"She's just been through an ordeal," explained Henry as we stood waiting at the bottom of the courthouse steps, waiting for Cadence to make her exit. "I want to show her some support."

"An ordeal of her own making," I said, shaking my head while turning my gaze heavenward. "Stubborn woman…"

Scowling, Henry looked at me askance. "You don't think she should have given up Quinn and the Underground, do you?"

"No, of course not," came the knee-jerk response. But then, I gave the question a moment or two more consideration and had to answer with an uncomfortable, "Well, perhaps. It's just –

she– she takes risks sometimes and doesn't always think about the consequences."

"I imagine since leaving Whiston all of her life has felt like one big risk," said my friend, shrugging. "Maybe she's become a little numb to the idea of consequences."

"Oh, I hope that's not true," I said, turning away from the steps to look at my friend in undisguised horror.

Henry let loose a chuckle. "Why?"

I rolled my eyes. "Can you imagine a fearless Cadence?"

He opened his mouth to respond, but then closed it, stepping around me with his arms spread wide. "I don't have to imagine it, she's right here. Hello you!"

I spun around to watch Cadence skip down the stairs, her smile dazzling, before she launched herself into Henry's embrace. "Cy, Henry!" She hugged him with enthusiasm. "You didn't have to wait for me!"

"Of course, I did! My favorite gumshoe lives to fight another day." Releasing her, he stepped back looking her over from head to toe. "Was it terrible? Did you survive? How are you, Cadence?"

Cadence heard Henry's questions, I was certain of it. But as she let go of Henry, her inky blue eyes met mine and I knew in a flash that she had no intention of answering them with words.

She closed the distance between us with two long strides, lifting her arms and locking them around the back of my neck, pulling me against her in a way that broached no argument. She kissed me like she'd been poisoned, and my lips were the only antidote. My hands curled into the fabric that covered her lower back as I held her to me. If I didn't hold her tight, I was certain I would've floated away, the ground already spinning under my feet.

With a last suckle at my bottom lip, she drew away from me and it was all I could do not to moan in protest.

"I'm much better now," she breathed the words against the corner of my mouth, resting her forehead against mine, her eyes closed tight. "Sinc, Chance, I missed you."

"I–" Before I could finish my sentence, her lips were on mine again. I melted into her, feeling quite lightheaded by the time she allowed me to speak again. "I missed you too, Cay."

"That doesn't look like nothing," chirped Henry from behind her, eyes wide.

Cadence, her arms still wrapped around my neck, craned her head back to look at him, her nose wrinkled. "Huh?"

"Ignore him," I cut in quickly, grabbing one of her hands from behind my head and holding it tight. "Are you ready to go home, darling?"

She nodded, looking down at her wrinkled week-old outfit and frowning. "I think I could do with a change of clothes at the minimum."

The three of us walked to the PT dock at the side of the courthouse complex, where Kace had already secured a vehicle for us. Remembering my promise to Brisbois, I phoned the office from the back of the transport, instructing Miss Taylor to give the Enforcement Office our full cooperation with whatever files they needed.

"They should be contacting you shortly about some data we received from Gwen Largent," I explained, nodding to Kace as he prepared to exit the PT and proceed us into Cadence's building.

"Yes, sir." I heard the woman on the other end of the line take a deep breath, and then the sound of quick footsteps and a door closing. Her voice lost its veneer of formality as she demanded. "Chance, are you alright?"

I followed Kace up the stairs, with Cadence and Henry chatting behind me. "Fine, why?"

"You have no idea the kinds of rumors that are flying around about you." Lily's voice teetered between irritation and concern, both of which touched my heart. "You've been out of the office for over a week, hardly anyone's been able to reach you, the last time you were here Director Aja—"

"I'm fine," I repeated, stepping back as Cadence moved past me to unlock her door.

"I'm your executive assistant, Chance – I know you about as well as anybody. You can't lie to me."

Considering the validity of that statement, I tapped my foot against the floor, waiting with the others in the corridor while Kace cleared Cadence's apartment. "Listen, I can't really say much. Just... everything should be back to normal soon, I promise."

"Good." The rolling of her eyes practically echoed down the phone line. "Now say it again like you believe it, and I'll buy it."

"Everything will be back to normal soon," I said, beginning to feel a bit like a corrupted story cube. Kace returned to the door and ushered us inside. I stepped to one side to allow Cadence and Henry to enter in front of me. "You have to have a little faith, Miss Taylor."

"Yes, well—" A muffled beeping, and Lily's voice became sharp and serious. "Looks like the EO is calling on the other line. Better go!"

Shaking my head, I pulled my mobile out of my ear, closing the front door behind me. Walking into the foyer, I pulled off my coat. Henry collapsed down onto the sofa in the waiting room and Kace prowled into the office, still on alert for potential threats.

Throwing my coat over the back of the nearest chair, I called out my beloved's name. Her voice rang out from the loft above me. "Everything alright at work?"

"Sounds like it," I called up to the loft, shoving my hand in my trouser pockets. "Brisbois is getting his hands on the information we received from Gwen Largent about Noll Hudd,"

"Excellent!" Cadence, beaming as she made her way back down the stairs in a fresh outfit, looked every bit as excited as a child about to receive a special present. "I hope we don't have to wait too long before he's ready to move."

"We—we need to talk about that, Cay," I said, probing the inside of my cheek with my tongue.

She paused at the bottom of the stairs, her hand on the railing as she stared at me. "Talk about what?"

I turned away, walking into the waiting room area, my hand coming out of my pocket to rub at the back of my neck. "Brisbois said you wanted to be there when they took Hudd into custody."

There was no immediate response to my statement. I looked over my shoulder at Cadence. One brow quirked upward, she still smiled, casting an inquisitive glance at Henry on the sofa as if he might be able to clue her into what I was getting at. "Yes, of course. What about it?"

I took a deep breath and let it out in a sigh. "Isn't that... don't you think that's unnecessary? Reckless, even?"

I watched her face darken. "No. No, I don't." Frowning, she leaned forward, one hip jutting out as her weight rested on her front foot. "I need to ask Hudd questions before he's had a chance to regroup. While he's knocked off balance. Nothing knocks you off balance more than being arrested – I can say that with authority now."

"And few people like being arrested less than armed gangsters," I said, stepping back towards her, glaring. "It's dangerous, Cay. You can't keep–"

She cut me off with a slice of her hand, her brows low over eyes. "This is *my* decision, Chance."

She put emphasis on my name, pushing it out from between her teeth like it was a curse; like it was a threat. Henry stiffened visibly, his attention flickering between us.

"Well, your decisions don't just affect you, Cadence," I said, stressing her name in the same way she had stressed mine.

Cadence crossed her arms slowly over her chest, her gaze digging into me, as if daring me to push her further.

I rolled my eyes, throwing one hand up into the air. "Fine. Fine! If you're going, I'm going."

"What?" exclaimed Kace, striding back into the room, alarm writ clear on his face.

"Chance–" started Henry, but he didn't get anything more out before Cadence cut him off, stepping on his words with her own.

"Absolutely not!"

"It's *my* decision," I shot her own words back at her, working hard to control my temper. I crossed the room towards her, pointing first at her, then myself. "Where you are, I am. That's what a partnership means."

"We're lovers, Chance," she said, each word dropping like an icicle into my heart. "Not partners."

Her words landed like a fist to my guts. My throat closed up with hurt, and I struggled to breathe for a moment, a strangled sound escaping from my closed mouth. Henry stood up from his seat on the couch, his brows drawn to a point.

I shook myself out of my shocked stupor, a ragged rush of air leaving me. "Well. I guess you're right. Partners listen to each other." Gritting my teeth, I clenched my hands into fists, feeling my nails digging into my palms. "And you're not hearing me, damn it." Looking away from her, my gaze landed on my coat. I reached for it, swiping it off the back of the chair on which it rested. "I won't let you push me to the sidelines anymore. I don't care the reason."

Cadence stepped towards me, shaking her head, scowling. "And how exactly are you going to stop me?"

I turned my back on her, shoving my arms into my coat sleeves. "By leaving."

Stunned silence in my wake, I strode through the flat, wrenching open the front door and walking out into the corridor. I heard Henry's footfall catching up with me from behind, but I didn't stop, not until I was almost at the landing for the stairs, when he called out, "Chance, wait–!"

"Henry–" As I turned to face him, I bit back my words and fought back my tears of frustration. Kace exited the apartment and moved past me down the corridor to the stairs, silent as a ghost. I shook my head and gestured back to the flat. "Could you... stay with her, please? Keep an eye out."

He lowered his hand, which had been outstretched towards me, and nodded. "Of course. You should get some rest." With a final shake of his head, he took one more step towards me, his expression earnest. "Chance, she's just trying to figure everything out. She loves you, she–"

"I know she loves me," I said, swallowing hard. "I'm just not sure she knows what that means."

Turning back towards the stairs, I found myself staring into the not unsympathetic face of Kace, standing a few steps below me, his hand on the railing of the staircase. "You ready to go, Mr. Hale?"

I nodded. We exited the building without another word, and I allowed myself to be led to the nearest PT station. The ride to my flat passed in silence, for which I was infinitely grateful, lost as I was in my own frustration and misery.

Maybe I wasn't cut out for this love business. Resting my chin in my hand, I watched the city fly by and succumbed to thoughts of Cadence. Did she really view me as nothing but an accessory? Was I a beloved toy and nothing more? I couldn't believe that. But that's certainly how she was treating me, intentionally or not.

When we arrived at *The Feathers*, I followed Kace through the apartment building foyer and onto the elevator. I had always thought that falling in love and being loved in return was the hard part of a relationship. That once achieved, everything else would fall naturally into place.

I couldn't remember the last time I had been proven so resoundingly wrong.

Stepping out of the lift, I swiped my finger over the bio lock on my front door, stepping back to let Kace perform his duties. He soon waved me inside and I strode past him and into my bedroom, loosening my tie as I went. Henry was right. I had been running on anxiety and adrenaline for days now. *And for what? A pernicious little voice in my head taunted. For a woman that loves you and doesn't trust you? What good is that?*

What good is love without trust?

Pushing my hands through my hair, I gave a strangled cry of frustration that turned into a decidedly mirthless grunt of laughter. I turned to sit down, only to find Kace lurking in the doorway.

"Mr. Hale?"

I threw up my hands. "What, what is it?"

He jabbed his thumb back in the direction of the living room. "I'll be out here, if you need me."

"I won't," I snarled, hardly recognizing the bitterness in my voice. The sound alone was enough to bring me back to my senses, and I lifted a hand to my face, pinching the bridge of my nose. "Damn it. Sorry, Mr. Morgan. Kace. Sorry." I tried to smile. "Been a strange time."

"No need to apologize, Mr. Hale. I..." He shifted his weight from foot to foot and looked away from me for a moment. "Relationships can be...complicated. But that doesn't mean... I suppose I don't know her very well, but if she's what you want..." Shaking his head, he rolled his eyes heavenward. "Just don't give up, I suppose. Sometimes it takes a little extra work, but if Cadence is who you want to be with, it has to be worth it, right?"

Honestly touched by the man's fumbling attempts at comfort and advice, I felt my smile take on a more genuine aspect. "Thank you. Thank you, Kace."

Kace stepped back from the door and threw his hand out towards the bed. "You should take Mr. Davers' advice, though. Get some rest."

I was soon left alone in my room with only my own thoughts for company. The evening was coming on quickly and I collapsed fully clothed onto my bed, lying flat on my back, limbs splayed out around me.

Rest. I shut my eyes and released a deep breath. I needed rest.

Cadence above me in the dim light, her hands sliding against my bare chest, staring down at me with that smile – that damnable, wicked summer smile that never seemed to go away. Except, I'd find out, except at the moment of utmost ecstasy, when she called out my name and it was like the first time I'd ever heard it. Every time, it was like the first time...

I opened my eyes, my body on fire, my skin so slick with sweat that my clothes stuck to me. Groaning, I rolled over onto my side, curling up into a fetal position. Had I slept? I must have – I dreamed, didn't I? The same dream I'd had for days now, the same damn dream. I balled my hands into fists, rubbing them against my forehead.

A knock at the door – surely the sound that had originally roused me from my fevered dreams. "Mr. Hale? Are you awake?"

Glancing at my watch, I noted that it was almost ten in the evening. "Yes, Kace, what is it?"

"Inspector Brisbois' been trying to reach you." The door creaked, presumably from Kace leaning his weight against it. "They're picking up Noll Hudd tonight. You said you wanted to be there?"

I scrambled off the bed and crossed the room, flinging the door open. "When?" I demanded.

Kace, jumping back from the suddenly ajar portal, grimaced at me. I'm sure I looked a sight – I certainly felt like I'd been through the wringer. "A couple of hours from now." He straightened, shaking his head. "I still don't think it's a very good idea for–"

I cut him off with a wave of my hand. "Did he tell you where?"

For a moment, Kace looked like he was about to argue with me. But whatever sensible words he had on the tip of his tongue, he swallowed down. "Yes, sir." He stepped back into the hall, giving me room to move past him if I wished. "We'll need to leave now if we want to make it – it's on the other side of Römer."

I took a deep breath as I pulled on the knot of my tie, fully undoing the constrictive piece of clothing. "Give me five minutes," I said, and I closed the door without waiting for his response.

Rushing into the bathroom, I dumped the coldest water I could into the sink, filling it before plunging my face straight into it, opening my stinging eyes wide. Cadence – Cadence would be there. What would she say? What would she do? What would I do?

I honestly had no idea.

The PT dropped us in District 86 after a solid hour and a half of travel. An industrial area of the city filled to the brim with block after block of automated manufacturing plants, District 86 pumped out all the goods the planet could desire – all day, every day. There were a few buildings meant for human habitation, but these were slapdash and temporary at best – offices for engineers and mechanics who might need to stop in and do some maintenance on the plants' constantly moving machines, all night convenience stores which catered to their late hours and need to eat, but little more than that.

Stepping onto a lift at the end of one of the public walkways, we were whisked up to one of the upper floors of these gargantuan factories. The lift deposited us on the far end of a huge dock, where the product created inside was picked up for distribution to the larger world. Most of the time, such a dock would be bereft of people, everything happening by means of auto-piloted transports and other robots.

That was not the story tonight.

Tonight, the dock was peppered with enforcement officers. I saw no EO cruisers, but there were several tactical transports waiting at the north end of the dock. There must have been thirty plus people scattered around the area, all wearing expressions more suitable for a funeral. I heard Brisbois' voice on the wind and pointed towards the transports from which it came.

"Shall we?"

Kace shrugged. "Suit yourself. I've given up trying to argue with you."

Kace and I made our way across the platform towards the transports, stopping several times to explain our presence to various EO personnel as we went. As if we were connected by some kind of invisible string, I was able to pick Cadence out of the crowd almost immediately. With Henry at her side, she stood in front of one of the black vehicles, surveying the scene with her usual intense interest. Her eyes moved over me as if I were a stranger at first, and I felt that familiar pang of hurt in my chest. But a second after her gaze passed, it was back. Her mouth fell open, and she pushed an EO officer standing in front of her out of the way.

"Chance?" Cadence shook her head as she made her way forward to intercept us. "What are you doing here? I told you–"

"I was invited," I said, continuing forward without slowing my step.

"It's too dangerous," she hissed, turning away from me to address my bodyguard. "Kace, how could you–!"

Kace held up a hand, shaking his head with closed eyes. "I've learned my lesson – it's better to go along with whatever crazy thing he wants, and just try to do my job."

"How is it dangerous?" I gestured to the dock around us as I walked. "I'm surrounded by enforcement officers, my bodyguard, Henry, and you. Couldn't be safer."

Cadence stepped in front of me, holding her hands up. I was forced to stop or plow into her. "Chance, please." Her lips were a firm line, her voice low. "We can talk about this later, but for now, you need–"

I took a single step forward, my face inches from hers. "I'm exactly where I need to be, Cadence."

We stayed there for a long moment, staring into each other's eyes, each daring the other to say something that couldn't be unspoken. Cadence broke first, dropping her hand to her side and swallowing hard. I took the external signal of discomfort as a sign that she hoped I wouldn't make more of a scene than I already had.

I nodded to her as I passed, smiling without warmth, the roiling in my belly a potent mixture of hurt, anger, and a smattering of attraction for which I could not account. She fell into step behind me with Kace, and I waved at Henry, who strode towards us.

"So, you are joining us then," he said, his expression stoic.

"You know me, Henry, chum," I answered, my words light but my tone funereal. "Man of my word."

"Speaking of..." Henry extended his hand out towards the opposite side of the dock. "Inspector Brisbois wanted to chat once you arrived. He's this way."

Brisbois was deep in conference with two tactically outfitted EO officers, both of whom held datapads up for the senior detective's consideration. As we approached, I slung my hands in my pockets, attempting to adopt a cavalier attitude.

"Hullo, Inspector," I chirped. "Fine night for it, isn't it?"

"Evening, Mr. Hale," said Brisbois, turning to face me with a grim expression. "Mr. Davers – Miss Turing," he nodded to Cadence, who stepped up beside Kace, careful, I thought, to keep his body between us. Brisbois said a few more words of instruction to his officers, and then sent them off with a nod before returning his attention to our little troupe. "Hope you're all wearing your comfortable shoes because we'll be waiting here a while. The shipment isn't due to come in until fifteen o'clock at the dock over there – the decommissioned one. We'll monitor the operation from here."

Brisbois gestured to the dock in question. There was a dock

between us, and the decommissioned loading zone, separated on either side by ten to fifteen feet of empty air.

"Fifteen o'clock?" I jiggled the thin gold band on my wrist to life, and frowned as the face proclaimed it to be just past twelve. "Then, why are we–?"

"The EO teams need to get in place early enough that Hudd's people won't be around to spot them," offered Kace, with an easy sort of confidence that did not go unnoticed by the Inspector.

I nodded. "Ah. That makes sense."

Brisbois slid his hands out of his pockets, looking my body-guard up and down with an appraising eye. At last, he proffered his hand towards him, palm up, asking, "Are you carrying, Mr. Morgan?"

Kace blinked once, slowly, and then shrugged, reaching his hand underneath his coat and suit jacket. "Licensed to, Inspector Brisbois," he said, before carefully withdrawing a sleek, handgun-styled Pulsar. He placed the jet-black energy weapon in Oliver's hand, the butt of the Pulsar facing the inspector.

My mouth fell open. "Kace!" I exclaimed, taking a step back.

Henry stared wide eyed at the device. "I didn't know you had that!"

Kace rolled his eyes and shook his head. "Well, neither of you ever asked." He gestured towards the weapon, which Brisbois was inspecting in both hands. "It's perfectly safe."

A sharp bark of laughter tripped from between Brisbois' teeth. Pointing the Pulsar at an empty space on the ground, he looked down the length of it. "For something that shoots out a pulse of energy with enough force to tear a hole through muscle and bone in less than a second, yes–' He looked up at us, passing the weapon back to its owner, wiggling his brow. "– I suppose it's relatively safe."

"It only does all that if you pull the trigger." Kace secreted the Pulsar back behind him, readjusting his clothes. "And if the safety's off."

Cadence frowned. "I didn't think lethal weapons were allowed in the hands of private owners on this planet."

"If they're duly licensed for work or sport, there are exceptions to that rule, Miss Turing." Brisbois gestured to Kace. "Mr. Morgan, as a personal security professional, has every right to apply for a license to carry in public."

"I don't use it unless I absolutely have to, Miss Turing," said Kace, pulling his jacket tighter around his body. "And I promise you, I know how to."

Looking at the EO officers gearing up around us, I realized that Kace's Pulsar was not the only energy weapon within sight. "I see you all aren't packing light for this party tonight either, Inspector.". I nodded to the general hubbub in which we stood – numerous people readjusting body armor and strapping on helmets, while others checked the energy readings on Pulsar-like rifles and the charges on their taser guns.

"Hudd and his ilk have proven dangerous to us before." Brisbois' pressed his lips into a thin hard line, clenching his fists. It occurred to me that what I was witnessing was the man on edge – something I didn't think I'd ever seen before. "I don't want to lose anyone tonight that I don't have to." He pointed his finger at each of us in turn. "Which means you all are going to be quiet, unobtrusive, and functionally invisible tonight, right? Remember, you're here only because I allow you to be."

Henry and I shared a glance, but it was Cadence who answered, nodding. "We'll be good, Inspector."

17

Chapter 17

The air on the factory dock had a bite of winter in it that I hadn't detected on previous fall nights. With Brisbois engaged in his operation, there was precious little for the rest of us to do but to keep out of everybody's way and try to keep warm. I lit a nix and offered one to Kace, but he refused.

"I think I'll see if I can be of any help," he said, buttoning his coat closed at the neck. "Sounds like they could use all the extra hands they can get."

"Suit yourself," I replied around the thin tube of herbs and paper perched between my lips. "Just don't go and make yourself indispensable. You work for Halcyon Enterprises, remember – can't lose you to the EO."

"No chance of that," said Kace, smiling as he walked away. "Their retirement plan is shit."

My eyes searched out Cadence before I could stop myself. A

few yards away, she sat on the running board of one of the black tactical transports, her hands clasped between her knees, her face a perfect blank. I noted that she wasn't bothering to breathe or blink – a sure sign that something was on her mind, taking up precious processing power.

I felt Henry move behind me. I glanced over my shoulder at him and found him watching Cadence just as I was. He looked from her to me, leaning forward onto the balls of his feet. "You could go and talk to her, you know."

"That hasn't been working out very well as of late," I said, blowing nix smoke up out into the night air. "In case you hadn't noticed."

He sighed. "She just–"

"Don't make excuses for her," I snapped, swinging around to face him fully.

"I'm not!" He took a step back, his hands raised defensively. But he soon lowered them, fixing me with a plaintive stare. "It's only... Look, speaking from personal experience, it can be hard to let someone else into your life when you've gotten used to going it alone."

Shaking my head, I looked over my shoulder at the subject of our discussion. "She certainly is independent."

Henry nodded. "Self-confident."

"Uncompromising." I shoved one hand in my coat pocket, scratching at my brow with the other as I sighed. "All things I adore about her." Pausing to take another drag on my nix, my eyes narrowing against the smoke, I said, "She knows her own mind. It's just lately she seems to think she should be able to tell me mine."

"And vice versa?" suggested my friend gently.

I paused and thought over his words. After a moment, I shrugged. "Well... you may have a point there."

Smiling, Henry closed the distance between us with a step, lowering his voice and tossing his head in the direction of our mutual friend. "Listen: have a little patience–"

I rolled my shoulders back as I turned back to face Cadence. "Not something I'm known for," I muttered under my breath.

Henry gave me a small shove just between my shoulder blades. "– and try again."

Propelled both by Henry's encouragement and my own desire to be on better footing with my beloved, I walked towards her, coming to a stop just in front of her. I dropped my nix onto the metal surface of the dock and ground it out with the toe of my shoe. "Hullo, Cay."

She did not grace me with so much as a glance. "Chance."

Swallowing down the fist-sized lump in my throat, I took up position beside her, brushing my shoulder against hers as I sat on the hard metal surface of the transport. "Cadence... are we really *not* going to talk about this?"

She turned to glare at me, but it lacked conviction. "I don't think the middle of an EO operation is really the time or the place, do you?"

I shrugged my concession. "Fine – then name the time and name the place. I'm all ears."

I felt her eyes on my face. I wondered what she saw when she looked there. Cadence stood abruptly, shoving her hands in her trouser pockets. "Tomorrow." Pausing to take a deep breath and let it out through her nose, she nodded. "At Lillit Park. We can have breakfast. Does that sound alright?"

"More than," I said. Then, without really knowing why, I reached out and placed my hand on her knee, squeezing her in a gesture of reassurance. "Everything is going to be alright, Cay. I promise."

She opened her mouth to respond but was silenced by a shout from Brisbois.

"Alright!" He stood at the end of the dock closest to the lift, a crowd of tactically outfitted EO members surrounding him. "You have your instructions! Let's get this bastard off the streets! Alpha team, move into position one and hold there until you receive the go from me. Bravo Team, remain in place here!"

A chorus of 'yes sir' pierced the air and the group scattered, many of them heading in our direction. Cadence and I scuttled out of the way, taking refuge amidst some discarded shipping containers and bioplastic crates. The two tactical transports, with engines silent as silk on silk, started up. Alpha Team piled into the vehicles, jostling each other as they went.

Kace and Brisbois broke off from the dispersing crowd, striding over to join us. "Well, what team are we on?" I asked.

"Bravo," Kace replied. "We wait and we watch."

There was a powerful gust of displaced air as the transports pushed away from the dock. I tried to keep a bead on them, but they disappeared into the darkness above our heads. "So, what's the idea? They swoop in, get the bad guys, and we just–"

"Provide support and reconnaissance," said Brisbois. He stood at the corner of the nearest shipping container, which provided him with a clear view of the manufacturing dock. "They're experienced officers, Mr. Hale. This should go off without a hitch."

With the Alpha Team dispatched, the dock felt deserted except for our little group of onlookers. Time passed with infinitesimal slowness, the night growing darker and deeper. There was no sign of our quarry.

Jiggling the band on my wrist, I watched the time tick over to twenty minutes past fifteen o'clock. I lit yet another nix, inhaling the smoke deep into my lungs as I stepped up behind the watchful inspector. "Is it always like this?" I whispered in Brisbois' ear.

Brisbois glared at me over his shoulder. "Like what?"

"Boring."

"Real life isn't a flicker, Mr. Hale," he sneered, returning his attention to the other platform across the way.

I sighed, careful to direct the smoke from my nix up into the air instead of directly into the back of the inspector's head. "Maybe they–?"

Movement caught my eye on the platform. I hushed immediately, watching as first one, then another, and then a handful of male-presenting bodies appeared from the shadows. Some of them arrived alone, some in pairs, but it seemed as if they issued forth from the very depths of the factory, from abandoned shipping containers, and from everywhere all at once. Their voices carried on the wind. They weren't being quiet, why should they? District 86 was practically devoid of life, and they had no reason to think anyone was around to hear them. Laughter rippled back to us, rough and boisterous as the group congealed into one mass.

A final figure stepped out from amongst the crates, moving past the other bodies on the platform to the edge. I saw the flare of a nix being twisted into life and placed between the person's lips as they looked up into the night sky.

"There he is," said Brisbois, leaning forward and touching his finger to the bud in his ear. "Alpha Team, the target has arrived. Be advised that he is not alone. I count...at least eight to ten additional hostiles on the platform."

"Copy, Bravo Team," came the reply.

I didn't recognize the man at first – the dark and the distance did their best to obscure him from my sight. But a cold wind blew a cloud away from the face of one of the moons, a shaft of silvery light illuminating the notorious Mr. Hudd.

The boss of a large criminal empire, Noll Hudd fancied himself an entrepreneur of the highest order, but in reality, he was a peddler of poison and perversion. He had no love for animanecrons, and never hesitated to use violence to get what he wanted. We had met the man several months ago, during our investigation into the death of Ani Rights activist, Elea Cerf. Elea had stolen the hearts of Hudd's wife and child while he had been serving time in the Anteries Penal District. He was not the type to let such a slight go unanswered. Now, standing on the 'decommissioned' dock, Hudd took a long drag on his nix, cupping the end to protect it from the wind. One of the other low-lifes loitering on the platform said something, and he nodded in response.

"What are we waiting for?" Henry asked quietly.

"We need eyes on the merchandise," whispered back Brisbois. "Otherwise, the most we can arrest him for is trespassing."

As if on cue, an Automated Transport puttered around the corner of the building, a shipping crate the length of a coffin, but twice as wide and twice as tall, clutched in its front-facing claw. Hudd and his men moved back from the edge of the platform to give the AT space to deposit its treasure. The transport slid its cargo onto the platform and released it from its jaws before shuddering back the way it came.

Hudd approached the crate and kicked at it. One of the metal panels on the front slid away and clattered onto the ground, revealing a keypad and computer screen of some sort. Barely illuminated by the dim light coming off the screen, Hudd punched something into the keypad. The crate groaned and hissed. The top split open, the panels sliding to the right and left like the skin off a snake. Hudd reached in and pulled out a long cylinder filled with dark, red liquid, which I was sad to say that I recognized as drogan -- the man who killed my father had been an addict, and I had nearly been killed by a small syringe of the stuff. If the crate was packed with cylinders of that size, all filled with drogan...

My stomach clenched. "Is that it?"

Brisbois nodded. "Yes." His fingers flew back up to his ear-bud. "Okay, Alpha Team, be ready to move on my mark. In five... four... three... two... on—"

A glint caught my eye, and I turned and looked down the platform -- away from the crate full of drugs, away from Hudd, and away from his men. A figure had appeared at the far end of the dock and was moving at a steady run through the crates, waving their arms.

I pulled at Brisbois, twisting him to one side so that he

could see what I was seeing. "Wait, Oliver, there's somebody else out there!"

But it was too late. Shouting on the platform. Hudd and his crew exploded into action, scrambling to ready heavily modified Pulsars and other weapons. Seconds later, Alpha Team descended from the heavens. But seconds were all that Hudd's people needed. The teeth clattering rattle of an automatic gun blasted through the quiet night, followed quickly by the sharp zings of energy weapons releasing their charges. The EO returned fire as they tried to land personnel on the platform. As I watched, an officer was hit in the chest and dropped down into the dark street below.

"Shit!" The expression on Brisbois' face was one I wouldn't soon forget, lit as it was by the flash of muzzle flare and firing energy weapons. Brisbois wrested his taser out of its holster and started forward, barking behind him, "Stay here!"

He ran for the side of the platform and jumped, clearing the gap, and landing on the adjacent dock with a slight stumble. He repeated this maneuver on the other side, energy blasts zipping past him, forcing him to drop in a low roll onto Hudd's platform. A few EO officers had managed to make it to the dock's surface and were taking cover behind the container of drugs. As I watched Brisbois dodge and weave across the field of fire, my gaze was drawn to a lone figure running in the opposite direction, across the dock.

In my bones, I knew who it was. It was the person who had warned Hudd of the impending EO raid. They were trying to escape.

I couldn't let that happen.

Dodging out from behind the safety of the shipping container, I ran towards the lip of the dock. I felt Cadence's hand miss the back of my coat as I sprinted away, and I heard her voice shouting my name.

"They're getting away!" I cried, running as fast as I could towards the firefight.

As I approached the gap, it suddenly looked a good deal larger than ten feet. But I didn't give myself time to hesitate. Blood screaming in my ears, I jumped.

I landed on the opposite dock so hard that I bit my tongue. Blood flooded my mouth and I stumbled, but I forced myself to stay upright and keep running. My eyes never left the figure who was running for the lift at the back of the dock, which would take them back down to street level.

They had warned Hudd that the EO was coming. People had died because of them. They couldn't get away with it.

Heedless to the shots going off around me, I attempted to mimic Oliver's landing on the decommissioned dock. Leaping over the gap, I tucked my body into a ball and managed, quite embarrassingly, to sort of bounce along the surface of the dock rather than roll along it. Still, it made me a difficult target to hit – or maybe no one was aiming for me as I hurried to my feet and kept running. I caught sight of Brisbois peering out from around the corner of the illicit crate, his mouth gaping, and his expression furious.

"Hale!" I heard Brisbois shout after me. "What the hell are you doing?!"

But I ignored him. There wasn't time for a debate. I ran across the dock and made one last leap.

And came up short.

The lip of the empty dock hit me in the stomach, and my vision went white. Instinctually, I reached out with both arms, my hands scrabbling against the smooth metal surface of the dock for some purchase and finding none. I slid back to the very edge. Dangling a hundred stories above the ground, my fingers screamed as they sought to hold my full weight.

There was a thud above me. The platform shook, and my left hand slipped. I gave a shout, terrified beyond speech.

A hand closed around my wrist.

I looked up and saw Brisbois leaning over the edge of the platform, holding on to me.

"I've got you," he grunted, every muscle in his body straining to hold onto the edge of the platform and hold on to me. "Don't let go."

Keeping my eyes fixed on his face, I swung my left hand up and grabbed hold of the arm that was holding on to me. He winced, gritting his teeth and shouting, "Hold on!"

With another shout, he heaved at me, pulling first the top half of my body, and then the rest of me, up over the lip of the platform. On my hands and knees, I crawled over him and onto the cold metal of the dock, gasping like a half-drowned man. As soon as I could, I forced my feet under me and stood, lurching to and fro as I searched for the figure that I had been pursuing.

"Damn it!" I whipped my head from side to side, seeking any sign of my quarry as I staggered forward. "They're gone!"

I turned back to face Brisbois, only to spin right into his fist. He bashed me hard on the jaw, hard enough to land me flat on my backside while he towered over me, shouting, "What the hell were you thinking?!"

"They were getting away!" I responded with equal volume, blood trickling down the corner of my mouth.

"You could have been killed, you idiot!" Incensed, Brisbois' fists were up and ready in front of him, his green eyes wide and wild. "I should arrest you for being a bloody fool!"

Chastened by his anger, my heart still pounding in my ears, I tried to scoff, pushing myself up on my forearms. "Well, if that were a chargeable offense, I'd have been behind bars years ago."

As I shakily got to my feet, Brisbois looked ready to strike me again. He settled instead for throwing his arms into the air, howling: "This isn't a joke, you stupid bastard!"

Before I could think better of it, I rushed towards him, wrapping my arms around his shoulders. "Thank you," I said, not trusting my wobbling legs to hold me if I let go of the man. "You saved my life. Thank you."

We stood that way for a long moment, Brisbois probably too stunned to process what was happening. But soon, he elbowed me away, scowling. "I didn't do it for you," he said, his voice a low growl. "I did it because for some unfathomable reason the woman I love, loves you."

Now it was my turn to be too stunned to process what was happening. I stared at him, still breathing heavily. "Oh," I managed at last. I pulled a half-grin, half-grimace across my face. "Er, well, I– thanks all the same, I suppose. Or...I'm sorry?"

The anger draining from him, Brisbois shoved his hands in his pockets. "Forget about it. We should take the long way back. Alpha team should have Hudd and his men in hand by now."

I gave a mirthless chuckle. "Sounds like–"

As I looked at him, the expression on the inspector's face shifted rapidly. His eyes opened wide, his brows drawing to a point. The color ran from his cheeks like paint on a watercolor canvas, his mouth dropping open. He lunged towards me, both arms outstretched.

"Down!" he shouted, his hands already on my back and shoulder, already shoving me down and behind him.

For the second time in as many minutes, I hit the ground hard, this time my chin bouncing against the filthy metal as I landed face down, my teeth clipping the side of my tongue. I rolled over and away from Brisbois, looking up just in time to see the bolt of energy rip through his lower torso.

Blood and viscera covered me in a thin spray, like a sticky mist from warm, crashing waves. The man dropped, first onto his knees and then backwards, his head landing with a thud against my thigh. I heard a scream. It wasn't until sometime later that I realized the sound must have come from me.

Scrambling forward, I grabbed Brisbois under both his arms and pulled him up into my lap, shouting his name and shaking him. "Oliver!"

Blood oozed out of his tightly closed mouth, running down his chin and covering his neck and chest. His wide eyes darted from side to side, the panic in them clear. I pressed my hand over the fist-sized hole just below his rib cage. Blood pumped freely around my fingers as I dug my fingernails into flesh that had never been exposed to the open air. As I held him, I felt his legs twitching uselessly against the dock, kicking as if he was trying to outrun what was coming for him.

"Shit!" I blinked the blood out of my eyes and shook him again. "Oliver! Oh God, stay with me. Stay with me!"

I heard the clang of the lift as it reached dock-level. I looked up to see EO officers running out onto the platform. "Help! Somebody help!" I shouted towards the approaching figures.

The body in my arms seized and shook and I held onto him tighter, beginning to sob as I begged, "Oliver, don't, don't die like this, don't, please..."

His eyes met mine. His hand jerked up and clamped onto my wrist, just as it had when he had pulled me back up onto the dock. I nodded in encouragement, a crazed smile twitching across my lips. "That's right, just hold on. Help is–"

His green eyes dulled. His hand loosened around my wrist, slipping down into his lap.

18

Chapter 18

I don't remember someone taking Oliver away from me, or me away from Oliver. I don't remember getting checked over by EO medical personnel. I don't remember giving my statement about Oliver's murder to an EO officer, although I was assured that all the former events did indeed occur. No, the next thing I remember after Oliver's passing is sitting against an empty shipping container near the edge of the dock, my knees pulled up to my chest, a half-smoked nix pinched between my fingers. Kace sat beside me, sighing heavily.

I glanced at the band on my wrist. It was two thirty in the morning. I brought the nix up to my mouth and inhaled robotically. I couldn't taste the smoke, but it felt good – cleansing. I knew it was my imagination, but I fancied that I could still catch the taste of Oliver's blood on my tongue.

Kace waited beside me. After a moment, he reached over and

took the nix from me, taking a long pull of it before flicking away the stub. "That's your last one tonight. I'm cutting you off."

I took a deep breath. I let it out slowly.

"It's my fault," I said. My voice sounded quiet and faraway. "He's dead because of me." I ground the heel of my hand into my eye, heedless to the fact that it was covered with Oliver's blood. "He saved my life, and now he's..."

"He did his job." Kace looked me over, and I turned away from his assessing gaze, not wanting to be perceived at that moment. "Did you see who–?"

"It was dark," I spat the words out with disgust. "My back was turned." Slumping further against the boxes, the tears flowed freely down my cheeks. "They were aiming for me."

"He did his job," Kace repeated, with more firmness this time. Someone from one of the command stations farther back on the platform called out to him and he stood, his hand coming down to squeeze my shoulder. "I'll be right back. Are you going to be alright? Should I get Henry?"

I nodded, waving him away without looking at him. The sound of his heavy footfalls receded into the distance. Taking in a shaky breath, I leaned my head back against the shipping container, forcing my stinging eyes to open and stare heavenward.

The minutes passed slowly. I'm not sure how long I stayed like that. But I know that when I lowered my head and looked in front of me, Cadence was standing there, her hands fists at her sides, her eyes wide and wild, her lips a firm line.

"How...*dare*...you?"

Each word struggled out from her, as if just speaking was

taking all of her willpower. I struggled to my feet, wiping my face on my sleeve. "Cadence–"

Face blotchy red, she vibrated with contained rage, shouting, "Anta, how dare you!"

She slapped me hard across the face, and I stumbled, barely managing to right myself as she continued to shout at me. "You have the nerve to lecture me about recklessness! And then you–" She struck me again, but this time rather than let me stumble, she grabbed me by my shirt and lifted me up so I was forced to look her in the face. "What were you thinking!" she screamed. "You could have died!"

Terror replaced the anger in her eyes, her own words echoing back to her in the night. "Tris, you could have died..." She dropped me onto the dock, her shoulders shaking as she struggled to breathe. "And– and– and I never would've been able to tell you that I'm sorry! I–I–"

Without waiting for her to finish her thought, I pulled her into my embrace, pressing her face into my shoulder, rocking her in my arms, pressing my lips to the top of her head. She allowed me all this, slowly relaxing in my grip and, even slower still, wrapping me up in her arms in return.

"Tris, is Oliver really gone?" she said after a few long, quiet moments.

"Yes," I nodded, fresh tears springing to my eyes. "Yes, Cay – I'm so sorry."

She pulled away from me then, looking into my face. Face contorted in pain, she lifted her hand to my cheek, wiping my tears away. "I can't cry," she whispered. "I can't cry with you, Chance. I can't..." Her hand, still wet with my tears, slid across her forehead as she shook her head. "I can't help it, I'm just...I'm so glad it wasn't you, and I feel so, so terrible that I'm so glad. He deserved better from me."

I gathered her up in my arms and held her to me, resting my cheek against hers. "From me too."

Gripping me tight, her lips at my ear, she said in a hushed voice, "It hurts. It hurts so much. And I didn't even..." A shudder ran through her. "Is this what it's going to feel like? Only worse?"

It took me a moment to understand what she was talking about. But when I did, when I realized what she was asking, there was nothing I could do but tell the truth. "Yes," I answered quietly. "When I die, it'll feel like this."

Suddenly, she released me. Stepping back, Cadence rubbed her cheeks, avoiding my gaze. "Oh no. No, no, no. I can't. I don't think I can–"

Whatever she was going to say was interrupted by the sound of a disturbance behind us. We turned to see Kace and Henry talking loudly and animatedly with a tactical EO officer, all three of them walking towards us.

"I'm telling you, you're making a mistake," said Henry, throwing his hands in the air, his face the picture of panic.

The officer glared at him, rolling his eyes. "And like I told you, sir, several times: I'm only following orders."

The trio came to a stop a few feet in front of us, and the EO officer, scowling, addressed me with an inclination of his head. "Mr. Hale? Would you mind coming down to the District Headquarters, and answering a few questions?"

Henry moved in front of me, clenching his hands into fists at his sides. "Yes, he minds!"

I shook my head, casting a confused glance at Henry. "No, of course not." I rubbed my blood covered hand down the front of my shirt, suddenly aware of how nightmarish I must look. "Right now?"

"Yes, sir."

Kace blocked my way, holding out his hands. "Mr. Hale, you don't–"

"It's a few questions, Kace," I said, moving around him as if he were a rock and I was a stream. "I'd say the least I owe them after tonight is some answers, wouldn't you?"

As a result of my colorful and misspent youth, this was not my first visit to the Enforcement Office District Station House. I noted that they'd changed little since my reformation: they were still small and antiquated buildings, stuffed to the brim with officers and offenders. District Headquarters were mainly administrative buildings -- places where officers received orders before going out on patrol, or processed prisoners before sending them to the Anteries Penal District. As I was led through a cluttered maze of computer stations and offices to an interview room, I caught the scent of sweat, starch, and vomit.

Ushered into the dingy, sound-proofed room, I was then left alone for several long minutes. I walked the perimeter of my little cube, but soon tired of the exercise, and collapsed into the cold metal chair opposite the door. I attempted to pull it up to the steel table before I realized that both items of furniture were bolted to the floor.

When the door opened again, I found myself confronted with a familiar face. She swept off her EO helmet as she entered revealing a high, tight bun composed of the thin yellow braids of hair that I had first noticed when we met beside Aldo Fogg's corpse. Her blue eyes were bloodshot and watery – she had been crying, although she'd done her best to erase the signs, her sharp cheeks dry and a little raw from rubbing.

She didn't look at me when she entered, turning away to press the toe of her boot against the button that resealed the door. I heard the lock click into place. Taking a few steps backwards, she said aloud, "Voluntary interview with Mr. Chance Hale, three o'clock in the morning, on the date indicated on this datafile. Mr. Hale has not been formally charged in any way, and therefore has not been informed of his rights at this time."

I waited while the blonde EO officer settled herself into the seat across from me. She placed her helmet on one corner of the table, and then took a palm-sized datapad from her vest pocket. Still, she didn't look at me, preferring to skim through something on her datapad with consuming interest.

I cleared my throat. The sergeant did not react, continuing to sit and scroll with one finger through the information.

"It's Sergeant Jenkins, isn't it?" I said at last, anxious to break what I saw as the unnecessarily tense silence.

She looked up at me but did not smile. Instead, she folded her hands on top of her datapad. "Good memory you have there, Mr. Hale."

A terse smile was my response. "It's a curse."

She pulled a stylus from her uniform's breast pocket and began writing on the datapad. I remained silent, watching her, and awaiting her questions.

They didn't come.

"Did you get him?" I asked hesitantly.

She continued to write on her datapad. "Noll Hudd, you mean? Yes, he's being processed at a different station."

"Well, at least there's that." I leaned back in my chair, a small wave of relief, brief as it was, washing over me.

"What can you tell me about Halcyon Enterprises' Defensive Technology Division?" Jenkins asked without warning.

I readjusted my seat in the uncomfortable metal chair. "Not a lot."

Now, she smiled, lifting her right hand to tap at the table. "You are the head of Halcyon Enterprises, aren't you, Mr. Hale?"

I glared at the sergeant. "Yes, of course." Sighing, I leaned forward across the table, splaying my hands wide across the metal. "DTD was shuttered earlier this year. We felt–"

"By whom?" she interrupted.

I met her stern gaze evenly, pausing for a moment before answering carefully. "By me." I sat up a little straighter. "I don't believe that we should be in the business of making weapons."

Nodding, Jenkins unfolded the datapad so that it was the size of a large optric frame. She slid the folded pad to the center of the table, indicating it with a nod. "Can you tell me what this is?"

I moved the datapad closer, tipping it up off the table to mitigate the glare from the overhead lights. In the image a black, forearm-length gun was held up in two blue-gloved hands. The barrel was shiny, almost wet looking, and the small trigger was nestled beneath a sizable charging pack. "It's an energy weapon of some kind," I pronounced at length, lowering the datapad.

Jenkins stared at me. She heaved a large sigh.

"What?" I said, widening my eyes.

The EO sergeant tucked one of her thin yellow braids behind her ear. "I know that you've only been Halcyon's CEO for the last year, Mr. Hale -- but you should know your own company's logo."

I reexamined the image, squinting at the side of the charging pack. Sure enough, imprinted in the plastic was a thick, bold, capital letter "H." Inside the letter were laser etched capital "E"s.

I pushed the pad away. "As I said, the DTD designed and manufactured weapons. They'd been doing so for over forty years, until I shuttered the division. I'm sure you can still find our old inventory in all sorts of places."

She stabbed a finger at the pad. "This gun is fresh off an assembly line."

The bottom dropped out of my stomach. A cold chill crawled up my spine and spread across the back of my pounding head. "That's...not possible."

She swiped at the picture, revealing a multi-page document, watermarked with the words ``EO CONFIDENTIAL''. "Read the report for yourself."

Scrolling rapidly through the document, which detailed the findings of the EO Weapons Lab, I shook my head, slowly at first and then faster. The lab's tests had been conclusive: the energy weapon in the picture was new, never fired, but definitely created within the last six months.

"Where?" I desperately pawed through the rest of the document. "What factory?"

"We don't know." Jenkins twisted her head around to gaze at the report. "There isn't a serial number on this one. Or any of the others."

I stared at Sergeant Jenkins. "No serial number? That's illegal, isn't it?" The rest of what she had said slowly seeped into my panicking brain. "Wait, did you say–?"

Her face was carefully blank, her blue eyes half-lidded. After a moment of silence, she reached forward and took the datapad out of my unresisting hands, tapping the screen several times.

"What others?" I croaked.

"These others." She returned the pad to the center of the table and waved at the image displayed there. "All newly minted, all untraceable, and all ready to be shipped out to whatever planetary conflict might need more firepower."

This new image stilled my heart. I recognized the crate in which the energy weapons were packed and stacked, recognized the vials of drogan that had been removed to reveal the weapons hidden beneath. The crate was the same one that Hudd had taken possession of earlier that evening. The one that had been meant for Aldo Fogg, the arms dealer and smuggler.

Aldo Fogg was trading in Halcyon Enterprise hardware.

I swallowed hard. "They must be knock-offs." I nodded, grasping onto this new thought like a shipwrecked man holding tight to a plank of driftwood. "They're fakes -- weapons meant to look like ours. Anyone can put a logo on something." Pressing my finger into the tabletop, I pleaded with the immovable sergeant. "I told you, the defensive technology division doesn't exist, not anymore. There's no way these could have come from us."

"It's all there in the report, Mr. Hale." Jenkins shook her head. "These are your guns. Inside and out."

"I don't understand," I confessed, collapsing back into my seat. "Our designs are proprietary. No one else could–"

She leaned against the table, lifting her brow. "Are you trying to tell me you knew nothing about this?"

Her question sent a shock of fear through me. I jerked upright. "Of course, I didn't!"

Jenkins retreated to her side of the table, crossing her arms over her chest.

"Now, hold on a minute," I said, holding my hands up in front of me. I attempted a smile, but it came out sickly and warped. "I am not some kind of illegal weapons supplier. I am the head of a major tech conglomerate."

The datapad buzzed and a notification flashed over the screen. Before I had an opportunity to read it, Sergeant Jenkins whisked the pad up into her hands, glaring down at the screen. Her expression became stony, and she let out an exasperated huff.

She folded the datapad and pushed away from the table. "Looks like you're both, Mr. Hale," she said as she stood. "Excuse me, I'll be right back."

Picking up her helmet, she strode towards the door, kicking at the button that opened the portal.

"I'm sorry," I said.

She froze, half-in the hallway, half-out of the room. She took a deep breath before looking over her shoulder at me. "For?"

"Inspector Brisbois." I forced myself not to look away from her. "I'm sorry."

Shock flashed across her face. She jerked forward, tension rippling across her shoulders as she gripped the doorknob. "Thank you," she muttered.

The door closed behind her with a crack.

19

Chapter 19

Halcyon Enterprises weapons. Was it possible? Had one of my own guns killed Oliver? My stomach twisted painfully at the thought as I stared at the tabletop without really seeing it. How many other people had been hurt by weapons designed by my employees, built at my factories, sold by... by whom?

I jiggled the band on my wrist, astonished to see that only five minutes had passed since the sergeant had left. How long would other days, months, years even, feel if I wound up in a penal district cubicle?

The door opened with a crack. I started, looking up expectantly for Sergeant Jenkins' return – even her displeasure was preferable to being alone and abandoned in that tiny room.

Rin stood in the doorway with a scowl on their face. "Come on, Chance," they said, jerking their head towards the hallway.

"Rin?" I asked in confusion, staring up at them with my mouth half open.

Rather than answer my question, they stared back at me. After a moment, they gestured out into the hallway again. "Don't make me pick you up and carry you."

I gaped at them for a few more seconds. They started forward, as if to make good on their threat, and the movement was enough to jolt me into action. I shot up from the chair, banging the back of my hand on the bottom of the table as I hurried to my feet.

Rin stepped back, waiting just long enough for me to exit the room before they set off through the station, shoving their hands deep in their overcoat pockets. I had little choice but to follow them.

"What's going on?" I demanded, bundling my coat into a tight ball under my arm as we walked.

Rin's pace did not slow. They rolled their shoulders back, talking at me rather than to me. "Henry called me. I explained to Sergeant Jenkins that you had requested representation and that your informal chat was officially over – unless they'd like to arrest you. They declined to do so."

I struggled to follow Rin, dodging a pair of EO officers hurrying the opposite way. "I have lawyers, you know. Or the company does."

They stopped so abruptly that I nearly plowed into them. Swinging around, their hand rose and fell, slapping against their side with a clap. "Then why didn't you call them?" They gave an exasperated sigh, rolling their eyes. "I mean, agreeing to an enforcement office interrogation? What the hell were you thinking?"

"That I had nothing to hide," I said sheepishly, cowed by their obvious irritation.

They clicked their tongue off the top of their mouth and turned away. "You can't really be that naive," they said, starting forward once more. "This is the EO. They have a way of twisting things."

Nodding, I hurried to catch up with them. "I'll keep that in mind next time."

"There better not be a next time," they cautioned, holding the door to the outside world open. I passed in front of them. "You look awful, by the way."

I gave a snort. "Good – nice to know I look how I feel."

The sun rose, the glare from the slanting rays almost blinding as I tripped my way down the station's steep front steps. Henry closed his arms around me before I was fully aware of him standing in front of me. As he squeezed the air from my lungs, it occurred to me how worried he must been – how close I had come in a single night to the end of my existence practically right in front of him.

"Henry," I said, wrapping him up in a tight embrace. "Love of my life. I'm so sorry."

He patted my back once, and then again before pulling away from me. He kept one arm tight around my shoulders. "Let's get you home," he said quietly. "Get you cleaned up."

Kace stood several feet away, talking in a hushed voice with the driver of an idling PT. Henry led me to the backdoor of the transport, and the four of us piled inside the spacious passenger cabin. No one spoke as the PT whisked us away into the Arrhidaean morning.

My ribs ached from where I had struck the dock. But the ache deep within my chest pained me far more – Oliver was dead. Cadence was nowhere to be seen. I flexed my hand inside my trouser pocket, longing to feel her fingers entwined with mine.

"Are you alright?"

I blinked myself awake from my navel-gazing haze. I looked across the cab to see Henry staring and grimacing at me in concern. I mustered up a smile and shook my head. "No, chum," I said simply. "No, I'm really not."

Henry nodded. "Is there anything I can do?"

I wanted him to tell me that this whole mess wasn't my fault. I wanted him to tell me that everything was going to be okay, even if it wasn't. I wanted to lean on his shoulder and cry, just like I had when we were children and my mother had passed away.

Instead, I turned away from him to look out the PT's window. "Where's Cadence?"

A pregnant pause followed my question. A blush colored my cheeks.

Kace cleared his throat. "She left the dock after you went off with the EO. I'm not sure where–"

"It's fine." Sighing, I pinched the bridge of my nose. "She'll turn up. Or she won't."

The PT pulled up to the transportation dock of my apartment building. We disembarked one at a time, each of us shivering a little in the cool autumn air. I started to walk towards the entrance but was stopped by Kace's hand on my shoulder.

"For once, would you let me do my job?" he said. "I'll call down when I've cleared your place."

A nod was my answer. Kace walked inside and out of sight, leaving the three of us to wait outside on the blustery PT platform. Another awkward silence threatened to take hold, but Rin, who seemed inordinately practiced in juggling tricky social situations, spoke up. They craned their head back, examining the building in which I lived.

"I've always wondered what a flat in one of these types of places goes for," they mused. "What is it? Four, five thousand credits?"

"Depends if you want a private floor or not," I answered ruefully.

"Private floor." Rin shook their head. "Damn rich people. Honestly, it's like you live on a different planet."

"Last time I checked, lawyers didn't exactly make a pittance," I parried, shuffling my feet.

"Check again. I work pro bono most of the time."

The band on my wrist buzzed, indicating a v-chat from Kace: ALL CLEAR.

"All's well upstairs. There's no need for you to come up," I said, hunching my shoulders against the stiff breeze. "I'm sure you have better ways to spend your morning." Addressing Rin with a nod, I added, "And you've already done more than enough for me."

Henry and Rin shared a look. The latter brushed past me, patting me on the chest as they went. "If you think I'm leaving without some high-end rich people's coffee in recompense for my services, you're crazy."

I scoffed in response, lifting a brow at Henry. "And you?"

Henry followed in his paramour's footsteps, smiling. "I'll take tea, but you're not going to get rid of me that easily either."

Shaking my head, I trailed after them. "Suit yourselves."

Rin chatted with us as we rode the lift up to my flat, but I wasn't listening to most of the conversation. Instead, I allowed my mind to wander over the details of what had happened over the last few hours. By the time we reached my floor, I again wanted nothing more than to crawl inside myself and cry.

The front door stood ajar. As I stepped into the foyer, Kace approached from the living room, one hand in his pocket. "You have a visitor," he said, his expression strange.

"What?" I said, wrinkling my nose.

Cadence stood up from the couch, suddenly and sharply coming into focus. She met my gaze with her usual boldness, although she was blinking excessively as she crossed her arms at the wrist. She waited.

"Oh." Swallowing in an attempt to wet my suddenly dry mouth and throat, I turned to one side. "Henry, do you think you and Rin could...?"

Henry drew me into another hug, smiling a little this time. "Call me tomorrow. I want to make sure you're okay, alright?"

"I will." I drew away from him, nodding at Rin as I went. "Thanks again, Rin."

"Look for my bill," they said, and then, breaking out into a wide smile, they waved, walking away towards the lift. "Just kidding. Get some rest!"

"I'll wait outside, sir," said Kace, already following my departing friends.

Patting his shoulder, I ushered him out the door. "Thanks, Kace."

Kace closed the door behind him, leaving Cadence and I alone. I didn't move towards her, and she made no motion to approach me either.

"Cay," I said, breaking the silence at last, running a hand through my hair. "If you have something to say, please just say it."

She opened her mouth as if to respond, but then shut it so sharply I heard her teeth snap together. I lifted my brows at her in question.

She swallowed – an affectation she adopted when nervous. Her eyes roamed over me, and her frown deepened. "Con, Chance, you look terrible."

I sighed. "So I've been told."

We stood there for a solid thirty seconds before Cadence suddenly closed the distance between us. Striding forward, she grabbed my wrist and tugged at me, sending me tumbling after her as she turned and walked with determination down the hall.

"Where are we going?" I stuttered as I was dragged through my own flat.

"You need to get out of those clothes," said Cadence over her shoulder without stopping. "I can't talk to you when you're covered in blood."

Looking down at myself, I winced. "Fair enough."

We barreled into my bedroom, Cadence calling for the lights as she entered. She pulled me towards my wardrobe, a large cherry wood and glass affair that stood nearly seven feet tall. She released me, but just long enough to survey me from head to toe before shoving my suit jacket off my shoulders and down my arms.

"Cay–" I was cut off when she spun me around to better facilitate her attempt to strip me. I acceded with a disgruntled harumph, until she forced me back around and began fumbling with the buttons of my dress shirt.

"Cadence," I repeated, wrapping her busy hands in both of mine.

She looked crestfallen, her gaze falling to the top of my feet. "I just... want to help."

Keeping hold of her hands, I led her over to the foot of the bed. "You can help by telling me what you're doing here."

She allowed me to deposit her on the mattress, her look of sadness deepening when I did not join her. I felt the need for distance as I returned to stand in front of my wardrobe – I didn't trust myself to be any closer to her – but as I watched her squirm in her seat, it took everything I had not to prompt her again.

She needed to say what she needed to say without help from me. It was important.

With her leg tucked under her bottom, she took a deep breath. She looked at me, and then looked away, blinking rapidly. "Oliver was a good man," she said quietly. The words came out tersely, in short spurts, as if forced through her teeth by sheer force of will. "I can't believe he's gone."

I took a deep breath through my nose and let it out slowly. I finished unbuttoning my shirt. "Neither can I." I threw the shirt to the floor, lacking the energy to walk it over to the incinerator. Blood had soaked through to my undershirt. "He was in love with you, you know. He told me so."

As I pulled my undershirt up over my head, a textured silence rippled back to me. I realized with a start what I had just said aloud. I ripped the shirt free and stared at Cadence, my eyes wide with concern.

Cadence looked as if I had just slapped her across the face. She sat ramrod straight on the corner of my bed and stared back at me. She shook herself and turned away, crossing her arms over her chest, her cheeks flushing pale pink.

"I'm sorry." I started towards her and then stopped, my hand closing uselessly in front of me. "Should... should I not have said anything?"

"No!" She shook her head, rubbing her arms in an attempt to self-comfort. "No. Tris, it just makes me miss him more." Looking around herself as if she had mislaid something, she dropped her hands into her lap. Her mouth hung open for a moment and then she finally said: "Do...do humans always fall in love so easily?"

The corner of my mouth twitched up in a weak smile. I balled the thin undershirt up in my hand. "Sometimes," I said, tossing the shirt onto the pile of clothes destined for destruction. "But you're a very special woman, Cadence. It doesn't take a genius to see that. And Brisbois – Oliver – he was quicker than most."

"Have..." As I watched, she rolled her lips under her teeth and picked at the fluffy duvet cover. "Have you ever been in love before?"

"Before you?" I undid my trousers, pushing them down around my ankles and stepping out of them and my socks. "Honestly? No. There was a time I didn't think I was capable of falling in love."

I glimpsed my reflection in the glass of the wardrobe and shuddered. Swathes of my body were caked in dried, flaky brown blood and the bruise on my torso was purpling nicely. Turning away, my eyes fell on Cadence once again.

Her gaze was unfocused as she stared off across the room. She tapped out a slow, steady beat against her forearm, the meaning of which alluded me. I couldn't remember when I had ever seen her look so lost. So, defeated.

I crossed the room and sat down on the bed beside her. She didn't move at my approach, didn't shift when my weight pressed the mattress down under us. Reaching forward, I rested my hand over her tapping fingers, stilling them.

I squeezed her hand lightly, leaning forward to look up into her downturned face. "But you changed all that."

She twitched her fingers around my hand, as if she wanted to hold it, but then she seemed to think better of it. She pivoted away groaning as she pushed her free hand back through her hair. "Frig, Chance..."

I waited. I watched as her breathing stilled and she remained perched like a gargoyle on the edge of my bed. She opened her eyes slowly. I wondered, not for the first time and not for the last, what thoughts were flying around inside her microscopically complex neural network. She then opened her mouth as if to speak.

No words, no sounds came from her lips.

"Cadence," I sighed. "You can tell me anything. Okay? Anything."

She moved her head to look at me. Her eyes were wide and

round – I don't think I'd ever seen her so obviously afraid. She nodded, slowly, and then spoke.

"I'm scared," she whispered. Reaching up with her free hand, she grabbed hold of my wrist and pulled my left hand to her chest. "I'm scared to be with you. And I'm scared to lose you." She scoffed, shaking her head. "I'm just so scared! And I don't know what to do. I don't know how to be with you. It's all very strange for me – I always know what to do."

I brought her warm appendage to my chest, mirroring her. "Do you love me?"

Cadence blinked once and then again. "Yes. I love you."

"And I love you," I said. Sighing, I leaned forward, resting my forehead against hers as I closed my eyes. "I think we both just need to figure out how to be in love with each other."

"Sarc, I don't think we've been doing a very good job so far."

A small laugh was my response. I straightened up where I sat, opening my eyes. "There's room for improvement, to be sure." Holding her hand tighter, I met her gaze steadily, my expression sobering. "How about this: I promise to be more careful and not needlessly put myself in harm's way. Okay?"

"Okay," Cadence said, nodding. "And I promise not to make decisions for you." She took a deep breath and let it out slowly. "We're partners, like you said. The things we do affect each of us. I can see that now. And you deserve to have input into what affects you."

"Thank you," I said. Lifting her hand to my mouth, I brushed my lips against her knuckles. "I don't want to clip your wings, Cay. I just want to fly with you."

Eyes locked, we sat there for a few long, silent moments.

Then, Cadence launched herself at me, knocking me flat against the mattress in an embrace. She answered my kiss with one of her own, pressing her lips against my bare chest. I shivered, and she took this as a sign to continue, hesitantly at first, but then with growing intensity.

"Cay," I said, voice hushed.

But she was lost in her own world, of which my body was the focal point. She lavished kisses across my collarbone, stopping when she reached my carotid to nip and suck at the sensitive pulse point. She slid her hands down to the hollow of my hips, pressing her thumbs into me with a firmness that left no doubt as to her intentions.

"Cadence," I tried again, putting a little more force behind her name.

She lifted her lips from my throat but did not move her hands. "Yes?"

I gestured down at myself. "Love, I need a shower, at the very least."

Cadence frowned and looked down at me for a long moment. Nodding and smiling her summer smile, she sat up, inched off the mattress, and stood beside the bed, kicking off her flats.

"Right," she said, reaching back and undoing her dress. "Let's get you into one then."

I watched dumbfounded as she began to strip. "What? I thought you couldn't–?"

The dress slid off her like bubbles sliding down skin. "Just because I don't do something, doesn't mean that I can't." She paused, hooking her thumbs on either side of her underwear as she thought. "Now, I can't swim. And a bath would be a bad idea.

But a shower?" Her underwear landed on the floor, followed quickly by her bra. "That's like standing in the rain."

Turning, she walked towards my washroom. I watched her go with my mouth gaping. It wasn't until she stopped in the doorway and looked back at me that I remembered to start breathing again.

She was a vision. And she wanted me. She loved me. The world had gone mad, and I hoped never to return to sanity.

Cadence gestured into the bathroom. "So...?"

I nodded enthusiastically, pushing myself up onto my feet and hurrying to follow her. "Yes. Yes, please."

20

Chapter 20

In the dim room, my eyes blurry with sleep, I struggled to make out the time on the thin gold band around my wrist. Once I determined it was just past midday, I gave a disgruntled sigh and slid myself out from between the sheets. Cadence was sleeping, a rarity, and I had no intention of waking her.

At least, I thought she was asleep.

As I crossed towards the wardrobe, I winced at the unmistakable sound of limbs rustling through bedclothes. "I'm sorry – did I wake you?" I asked over my shoulder.

"No," answered Cadence unsatisfactorily.

Not wishing to pursue the matter, I shook my head, freeing a pair of pants and trousers from the innards of the wardrobe, putting on the former and shaking out the latter.

"Chance?"

I turned, my feet in the legs of the slacks. Cadence had sat up in the bed. She hugged her knees to her chest. "What are you doing?"

"I need to go into the office," I said, pulling the trousers up onto my hips.

"Now?" She blinked and then leaned back against the pummeled pillows. "I find that highly unlikely." Her head fell to one side as she watched me dress. "Is this your way of getting back at me for walking out on you before?"

"No," I said, shaking my head ruefully as I pulled a dress shirt and suit jacket out of the wardrobe. When I turned back around, Cadence's eyes were burrowing into me, and I collapsed under her questioning stare with a groan.

"Honestly," I repeated in earnest, moving back to the bed and holding out my hand to her. "I need to go."

She took my hand, but instead of just holding it, used it to tug me down onto the bed with her. "Why?" she urged again, her eyes never leaving my face.

As succinctly and clearly as possible, I told her what I had learned during my interview with Sergeant Jenkins. "Someone at Halcyon was selling weapons to Fogg," I said. "The EO seems to think that someone was me."

"But we know that's not true," said Cadence, her gaze falling away from my face.

I nodded. "Correct. Not that the truth lets me off the hook." I chewed the inside of my cheek. "No, if someone's been using Halcyon specs to manufacture and sell weapons under my nose, I need to find out who, and put a stop to it as soon as possible."

"Alright," said Cadence, tossing off the bedsheet and scrambling towards the edge of the mattress. "I'm coming with you."

I shook my head. "You don't–"

"Partners, remember, Chance?" She stood, unabashedly naked and radiating determination. "Besides, I signed a contract with the EO, with Oliver, and I gave you my word. I'm going to see it through to the end." Swiping her dress up off the floor, she glared at me once before heading for the washroom. "I'm coming with you."

I knew better than to argue with her when she got that look in her eyes.

We dressed quickly and I called Kace, unsure if he was literally right outside my front door or down in the lobby of the apartment building. He was only too happy to arrange for a Halcyon Enterprises PT to pick us up from my apartment building and take us to the main campus. On the flight over, Cadence would occasionally ask me questions about the weapons I had seen in the optrics, about what precise words Sergeant Jenkins had used to describe them, and so on. But on the whole, she remained silent and contemplative, which suited my mood as well, if for slightly different reasons.

It had occurred to me that I had never taken Cadence into my office. We had met several times on the larger Halcyon Enterprises campus, for meals or some other activity, but I'd never taken her to the building, let alone the office, where I worked. As we rode the executive lift up the tower, I wondered what she would make of it.

Stirring me from these thoughts, Kace leaned forward and pressed the button for the security level. I gave him a questioning glance and he smiled at me. "Time for me to report in," he explained. "You're safe enough in here without me. But if you try to leave the building without telling me, I will track you down."

"I don't doubt it," I said.

We reached the security level and Kace stepped out, nodding goodbye as he went.

Even though I knew I would need her help, I wished that Miss Taylor would be miraculously and unaccountably away from her desk when we entered the waiting room. But, true to form, she was there, working with that single-minded determination that both admired and baffled me. She had, it seemed, broken into what she thought was her "secret stash" of chocolate-covered biscuits in the desk drawer, which I stole from frequently, and was currently biting into one when we entered.

Seeing us suddenly appear, Lily shoved the rest of the biscuit into her mouth, chewing quickly as she stood up from her desk. She brushed the biscuit crumbs off her blouse and trousers as she rose, missing the slight smear of chocolate at the corner of her mouth. She cleared her throat as we approached and gave a nod, clasping her hands in front of herself.

"Good afternoon, Mr. Hale," said Lily with far more formality than she usually greeted me, gluing her eyes to the young lady on my left. "We weren't expecting you in the office today."

"Miss Lily Taylor–" I stood to one side, throwing an arm towards Cadence, and ushering her forward. "Miss Cadence Turing."

"It's a pleasure to meet you," said Cadence, stepping closer and proffering her hand in greeting.

"Oh! Hello!" Lily leaned forward and took Cadence's outstretched hand. Her sparkling eyes devoured the other woman.

"It's *so* nice to finally put a face to the name." She relinquished Cadence's hand and turned to me. "I wish you'd let me know you were coming, Chance, I could've arranged a tour for you two, a late lunch, something–"

"Sadly, this isn't a social visit." I rocked back on my heels. "We need to do some digging, Miss Taylor."

"Not literal digging," Cadence added. "Research."

"Ah!" Lily's face brightened. "My specialty." She locked her workstation and stepped out from behind her desk, sweeping her hand out to indicate my closed office door. "Shall we?"

Cadence nodded and followed her eagerly, leaving me to bring up the rear as we entered my executive suite. I had made a few distinct changes to the place when I had taken over the space from my father. His taste had tended towards decidedly old-Earth -- lots of polished wood and ornate furniture -- while I preferred a more modern and minimalist style. He preferred to work in low light, covering the floor to ceiling windows with thick, heavy curtains. I had no curtains at all, adoring the stunning views of Römer and basking in the sunlight whenever I could. The city looked particularly beautiful in the midday autumn light, and I felt a thrill of pleasure go through me as we entered my sanctum sanctorum, casting a glance towards Cadence to see if she was similarly affected.

If Cadence was struck by the elegance of my office, she didn't show it, her attention fully captivated by Miss Taylor, whose steps she dogged closely. "How long have you worked for Chance, Miss Taylor?"

"I've been at the company for the past ten years," answered Lily, settling down into my chair with an unsettling ease. "But I became Chance's executive administrator when he took over the company earlier this year."

"I see." Cadence folded herself into one of the plush chairs in front of the desk. "And what exactly does an executive adminis-trator do?"

Punching in a few commands, Lily leaned back as the work-station came to life. "Basically, anything that keeps Mr. Hale and his work on the right track. I arrange his schedule, coordinate meetings with other executives, plan events, write up board reports...all kinds of things really."

"Sinc, that is very impressive," said Cadence, nodding enthu-siastically. "You must work very hard."

"Thank you," said Lily, smiling. She leaned forward onto the desk, resting her chin on her hands. "Of course, being Chance's admin also has its own unique challenges. But he's a wonderful employer – funny, considerate of others, hardworking when he wants to be. But I don't suppose I have to tell you Chance's good qualities, do I, Miss Turing?"

"He has so many," said Cadence with an earnestness that caught me quite off-guard. "It's nice to know that other people hold the same high opinion of him that I do."

I felt a blush start to creep its way up my neck and onto my cheeks. "If you two are done?"

Lily smirked, flexing her fingers. "Well, what kind of infor-mation are we looking for?"

I went around the desk to join her, leaning down to rest my hand on the edge of the dark wood. "The Defensive Tech Divi-sion." I looked at Lily, furrowing my brow. "I assume that even though we shut them down, we kept on the employees, correct?"

She rested her hands on the edge of the desk. "As many as we could, yes."

I nodded. "I need to know the name of any former DTD employees who could have access to the old DTD files – especially manufacturing specs, factory contracts, things like that."

Lily scoffed. Sitting back in the chair, she crossed her arms high over her chest. "Well, that's easy: none of them." She answered my questioning glare with a sigh. "To access any proprietary information, you would need special internal permissions. Someone would have to okay it."

Cadence crossed her legs, balancing her clasped hands on top of her knees. "Someone such as...?"

"Chance, for example," said Lily. Then, after a moment of further consideration, she added: "I suppose the head of IT, or even the Security Director could as well. But besides them–"

Cadence cut her off with a question, pointing to the floating screens that surrounded her. "Can you access the DTD files from this terminal?"

Lily nodded. "Of course. But only after Chance puts in his authentication codes."

Taking my cue, I leaned down and entered a series of passwords and codes, including some biometrics, until the machine granted Lily access to the drives she required. Humming a lilting tune to herself, Lily swiped and selected her way through a dizzying labyrinth of folders and machines, until an extensive list of files filled the screen to her right with a high-pitched beep. She swiped the window onto the center screen and enlarged it. "There. That should be all the old DTD information and specs."

"Alright. Alright, good. Well, next we need to know who

most recently accessed these files... aside from us, of course." I waved at the screen, looking at my admin pleadingly. "Miss Taylor, could you–?"

"I'm an executive admin, Chance," said Lily with a scowl, shaking her head. "I'm not a systems administrator. I can get you the metadata for these files but..." Lily punched in a few commands on the keyboard and brought up a screen filled with code. "...this all looks like gibberish to me."

"May I?" Cadence answered Lily's questioning glance with a shy half smile. "I know a little something about computers."

Lily pushed herself away from the desk and stood, indicating the chair with a wave of her hand. "Please do."

Cadence gave a nod of thanks and took up the seat, pulling herself up to the laser projected keyboard with a hum. She sat still for a moment, looking over my tech set-up before nodding again and starting to type with a flourish.

The three of us were silent as Lily and I watched Cadence work her binary magic. Lily stepped over to me on the other side of the desk, watching Cadence and nodding in approval. "Beauty and brains," she murmured, looking impressed. Lily leaned over to me, her hand at her throat. "Chance if you need the name of a good jeweler, I know a place that does these engagement necklaces that are to die for–"

"Don't help me, Miss Taylor," I sighed, shaking my head from side to side and grinning nervously. "I'm doing just fine on my own."

A loud harrumph was her response. "I find that very hard to believe."

"Well," said Cadence, interrupting my less-than-gentlemanly

retort. "I've managed to pinpoint the address from which the files were last accessed." She grimaced at the computer screen and sighed. "I don't think it helps us very much though."

"Oh? Why not?" I asked.

Cadence looked up at me, frowning. "The files were most recently accessed from a computer in this building."

Lily moved towards the desk, her excitement tangible. "Can you pinpoint the exact computer?"

Cadence gestured to the screen. "It has an internal address, yes." She shook her head, straightening in my chair. "But it's meaningless to me... you'd need to match it against your own list of active terminals."

"Miss Taylor—" I started, but as usual, my right-hand woman was already well-ahead of me, her finger at the bud that seemed to rest perpetually in her ear.

"Yes, hello?" she said, her eyes shining with excitement. "I need someone from IT over here right away, please." She nodded, beginning to pace around the office as she continued speaking. "Yes, absolutely, the highest priority."

"Psst."

Blinking in surprise, I returned my attention to Cadence, who was watching me with narrowed eyes.

I looked between her and the still occupied Lily Taylor, and then back again. "I'm sorry, did you just 'psst' at me like I'm some kind of cat?"

With a none-too-subtle jerk of her head, Cadence moved over to the large windows that lined one side of my office. I followed, bemused. Cadence stepped close to me, her lips directed towards my ear.

"What exactly is the plan here, Chance?" she asked, her voice a low murmur.

"What do you mean?"

She looked over her shoulder at Lily, who was still deep in conversation with our Information Technology department and rolled her eyes. "Let's say this works, and you link this computer to a person, one of your own employees – what then?"

"Then we inform the EO," I answered, folding my arms over my chest.

Cadence gritted her teeth for a moment before huffing her bangs out of her eyes. "What if–?"

"They're sending someone over," said Lily, crossing the room to join us.

I looked back at Cadence, but she turned away. I shook my head, returning my attention to my assistant. "Any idea how long we have to wait?" I asked.

Lily shrugged. "They said they already had someone on this floor, so they should be here any moment."

As if summoned by magic, a knock echoed through the office. We turned as one body to see my door open and a head appeared around the edge.

"Mr. Hale?" A young woman, who couldn't have been more than a few months out of her teenage years, peered into my office. "You put in a call for IT support?"

"Yes," I answered, walking towards the door, and opening it all the way to usher the young lady inside. "Thank you for coming so quickly. What's your name?"

She examined my outstretched hand with unaccountable

suspicion before taking it, shaking it once quickly before releasing it. "Bethany Howell, sir."

"Miss Howell," I said. "We need to know which computer in this building matches–" I hurried back to my desk, sliding behind it and enlarging the address we had found. "–this internal address." I stood back, allowing her room to access the computer. "Could you do that for us?"

Annoyance squirmed across Bethany's tight-pressed lips. "I wish you'd said so over the phone, sir." She sat down at my desk with a grumble. "I could've done this from my desk, you know."

I stared at her for a moment, taken aback by her brusqueness. Blinking, I shook my head from side to side. "I promise you, next time, I will keep that in mind."

Ignoring my sarcasm, Bethany focused on the task at hand. Her typing speed rivaled Cadence's, and it seemed like mere moments before she gave a nod, sitting back in my chair with a disappointed huff.

"The terminal listed is in Director Aja's office, sir," she announced.

"What?" exclaimed Lily, hurrying over from the windows with Cadence in tow. "Director Aja?"

"That can't be right," I said, coming around the desk so I could look over her shoulder. "Are you sure?"

Bethany looked at me as if I had just asked if the planet was still spinning. "Yes, sir; you can see for yourself." She indicated one of the several windows open on the center screen, leaning forward to enlarge it with a swipe of her hand. "It's a personal machine, but we needed to give it an internal address so that it could access the network."

I stared at the screen without really seeing it. My mind reeled with the implications of what it was hearing. I shook my head and looked again, my hand coming up to worry my lips.

"Who is Director Aja?" asked Cadence, looking between the three of us for an answer.

Lily was the first to respond, her face grim. "Sandra Aja -- she's our head of security."

Cadence nodded. "Ah. That would explain the rather impressive digital camouflage covering her tracks."

Bethany glanced between us all, her brow lowering, a worried frown forming on her face. "Sir?"

I plastered on my most reassuring smile and stepped back from my desk, giving Bethany the space to take her leave. "Thank you, Miss Howell, that's all for now."

Bethany stood, still frowning, and hurried for the door. Standing in the frame, she turned back, her hand on the handle.

"You want this shut?" she asked, somewhat petulantly.

I smiled politely. "Yes, please – thank you, Miss Howell."

Waiting until the sound of Bethany's footsteps had faded fully into the distance, I turned back to my two female companions. I held up my hands in front of me.

"Let's not jump to any conclusions," I said. "There's all kinds of legitimate reasons why Sandra would have accessed those files."

Neither woman looked impressed with my defense. Cadence rolled her eyes, gesturing to the computer with one hand, her other tapping a frantic pattern against her thigh. "Then why go to all the trouble of obfuscating the fact that she'd done so?"

"Well, we can stand here wondering, or we can go and ask

her," I said, heading for the door. "Kace is over there right now, let's just–"

Cadence rushed forward, her hands outstretched as if she were prepared to wrestle me. "I don't know if barreling over there with a bunch of accusations is a good idea, Chance."

"Questions, not accusations," I said a tad defensively, stepping back from her. "And why not?"

She gritted her teeth. "If this person is the one responsible for supplying Fogg with weapons, then it's very likely that's not where their involvement in this stops."

Her meaning hit me like a fist to the stomach – Sandra, a murderer? It was unthinkable. But how many times had Cadence proved the unthinkable to be the truth? I realized then that if Sandra had killed Fogg, had perhaps killed Brisbois, that would mean she had also tried to kill me. A wave of nausea roiled my empty stomach. Licking my lips, I shook my head violently from side to side.

"No. No. You don't understand: Sandra Aja is a friend, Cadence." Seeing that my love remained unconvinced, I threw my hands up in the air. "She's the one who insisted on assigning a bodyguard to me in the first place! Why would she do that if she had tried to kill me? If she'd killed Fogg?"

"What?!" Lily stared at me, aghast. "Chance, someone tried to kill you?"

I grimaced and waved away Lily's perfectly justified concern. "It was a while back now -- I'm fine," I said.

"Anno," started Cadence, her volume rising. "I don't know, Chance. I don't have all the answers yet, but caution is warranted under these circumstances!"

Proffering one hand towards Cadence, I gestured to the door with the other. "Come with me -- talk with the woman, you'll see how ridiculous this all is."

Cadence looked from my hand to me. In a frustrated burst of Animatum, she started towards the door, brushing my hand aside and leaving me to hurry after her.

"What do you want me to do?" called Lily from behind us.

Cadence stopped and turned back around, one hand on her hip. "You should call the EO. One way or another, they'll need to know what we've learned."

"Hold on: let's be smart about this," I countered, looking first at Cadence, but then turning my attention to my assistant. "Miss Taylor, contact our legal department and loop them in -- I'm sure they'll have their own ideas about how to proceed."

"Right," said Lily, moving towards my computer.

I answered Cadence's questioning stare by raising my shoulders up around my ears. "I've learned my lesson. I've already been in one EO interrogation room -- I don't fancy going into another." I gestured to the office door once more. "Now, shall we?"

21

Chapter 21

Sandra's office was two floors below my own on the security level. Cadence and I did not speak as we rode the lift down. Walking down the hall towards Sandra's suite, I picked up my pace so that I could lead Cadence in, looking back at her as I cautioned, "Now, let me do the talking, please. I still think there's an explanation for all this that isn't sinister."

"If that's what you want," replied Cadence with an evenness that grated.

Stepping into Sandra's office suite, I was surprised to find her executive assistant, Adam, absent from his usual spot behind his desk. A growing sense of unease put a hitch in my step. I made for the unusually closed doors of Sandra's main office, raising my fist to knock.

"I don't think you understand what you're asking me to do,

director." Kace's voice was muffled, but unmistakable through the closed door. It was also raised as if in anger.

"I understand perfectly what I'm asking you to do, Mr. Morgan." Sandra's words were softer, likewise muffled, but the edge of irritation in them was difficult to miss. "The question is: do you have the balls to do it, or am I going to have to find someone else?"

I turned to Cadence, about to suggest we wait until they were finished, only to find that she was not at my side any longer. Instead, I looked down to discover her head at the level of my hip, her fingers prying open the electronic lock on Sandra's door and pulling at the wires inside.

"What are you doing?" I hissed, instantly crouching down beside her.

"Shh!" said Cadence without looking at me, gaze intent on her work.

The tip of my tongue coming out to wet my lips, I glanced at the empty desk behind us. "Cay, her assistant could be back at any moment, we can't–"

But it was too late. There was a soft mechanical whir and the door slid inward a millimeter. Cadence replaced the cover on the lock and smiled at me. "Come on," she whispered.

Cadence, still crouched, snuck inside the occupied office. Keeping low, I followed her quickly, half-panicked that I would be left alone to face the questions of Sandra's returning assistant if I remained where I was.

Sandra's office reflected her personality. Refined and comfortable, the space was more like a family sitting room than a place of business. The walls were painted a warm mustard yellow, and the furniture was done in lush oranges and browns. An interior wall jutted out into the room a few feet past the door, giving the illusion of an entryway-- and it was behind this that Cadence and I hid. From our vantage point, Kace was clearly visible in the center of the room, his body turned towards the far edge where Sandra was standing.

"Chance Hale is a good man–" said Kace, but he was cut off by a shout from Sandra.

"I know!" Frustration roughened her voice and as she walked across the rugs that covered the floor towards Kace. I could feel her stomps reverberate up my spine. "I know, goddamnit -- that's the problem. He's a good man. Empathetic. He leads with his heart, not with his head." As she stepped into view, she threw up her hands, the muscles in her face tight. "He shut down the defensive technology department out of pure bleeding-heart sentiment. Who's to say he won't start it up again for similar reasons?" She shook her head. "We have to be prepared. If the IPC votes to move forward with military intervention on behalf of the animanecrons, which is just a matter of time, Chance may be inspired to get Halcyon back into the defensive smart tech business. And if he does that, he's going to find out that DTD was never as shut down as he would have liked."

Kace took a step closer to Sandra, a grimace darkening his face. "You mean he'll find out what you've been up to."

"What we've been up to," countered Sandra, lowering her brow and firming her lips into a hard line.

Kace gave a cough of disbelief, his hand coming up to his chest. "Me? I never wanted any part of this – of arms dealing, I told you from the beginning–!"

"And I told you–" Sandra crossed the office to Kace and, standing up on tiptoe, wrapped her arms around his shoulders. "–when you're with me, you're with me all the way."

My breath stilled in my chest as she captured his lips in a passionate kiss. I glanced at Cadence, but her attention was transfixed on the couple in front of us, her face grim as they embraced.

They stayed that way for several long moments, lost in each other, until Sandra broke the kiss, resting her cheek against Kace's. She caressed the back of his head, murmuring low into the shell of his ear. "Kace, baby, everything's going to be okay. We just need to get Chance out of the way and then–"

"Why?" begged Kace, drawing away sharply, lines of pain gouged deep in his cheeks.

"I just told you–" started Sandra before she was cut off by Kace shaking his head.

"Killing him?" His Adam's apple bobbed in his throat as he struggled to swallow. "Killing Fogg? That was never, ever part of the plan."

Sandra sighed, weaving her fingers through Kace's hair. "Fogg was a liability." She forced Kace to look her in the eyes. "Understand? Chance is a liability."

Seeing that her lover remained unconvinced, Sandra tutted softly. "Sweetheart, we've made enough money that we can go anywhere. Live however we want. But now we've got to get out clean. With Chance dead, we can lay the whole thing at his doorstep. Fogg's murder, the weapons smuggling, all of it – no one will think twice about it!"

He wrapped his hands around her wrists and pulled her hands away. "I will," he said, so quietly that I struggled to hear him.

Sandra's face clouded with confusion. She shook her head, as if to clear her vision before speaking, but Kace cut her off before she could say a word.

"I won't do it, Sandra," Kace said. "I can't. I can't kill him."

Sandra closed her jaw with a snap, making the muscles along her chin jump beneath her skin. Her hands fell limp at her sides, hanging there for a moment before she slowly curled them into shaking fists.

"Fine." She spat the word at his feet and turned away from him. "Fine! I'll do it myself."

"Sandra." He dug his fingers into the back of the chair in front of him as his face crumpled in pain. "No, honey." Shaking his head, he forced his eyes open. "No, this has to stop."

"It will," said Sandra, drawing out the last word in an attempt to soothe her lover. She reached back and put her hand on top of Kace's, pleading. "I've brought us this far, Kace. Let me take us all the way."

Kace yanked his hand out from under her own. "I'm telling you no, Sandra." He pulled himself up to his full height. "I won't let you kill him."

From my place behind the interior wall, I watched Sandra's expression harden. She turned her back to Kace and stalked away. Then, just as quickly, her body relaxed. She smiled -- a sickly, warped, oily smile that made my skin crawl. She sighed and looked at her nails, as if bored.

"And just how, may I ask, are you going to stop me?" she said, each word clipped and polite.

"I'll go to the EO." In a sudden burst of movement, Kace shoved the high-back chair out of his way and strode towards Sandra. "Goddamnit, I don't want to, but I will. I'll tell them everything. Please don't make me do that, Sandra."

Sandra laughed mirthlessly. "You never were very bright, Kace." She moved back towards her desk, still smiling. "No one at the Enforcement Office is going to believe you. Why would they? And the one person who would've?" She turned to face him, leaning forward at the waist. "I blew him away."

My vision blurred as rage settled in my chest, constricting my breathing. It was only the sound of my name in Kace's mouth that brought me back to reason.

"I'll...go to Chance," Kace said, sounding as if every word was painful to him.

"Your word against mine, love. Your word against mine. He's known you for all of a couple weeks." Sandra rolled her shoulders back, smirking. "He's known me for a lot longer. Who do you think Chance will believe?"

Kace took a deep, shaky breath. "You. He'd believe you."

"That's right," said Sandra, a smack of satisfaction to her words that left me nauseous. "Now, let's–"

In a swift motion that spoke to consistent practice, Kace unholstered his Pulsar and pointed it at the center of Sandra's chest.

"I'm not going to let you do this." Kace flicked the safety off with a twitch of his finger.

Sandra looked from the barrel of the Pulsar to Kace's face and back again. She licked her lips and took a small step back.

"Kace–" started Sandra, but he cut her off with a sharp, miniscule shake of his head.

"You know me, Sandra." His voice was hushed, but even in the whisper, I could hear the tremble in his words. "You know that I wouldn't point this at you if I wasn't ready to use it." He took a short, sharp breath through his nose. "If I wasn't–"

"You don't have the guts." The words hissed out between Sandra's clenched teeth. She stayed perfectly still behind the desk, her face a mask of rage. "Come on, do it. Shoot me. Fucking coward. Do it!"

22

Chapter 22

"Wait!" I shouted.

Before Cadence could stop me, I rushed out into the room, stumbling to a halt between Kace and Sandra. I stretched my hands out in either direction, glancing between them as if I were refereeing a lawnball match rather than trying to stop a violent confrontation. "Wait. Nobody else is dying today. It's over."

I tried to catch Kace's eye, but he looked through me, not at me. As I glanced down at the Pulsar now pointed at me, I noticed the tremor in his hand. I took a shallow breath and stepped slowly towards him. When I was less than a foot away, I lifted my hand, palm up, and beckoned.

"It's over, Kace," I repeated quietly, even as the barrel-end of the Pulsar was now inches from my chest.

No one in the room moved. With a flicker, Kace refocused his eyes on my face. He swallowed, parting his lips.

There was no going back now. He had a decision to make.

As carefully as one would handle a bird with a broken wing, Kace placed the Pulsar into my outstretched hand. I closed my fingers around the barrel and nodded, holding his gaze for another minute before I turned to face Sandra.

"We heard everything, Sandra," I said.

The panic faded from Sandra's eyes, replaced by an icy disdain that made me shudder. Her body relaxed as she leaned her hips back against her large desk. Sandra crossed her arms over her chest and her feet at the ankles. She jutted her chin out towards the portal through which we had entered. "I know I locked that door."

Cadence stepped out into the room, moving to stand a few feet behind me. "Sarc, you'd think the Director of Security would have something a little higher tech securing her office."

Sandra's dark brown eyes scanned Cadence up and down. She smacked her scowling lips, hugging herself tighter. "You must be the infamous Cadence Turing."

"I'm pleased that my reputation precedes me," she responded coldly.

"Not much of one," said Sandra with a snort. "I'd put most of your so-called success down to dumb luck. You're no detective – just a nosy amateur."

Cadence put a hand to her chest and gave a sharp bow. "You'll forgive me if I don't take the critique of a double murderer to heart."

Sandra stood up and shook her head. "Listen, Chance – it's nothing personal."

"Trying to kill me and frame me for an illegal weapon

smuggling scheme?" My heart still pounding in my chest, I passed the Pulsar from hand to hand. "It feels a little personal, Sandra."

She dug her fingernails into the fine fabric of her blouse. "It's just business." She stressed each word before tossing her head back with a groan. "You know, your father would've understood that. Hell, he probably would've gone in for a slice of this little venture with me. Of course, I never would've been able to run a shadow business from within his own company under his very nose either. So, I guess the apple falls pretty far from the tree."

She was right, and it rankled. I shoved the energy weapon away from me and back at Cadence as I growled, "I am not, and will never be, my father." I gritted my teeth and shook my head. "I'm sorry you don't seem to appreciate that."

"Oh, I appreciate it," Sandra sneered. "I appreciated it the minute I realized the opportunity you had left exposed by closing down the Defensive Technology Division." Glaring at me, she shook her head, her voice rising in volume. "Halcyon Enterprises' weapons were some of the most sought-after defensive tech across the settled spheres and you were going to throw all that money away for what? Principle? Ethics?" She gave a derisive snort. "Idiotic. Do you know how simple it was to download the specs I needed? Then it was just a matter of paying off the right people in the manufacturing district to get an automated factory for a few months and I was in business."

Cadence looked at her askance, disapproval clear on her face. "The business of death."

Sandra shook her hair out of her face, scowling. "Oh, please —

save me the sermon. People are going to kill each other whether you give them weapons or not."

"Why Sandra?" I demanded. "Don't tell me it was just the money."

Her face grew hard. "You wouldn't understand." Sandra's hands curled into fists, her words coming out between clenched teeth. "Money isn't just about what you can buy. It's about the wheels it can grease. The power it can give you over other people. The doors it can open. Opportunities that never would've been within your reach suddenly become attainable." Forcing herself to relax, she focused her attention on the floor. "I did what I had to do."

"You did what you wanted," I answered, words thick with disgust.

Sandra rolled her eyes, clicking her tongue off the back of her teeth. "So, what's next?" she demanded. "Fire me?"

"Fire you?" I spat the words back at her incredulously.

She lifted her brows.

I cast about myself, struggling to find the words. "Sandra, you've – you've killed two people! We're a little past haggling over your severance package at this point. You're going to jail for the rest of your life!"

"Oh, am I?" Sandra laughed, rubbing her temple with one hand. She flicked her gaze from face to face. "My God, you are all so stupid. So goddamn naive." Shaking her head, she leaned forward at the waist. "This isn't a flicker, children. The movie doesn't end here. Innocent until proven guilty, remember? That's 'proven.'" She tossed her hand into the air. "What evidence do you have that I killed anyone?"

"You just confessed!" I shouted, incensed.

She widened her eyes pointedly. "And? Is this a courtroom?"

I looked around, flinging out my arms towards the two other people in the room with me. "We all heard you!"

"Hearsay. Libelous hearsay and circumstantial evidence, that's all you have." Sandra shook her head. "You'll never get a conviction for that. It'll never even get to court."

Cadence stepped forward, clenching her hands. "We'll find evidence. You're clever, Director, but you're only human. You'll have left something behind, made a mistake somewhere–"

"You're right, I'm sure," said Sandra, trailing her fingertips along the edge of her desk as she walked behind it. "And by the time you find your smoking gun, you know where I'll be?" She settled down into her chair, lifting a brow. "Literal worlds away. Enjoying a well-deserved early retirement somewhere. Somewhere, where a lot of money buys a lot of privileges and the interplanetary extradition laws are a veritable nightmare."

Horror filled me. I could see it all happening, just as she had said. I couldn't keep her here. All my money, all my power -- and I was helpless. None of it could bring this woman to justice. I looked at Cadence, looked down at her right hand, which still held Kace's Pulsar. I jerked my head away, ashamed by the darkness of my own thoughts.

Sandra grinned. "I'm going to get away with it, children. I was always going to get away with it." Her veneer of amusement dropped abruptly and, frowning, she jerked her chin towards the door. "Now get out of my office."

"You're bluffing," I said weakly, not believing it myself, but wanting it to be true all the same.

"It's a damn good bluff then," answered Sandra. "Even your girlfriend is buying it. Think about that – even the android knows I'm right."

"Cadence?" I said her name quietly, pleadingly. I swallowed hard and took a step towards her. "Cay?"

My beloved remained silent, but the way she refused to meet my eyes spoke volumes. Cadence moved back from me, her eyes fixed on the floor. The swirling dread in my stomach coagulated into a solid mass. This couldn't be how things ended. But if Cadence could see no way out, no way forward...

I looked at Kace, who was staring at me, his face unnaturally pale. He opened his mouth to speak when a loud crack made us both jump. We turned back to see Cadence standing tall, staring at Sandra, the mangled remains of the Pulsar in her closed fist. She took a step towards the desk, releasing a sharp, short breath out of her nose.

"You confessed once." Cadence lifted her chin, looking down her nose at the woman behind the desk. "You're going to do it again. To the EO this time."

Sandra laughed. "Did you fry a circuit board, sweetie?"

Cadence made no move to respond, staring at Sandra while her head tilted incrementally to one side.

After a full minute of Cadence's unrelenting scrutiny, Sandra scoffed aloud. "And how do you plan to get me to do that: beat it out of me?"

"No," said Cadence. She relaxed her hands at her sides, the mangled pulsar falling to the floor. She smiled. "But what Gwen Largent is going to do once she gets her hands on you, I couldn't say." Her smile dimmed and she looked up towards the ceiling. "I could guess, but I try not to guess if I can help it – it's destructive to the logical faculty."

"Gwen Largent," repeated Sandra, amusement coming off her in waves. She leaned back in her chair, steepling her fingers in front of her face. "Alright, I'll play along. Even if you could get to Gwen Largent... why would she be interested in anything you have to say?"

Now it was my turn to adopt an air of snide self-assuredness. "Didn't you know?" I sneered. "We're good friends now." I took several steps towards Sandra, keeping my eyes fixed on her face. "Yes, we've had several long chats about Mr. Fogg and his business. How it ate into her profits. How she could never figure out where he was getting his supply, or how to stop him from crippling her business."

Sandra swallowed hard, lifting her chin to glare at me through narrowed eyes. "You're lying."

I threw my hand out towards Kace without looking at him. "Ask Mr. Morgan – he accompanied me to Gwen Largent's private residence."

Kace looked from Sandra to me and then back again. He nodded. "That's right, Mr. Hale. I did."

Sandra bolted up out of her chair and started towards him. "Why didn't you tell me?" she demanded.

Cadence crossed the room and intercepted her. "The bottom line is this: you may be able to outrun the law, but Gwen Largent is not, and has never been, the law." Cadence stood akimbo, shaking her head. "She's not concerned with extradition and jurisdiction. Once we tell her who Aldo Fogg's unseen partner was, she will hunt you down to the end of the system. She won't stop."

"You wouldn't." Seeing nothing but cold determination in Cadence's stare, Sandra turned to me. "Chance–"

I cut her off with a scowl and a scoff. "Oliver Brisbois was one of the finest men I've ever met. And you shot him down in cold blood right in front of me." Reaching into my pocket, I pulled out a palm-sized holopuck and shook it at her. "I'll call Miss Largent right now, and I'll do it with a song in my heart."

She swallowed hard. "You're bluffing." Pointing her finger at me, she sneered. "My death would be on your conscience. My blood on your hands."

Once more, I had to acknowledge the truth in her words. If I gave her name to Gwen Largent, I would be responsible for what happened to her. Maybe not in a court of law, but in my own mind, by my own moral judgment, I would be just as much her executioner as anyone. I looked to Cadence, who met my gaze evenly and openly. I looked down at the device in my hands and was struck, suddenly, by the memory of Brisbois' hand in my own. The strength in it as he pulled me to safety.

Without another moment of hesitation, I punched in Gwen Largent's number. "Oliver's blood was on my hands."

The holopuck cycled through its loading screen, waiting for the party I had called to answer and complete the connection. With an abruptness that very nearly made me jump, Davida's digitized face came into focus. "Hello?"

I didn't bother to look down at the puck as I said, "Yes, hello – is Miss Largent available? This is Chance Hale."

In my periphery, I saw Davida smile, her expression colored

with vague confusion. "Oh, good afternoon, Mr. Hale. Miss Largent is indisposed at the moment, but I can have her call you back. May I ask the reason for your call today?"

I kept my stare fixed on Sandra. "I have some further information about Aldo Fogg, which I think she will find illuminating."

There was the clicking sound of an old-fashioned keyboard, and Davida repeated slowly. "Aldo Fogg – Okay, I'll let her know."

"Thank you," I said, nodding. "Goodbye."

"Have a good day," she said, reaching forward to end the call.

The holopuck flashed off and I dropped it onto the desk with a clatter. "Still think I'm bluffing?" I asked Sandra.

The blood had completely drained from Sandra's face, leaving her sallow. She braced herself against a chair. For a moment I thought she might be sick. "If I turn myself in to the EO..." Sandra's words came out slowly and she didn't look at me when she spoke. She stared at the holopuck with wide eyes. "If I do that... can you guarantee that she won't come after me?"

"I can arrange it," I said, hoping that it was true. Gwen Largent had taken a liking to me, and we had managed to strike a deal in the past – but that was when I could offer her something she wanted. What she would want when Sandra's involvement in Fogg's activities became known... Well, it would require some truly acrobatic feats of negotiation to dissuade her from that. But I would certainly try my best.

Sandra pressed her teeth into her bottom lip. She breathed in and out through her nose, struggling with her decision. "I... I don't know that I can trust you."

Scowling, I shrugged. "At this point, what other choice do

you have, Sandra? Either I follow through, and you're safe behind bars or–"

"You're dead," said Cadence.

Sandra looked up at Cadence, and I saw the defeat in her eyes. But I felt no sense of relief, no sense of triumph. She had been a friend, after all. That made two that I had lost in less than a day. I looked at Kace, whose deep brown eyes were filled with tears. I knew then that we had all lost in this game.

23

⸎

Chapter 23

Press conferences and endless meetings with my public relations department filled the next month. Never have I spent so much time in front of my board as I did then, as we collectively attempted to survive the fallout that accompanied the arrest of a hitherto-trusted executive for double-homicide and an illegal smuggling ring involving our own DTD weapons. When I wasn't explaining to the public, or the shareholders, or Halcyon employees, what had happened and how we were going to move forward, there was also the Enforcement Office to battle. Sergeant Jenkins was a surprising ally in that fight, and through the ensuing weeks Cadence and I were even lucky enough to attend a promotion ceremony for her, where Sergeant Naomi Jenkins became Inspector Naomi Jenkins.

However, even with Sandra's confession, Cadence and I were called multiple times to give statements. We even had to appear before a judge a time or two with, seemingly, an entire firm of lawyers loitering around the edges of the courtroom.

One of those lawyers, I noticed, was Rin Murata. After one of my many court appearances, I caught up with them outside the courtroom, calling their name and waving as they walked away further into the building. They stopped, turning and smiling at the sight of me.

"Chance," they said, nodding in greeting as I approached. "You did well in there."

"Thanks," I responded, slipping my hands in my pockets. "Didn't expect to see you – everything alright? I hope Cadence and I didn't pull you into–"

They shook their head, cutting me off with a slice of their hand. "Oh no, nothing like that. Henry just wanted me to keep an eye on you is all. Make sure you're holding up okay."

Clicking my tongue off the top of my mouth, I nodded knowingly. "Ah, that makes sense. I really should call him..."

"You should," stressed Rin, still smiling. "He's no fun when he's worried, and he worries about you and Cadence like a mother hen."

"Well, he's a good man."

"Oh, I'm well aware," said Rin, blushing a little as they adjusted their glasses on their nose.

I smiled knowingly and reached out to shake their hand. "Well, I won't hold you up any longer. Just wanted to say thank you again for everything."

Rin took my hand and jerked me forward into a surprisingly intense hug. "Stay safe, Chance. And let's all get together soon!"

They released me and waved as they went on their way. Dazed, but happier than I'd been in several days, I wandered out of the building, to where more unpleasant business awaited me.

I didn't forget my promise to Sandra – I called upon Gwen Largent as soon as I could, meeting with her again in her greenroom.

"Two visits in the span of a month," quipped Gwen, settling down into her customary chair. "I feel like a very special woman indeed, Mr. Hale."

I took my own seat, crossing one leg over the other. "You certainly are, Miss Largent. But I think you knew that already."

"Flattery..." the older woman smiled, but there was a tiredness in the expression. "How I've missed it."

I dropped the charm immediately, seeing as it was not to her taste. I leaned forward, unbuttoning my suit jacket. "I won't waste your time, Miss Largent. I have a simple question to ask you, and then a proposition to put to you."

Her eyes brightened. She likewise leaned forward in her seat. "Alright."

"Are we friends?"

If my question surprised her, Gwen Largent did an excellent job of hiding it. She waited a beat, as if expecting there to be more and then, shaking her head, repeated the last word of my query back to me.

"Friends?" Gwen smiled, a warm, full smile this time, and rested back in her seat, shaking her head. "No, Mr. Hale. No, we are not friends." She rested the side of her temple against her fingertips. "I hope I don't offend you by saying that."

I returned her smile with one of my own, folding my hands in my lap. "Not at all. In fact, I'm relieved."

She raised her brows at me. "Oh?"

"I make it a rule never to go into business with friends," I said by way of explanation. "And the proposition I have for you is this: you have a perfectly legitimate enterprise through which you buy, sell, and distribute defensive technology, is that not so?"

Gwen blinked slowly, thinking a moment before responding. "Yes, I do."

I placed my hand flush against my chest. "I'd like to contract with your company. Or, rather, Halcyon Enterprises would."

The mature woman shook her head, her knowing smile still perched on the edge of her lips like a bird on the edge of a feeder. "But Halcyon no longer makes defensive tech, Mr. Hale."

"This contract would be exclusive, Miss Largent," I said, continuing as if she'd never spoken. "If we were to ever start production again on defensive tech, of any kind, you would be our exclusive distributor. Anyone who wants our product, would have to go through you."

Gwen folded her hands in her lap, squirming deeper into her wicker chair. "Intriguing!" Nodding, she clicked her tongue off the top of her mouth. "And extremely attractive to boot. But you and I both know that you don't get something for nothing. So, what is it you want, young man?"

"Sandra Aja." I leaned back in my seat, brushing some pollen off my knee as I continued. "She's going to be serving life in the Anteries Penal District by the time the dust settles. I'd like to ensure she survives to serve her full sentence."

Gwen nodded slowly. She licked her lips and, lifting her brows, turned to the small table beside her. She lifted a tisane glass filled with some translucent pink liquid and sipped at it. "I see," she murmured around the rim of the glass, more to herself than to me.

I waited patiently while she drank her herb-infused beverage, feeling privileged to have this rare opportunity to watch the wheels within a crime mogul's head spinning. She swallowed once, then again, coughing a little into the back of her wrist before shaking her head. She replaced her glass on the table with an expression on her face that defied translation. She returned her attention to me, and I immediately broke out in a shiver.

"Unmolested?" asked Gwen, her tone light.

"Unmolested," I repeated firmly. Consciously relaxing my taut jaw, I took a deep breath. "Leave her be, Miss Largent. Let justice have its way."

She turned back to look at me, her passive face unchanged. "And what about my justice?"

Rising without preamble, I reached into my breast pocket, removing a palm-sized datapad. I turned it on with a quick scan of my thumbprint. "I have an exclusivity contract here. Drawn up by our lawyers this morning." I passed the pad to Gwen, doing my best to mask my disgust at the situation. "This is a one-time only offer, Miss Largent. Now or never."

She took the pad from me and began to scroll through the document, pursing her lips. After a moment, she set the data-pad down and turned to look back up at me, a smile playing around her wrinkled lips. "There's nothing in here about Sandra, of course."

I frowned. "Certainly not."

"So, you'd take me at my word?" she pressed.

I let my head fall to one side as I shrugged. "Who are we if not our word, Miss Largent?"

She narrowed her eyes. "Who indeed?" She gestured to the datapad with one hand. "I'll need my company's people to look this over, you understand."

Bending forward at the waist, I gave a curt bow of acknowledgment. "Of course."

"But I'd say you had a deal, Mr. Hale," said Gwen, grinning and offering her hand to me.

I shook it, but before I could withdraw my hand she wrapped her other hand around my extended wrist, pulling me closer. Her voice low, her smile sinister, she said, "I must say, I find your concern for a woman who attempted to kill you confusing, Mr. Hale." She caressed the inside of my wrist, making the skin writhe there. "You are a curious young man."

Not one to be outmatched, I favored her with a grin of my own. "I made a promise, Miss Largent." Straightening, I pulled my hand free from her grip. "And my father taught me that a man always keeps his promises."

Gwen sat back in her chair, still smiling. "Do take care, Mr. Hale."

I buttoned my suit jacket and glared at her. "You as well, Miss Largent."

With Sandra's safety secured, my thoughts turned to her partner – her lover – my bodyguard – Kace. Through everything that had happened since that afternoon, I had seen extraordinarily little of Kace Morgan. At first, I was relieved by his disappearance. But, as the days ticked by, I found my thoughts returning to him – truth was, I was worried about him. When I finally caught sight of him with one of the Halcyon Enterprises lawyers as I left my most recent deposition, I broke away from my own pack of legal wranglers to speak to him.

"Kace!" I shouted, waving as I jogged towards him.

He looked up at the sound of his name and widened his eyes when he saw me approach.

"Sir," he said, taking a step back.

I rolled my eyes. "What did I tell you about that? Makes me sound like an old man." I gestured back to the courthouse. "What are you doing here?"

He swallowed and dropped his gaze to the ground. "Testimony," he said thickly.

Cursing my lack of tact, I swallowed, wincing. "Right." I sighed. "Well, what are you doing after?"

His head jerked up. He examined me for a long moment before asking, "Why?"

I was about to answer, when one of my entourage called out to me. I turned and tried to wave them off, but I couldn't ignore that I did have other matters to attend to that would not wait. I began to walk backwards towards them, gesturing to Kace as I spoke, "You have my number, right? Give me a call and we'll meet somewhere."

He exchanged a look with his lawyer before shaking his head. "I don't think–"

I stopped backing away and sighed sharply. "Look: I'm worried about you, Kace. Just want to make sure you're alright." I tried on a smile and found it fit, throwing in a wink for good measure. "And last time I checked, you were still my bodyguard.

And frankly, you've been shirking your duties -- but I'll let it slide this time, if you agree to meet up with me?"

The ghost of a smile flitted across his lips. Kace nodded, his tense shoulders relaxing ever so slightly. "Sure. Yeah, okay."

24

Chapter 24

Lillit Park was the largest biodome in Römer. It boasted over a thousand distinct species of flora, a Zen Garden, moss garden, bird marsh, pollinator meadow, reflection pool, and too many other features to take in during one trip. The dome was sunk deep into the ground, creating a bowl-like valley into which visitors descended via gleaming walkways from above. Everything was meticulously maintained and protected.

Due to the gorgeous weather, the park was particularly busy that week – the last gasp of a warm autumn before our traditionally-frigid winter. I waited for Kace on the third-level walkways, closest to the interior of the park. Looking over the multi-colored reserve beneath me, I propped my foot on the bottom rung of the walkway's railing, keeping my hands in my trouser pockets. The sound of my name roused me from my contemplation of the scenery. I turned to see Kace approaching through the crowd of visitors. Stopping a few feet away from me, he mimicked my casual stance, although the tension in his shoulders was hard to miss.

"Si–" He stopped himself, smiling ruefully before nodding to me. "Chance."

"Glad you came, Kace." I returned his nod, but made no move toward him, treating him as I would a skittish animal. "How are you holding up?"

"Fine," he answered flatly, his smile unwavering.

We stood there for a few quiet moments, staring at each other. I allowed the growing silence to turn awkward. Scratching the underside of my jaw, I looked him up and down, flashing a pained grimace.

"My God," I groaned. "You are a terrible liar. Remind me to never gamble with you."

A laugh exploded from Kace and, hollow as it was, it seemed to surprise him as much as it did me. His smile softened, faded, and then melted away completely into a soggy frown. He pulled at his chin and turned his face away, even as he closed the distance between us with a few meandering steps. He leaned against the railing and stared into the bottom of the biodome, blind to the cacophony of color that assailed him.

I knew there was only one thing, one person he was seeing in his mind's eye. With a groan, he pushed a hand back through his hair.

"I miss her," he said at last. "Is that... is that messed up?"

I leaned back, resting my elbows against the railing. "No. Not at all." Looking up into the cloud speckled sky, I asked, "Do you want to talk about it?"

After a moment, Kace nodded. For the next hour, as we watched our fellow Römerians enjoy the beautiful day, Kace talked. He talked about how Sandra and he had first met, almost ten years ago. He talked about how proud he'd been when she'd gotten her first job with Halcyon Enterprises. He talked about how amazed he was with how quickly she had climbed her way through the ranks of the company. He talked about the plans they had made, and how those plans had grown dusty and then soured and twisted into something else in Sandra's mind. He talked about his complacency. He talked about her coming back to his apartment the night of Fogg's death, and the look in her eyes. He talked about his growing fear of her, of them, and of what had become of their dreams.

"I want you to know–" Kace stopped, shaking his head fervently but still not looking at me. "No, I need you to know, that everything illegal that happened, the weapons manufacturing, selling them on to Aldo Fogg, the–the killing–" He closed his eyes and took in a deep breath through his nose. "I had nothing to do with any of that."

"I understand," I assured him. "And so does everyone else. That's why the Enforcement Office is accepting your cooperation and not pursuing charges."

He let the deep breath out through his mouth, opening his eyes again slowly. "But I–I didn't do anything to stop it, either. I knew, I knew what was happening, and I just...I couldn't...I should've walked away from Sandra a long time ago," finished Kace, hanging his head low.

I shook my own head, turning around to mimic his position

on the railing. "What could you have done? You were in love with her."

He heaved another sigh, twisting his lips into a grimace. "No. I was in love with a version of her that didn't exist anymore -- I just didn't want to admit it. I thought... I thought I could get her back." He straightened, standing and looking at me askance. "But she was gone."

I reached out and squeezed his shoulder, "Kace, I'm sorry."

"I'm sorry too," he said, shifting his weight from foot to foot. "I shouldn't have let things get as bad as they did. If I had, Inspector Brisbois would still be alive."

I let out a breath, the corner of my mouth crooking up into a rueful smile. I dropped my hand from his shoulder. "We could bat the responsibility for that back and forth all day... But he'd call us both morbid bastards and tell us to move on."

The ghost of a smile fluttered across his lips like the shadow of leaves against the ground. "Yeah. I suppose so. Well..." He stuck his hand out towards me, looking me straight in the eye for the first time since he had started talking. "Thanks for letting me have my say. I appreciate it."

I took his hand firmly with both of my own. "Of course. What's next for you?"

"Honestly?" Kace shook his head. "I have no idea."

"Well," I said, releasing him. "I may have a thought about that."

I reached into my jacket pocket and pulled out an unsealed envelope. I handed it to Kace with a small smile.

Kace took it, turning the envelope over in his hands. "What's this?"

I nodded to the cream-colored paper. "Open it."

His eye caught on the embossed Halcyon Enterprises logo in the upper left corner. He looked back at me, questions clear in his eyes. I indicated the envelope with a wave of my hand. Kace hummed in suspicion, but then slid out the thick bundle of folded papers. Working them open, he scanned them, casually at first, but then with growing intensity.

I moved to stand beside him. "You'll have to forgive the paper contract – old-fashioned, I know, but I was in an old-fashioned sort of mood when I had the HR people draw it up." Taking a step back, I looked up at the taller man from under my brow. "Now, I should warn you -- I've been told I'm not the easiest person to work with."

Kace looked over at me, wrinkling his brow in confusion. I smiled. "And this would mean I'd have to find a new bodyguard." I frowned exaggeratedly. "Or, I suppose, you would have to find me a new one, as my new Security Director."

"Chance!" Kace stared at me, aghast.

Beaming, I rocked back and forth on my heels. "A 'yes' would be sufficient."

It was like I'd cast a spell on the man, freezing him to the spot. The world continued around us -- people walking by, talking, laughing, children running through the park and screeching in unbridled joy as the birds chirped in the trees. But Kace did not move. He stood there, staring at me. For a moment, I started to worry that I had done some permanent damage to him.

A particularly loud shriek from a child broke through whatever was going on in the man's head. He shook himself into action, folding the contract back into a neat package. "I-I can't accept this, Chance."

"Why on the sphere not?" I asked, leaning forward.

His tongue clicked off the back of his teeth. "My girlfriend tried to kill you." Swallowing hard, he pressed his hand flat against his chest. "And I—"

I took the fist that was holding the contract and pressed it to his chest, looking him in the eye as I spoke. "I need someone on the board as Security Director who I can trust to look out for every person in the company." I tapped the back of his hand and smiled before stepping away. "I need someone who leads with their heart. Like me."

A flurry of emotions passed over Kace's normally stoic face. I thought I saw the hint of tears in his eyes. He swallowed and took a step back. "I appreciate that, Chance." At length, he shook his head once more, a laugh escaping his lips. "Wow. I honestly don't know what to say."

"Think it over," I said, still smiling. "Sign it when you've decided that I'm right."

Kace grunted in annoyance, tapping the folded-up contract against his palm. "Always so damn sure of yourself."

I ran my hand through my hair. "It's part of my charm."

Kace looked as if he were about to say something more when something past my shoulder caught his eye. His mouth snapped shut, his half-hearted scowl curling up into a grin. I turned to follow his gaze.

She would stand out in any crowd – at least, she would for me. Strolling through the steady flow of bodies, Cadence moved towards us, a look of utter rapture on her face as she looked up and around herself. She had one hand on top of her head, holding a floppy straw hat in place as she craned her neck back, her hair flowing loose behind her.

How hopelessly I was in love with her.

Cadence, looking down and seeing us, stopped walking. She rocketed onto her tiptoes, waving wildly at us, smiling from ear to ear. "Cy, Chance! Kace!"

I waved back at her, and she started hurrying towards us through the crowded walkways. A laugh from behind me redirected my attention. I looked back at my former bodyguard, a slight blush coloring my cheeks.

"Well..." Kace nodded towards the approaching Cadence. "Your charms appeal to someone, at least."

I dusted some non-existent lint off my shoulder and glared at him half-heartedly. "I can trust you to stay unobtrusive, as usual?"

He nodded, tucking the contract into his suit jacket. "As usual."

Cadence skittered to a halt in front of Kace, momentarily ignoring my presence. "Xio, Kace, it's so wonderful to see you!"

Kace laughed a little at Cadence's enthusiasm but returned the greeting all the same. "It's good to see you too, Miss Turing."

She rocked up and down on the tips of her toes. "I was hoping we'd get an opportunity to talk about your past investigative experience–"

"Ah ah ah," I chided aloud, real panic creeping into my voice. Stepping between them, I stared at Cadence beseechingly. "No – no business talk today. You promised, Cay, remember?"

To her credit, Cadence did look chastened, nodding quickly as she ceased her excited swaying. "Right. The Date." The way she said the word, a capital letter was more than implied - it was insisted upon. She peered over my shoulder at Kace and shrugged. "Maybe later?"

"Absolutely," he said, grinning, before stepping away to allow us our privacy.

When Kace was a respectable distance away, Cadence turned her full attention to me, smiling her sweet summer smile. She gave a firm nod, brushing out the skirt of her dress. "Sinc, I am ready for the Date to commence." Then, her smile wavering ever so slightly, she leaned forward, her voice quiet. "Urio, is it normal to be a little nervous?"

I matched her stance and her volume, nodding seriously. "Perfectly. Although I hope it's nervous excitement and not dread."

Cadence considered this for a moment before straightening. "I believe it is. Sometimes I find emotions difficult to parse."

"You're not the only one," I admitted. My own chest ached with a bubbling mixture of feelings that threatened to pop and spill out of me in a long, ill-advised ramble. Looking at her in the warm autumn sunlight, I wanted to tell her again how much I loved her. I wanted to promise her that I would never leave her. I wanted to swear to do everything that I could to make her happy. I wanted to share my life with her, however much of it I had left.

Cadence tilted her head and stared at me, her smile softening. She reached out and took my hand.

I smiled back. "Come with me." Her hand was warm and soft in mine, and I squeezed it as I led her along the path. "There's something that I absolutely don't want us to miss..."

About the Author

Robin Jeffrey was born in Cheyenne, Wyoming to a psychologist and a librarian, giving her a love of literature and a consuming interest in the inner workings of people's minds, which have served her well as she pursues a career in creative writing. She holds a BA in English from the University of Washington and a MS in Library Science from the University of Kentucky. She has been published in various journals across the country as well as on websites like The Mary Sue and Introvert, Dear. She currently resides in Bremerton, Washington. More of her work can be found on her website, RobinJeffreyAuthor.com.

Robin would like to take this opportunity to extend her sincerest thanks to everyone who made this book possible. To her endlessly supportive family and friends, to the authors who have mentored her, and to all the readers that have given her work a place on their shelves: thank you, from the bottom of her heart.

Reviews are the lifeblood of authors everywhere. If you enjoyed reading *LOS: A Cadence Turing Mystery*, please consider taking a few moments to leave a review on Amazon, Goodreads, or wherever you'd like to share your thoughts! You can also sign up for Robin's newsletter or follow her on social media - she'd love to stay in touch!